THE LAST VIRUS

Letters & Diaries from the inhabitants of Sector 4 in the city of Ayla

Major Caleb Adams

"hate is not for Humans" – Kenji Goto

James Foley, Steven Sotloff, Kayla Mueller, Marie Colvin, Hevrin Khalaf, Ruqia Hassan, Kenji Goto, Serena Shim, Charlie Hebdo, Theo van Gogh, and of course all the others

Printed in the United States of America

First Printing: April 2020

ISBN-13 978-1-7334716-3-3

CONTENTS

1 THE ASSASSIN

12th Day of Rabi al-Awwal

It is the twelfth day in the month of Rabi al-Awwal. It is necessary for us to follow this calendar. Our lives are dependent upon it. By their holidays we are most active. Those days that they pay homage, we give hell. Their God we know better than we know ours. It is necessary.

I am seventeen and I am an assassin. I have no family and I have disremembered my past. It is better for me this way. I am given my training and I am given my missions. Of the invasion, it was swift and came out of nowhere. It was like waking one day and suddenly finding the sun rising in the west. The man says empires they come and empires they fall. He says the last generation of an empire is the one that always suffers the most—paying the debts for all of the sins that have been accrued. He said the one we were born of is now in the annals of history. He said those pages have been turned, ripped and burned. He says it's all become oral history now. He says that is why I should write down all I have seen and all I have known. The man is clever with the language. He didn't say to write down all that I will see and all that I will know. The man understands I have no future.

We have been here in the freight tunnels for a little over two years now. Before that, we were nomads, sewer rats. Underneath the streets once ours, we ate and slept in their Caliphate filth. When we were found, as invariably we always were, we had to run from poisonous gas, automatic fire, and rocket-propelled grenades. And then before that, the man and I were hidden away in the cellar of his shoe store, rationing jarred and canned kosher food. Here in the freight tunnels, we have been the safest we have ever been. The reason is that the freight tunnels lie forty feet below the sewers. They have not realized we have descended into another ring of hell. The man says they will figure it out. There is no reason to believe he is wrong. Here though, at least we are organized. Here, at least we have assembled a resistance, assembled weapons, assembled some dignity. Here, at least we are able to kill. And that has made this a life now worth living.

There is a man I trust. He is the one I spoke of above. It's difficult to trust anyone. That comes from being in the sewers. There they had informers who would walk among us. I never blamed them though, the informers, that is. Their families were held hostage above. What choice did they have? But they were also fools, as eventually they too were slaughtered.

The man, he talks of his God now and then. The man is a Jew. A prized possession in this world, worth a purse of a thousand gold coins to him that captures one. He says his people have always been persecuted. I admire that he is a Jew. Not because of his beliefs, but because of his resolve and fortitude. They are fighters, the Jews. They are a proud people. When they are caught, they do not renounce their faith. And for this, they are tortured to a great extent. If captured, I would say, "In the name of Allah, the Merciful, the Compassionate, He is the one God, the Everlasting refuge, who has not begotten, nor has been begotten, and equal to Him is not anyone." I would say this or anything they wanted in order to spare me any more pain before death was to befall me.

I myself do not believe in God. The cross around my neck is more of a flag, like that of a country. Mass I attend to serve my body and not my soul. The cube of bread which impersonates a wafer I take only because it is food. The wine I drink only because it is from water. The son of our God some tell me will return. I think that if we do have a God and He is sending his son, then our God is a fool. His son should not come alone. What can one son do? Our God needs thousands of sons to defeat those above us. And all of those sons should bring ammunition and weapons. And with that, they should also bring food, batteries, and pillows for our heads. It is when I see this that I will believe.

There are cities and countries new, but these cities and countries are the same. What I once knew to be America is now Ummah. What I once knew to be Chicago is now Ayla. The man says it doesn't matter. He says the only thing I need to know is how to roll them off of my tongue. The man is right. My life is now dependent on the Arabic that I have been taught.

"Be ready," the man has said to me on more than one occasion, "this may last a thousand years." I wonder what he means by a thousand years. What may exactly last? What is there that the world can return to? Does he foresee a future where we no longer live below ground? I do not see that. I do not see that even in his thousand years. I am only glad that we are no longer in the sewers. They are a fetid bouquet of the Caliphate's waste. It is a stink that never leaves your tongue. You taste it when you awake. You taste it with the food you eat, and you taste it as you think. You can even taste it when you dream.

In the day I work as part of a bomb-making team. It is my first job. I have become quite proficient. I construct improvised explosive devices out of most anything that can detonate, maim, and kill. I take great pride in this work. It is tedious work that requires the utmost concentration. I have that kind of will and I have that kind of spirit. My second job is as a postman. That is what they call it. They send me out with a handler. He walks me around Ayla. We walk through their souks, we walk by their mosques. My Arabic is still something to be desired, but it is passable. To speak it properly I need to concentrate. I need to roughen my tongue as with sandpaper. When we are not gathering information, we are laying down those devices I have built.

The ones who have lived the longest on this earth are the weakest among us. This is because they fear the most. You cannot fear here. It would be debilitating and unconstructive. Death is something you have to accept. Not to accept as something that is inevitable but to accept as something that can be immediate. You must imagine that it can arrive while you are gathering thoughts for your next sentence. You must imagine it can interrupt you while you are eating that cube of bread. I imagine it all the time and hence I have no fear.

Those who have no future have religion. That is what the man has told me. This, he says, is how God recruits his followers. I asked him which God. He said all gods. He said they all work off of the same principle. I asked him that even after knowing this, why does he still believe in his God. "Because I have no future," he replied.

27th Day of Rabi al-Awwal

This morning I was ordered to Souk #2. I was told to purchase a half kilogram of baklava from the old woman with two fingers on her left hand. When I was given the baklava, I was to kneel and remove my backpack. It is a simple ruse. We have done it many times before. One backpack we hide inside another. So, after sliding the smaller backpack under the folding table of the old woman, I am to place the baklava inside the larger one. I then stand, and I look no different than I did before.

We were then instructed to sit ourselves and our baklava on a bench across from Souk #2. When the man whom we were shown a picture of came by the stall, I was told to detonate the explosives. He came with his daughter. She was five or six. This I was not told. Of course I was not told. They should have had more faith in me. I was not moved by her presence. We all suffer here. We all die here. Age is of little relevance.

It happens so fast. Like lightning and thunder. There is a flash, and then there is a sound. There are body parts being spit out in all directions. There are people rushing toward the blast to assist. I removed the vest of explosives concealed under my burqa and set it inside the second backpack. Sixty seconds I counted. Then, I got off the bench and ran toward Souk #2, flailing my arms and screaming like I was supposed to. His legs were no longer there, and he was bleeding out. I wanted to uncover myself and spit on his face. His daughter was already dead. This is war. There are many casualties in war. It was not my fault she was born of such a wretched man. To hell with him, to hell with the Caliphate, and to hell now with the little girl.

I waited for the men to push me aside. They did and I fell, quickly removing the second backpack and leaving it on the ground amidst all the chaos and confusion. Another wave of men then came running up. What fools. Have they not learned? I hurried my steps, through the smokescreen, through the gathered crowd. I smiled. I could barely hear as the first blast had beaten so loudly on the drums of my ears. I reached into an inner pocket of my burqa and depressed the trigger of the second device. We were not far enough away from the explosives. I should have judged the distance better. The blast wave rudely pushed us in the back. My body flung forward. That's all I remember.

I awoke in our infirmary. Only the man was there, sitting in a chair beside where I lay.

"My handler?" I asked.

"With heaven's help, he brought you here."

"May I see him?"

"When you die, you can look around for him."

The man then pulled back the sheet that was covering my unclothed body and looked me over. Not a lecherous look as I have seen others give me, but the look of someone who wanted to make sure that I would live another day. The cover he threw back over me and began to leave. When he was near the exit, he nodded over to a stand right beside me. I turned my head. There he had left a stem of grapes for me. I was grateful, for the grapes, that is.

13th Day of Rabi al-Thani

"May I ask you a question?" I said.

"Yes, you may," the man answered.

"Did you expect it?"

"Did I expect that one day I would know what it was like to be a feral dog living in tunnels below a city where I once dwelled quite comfortably?"

"That is not what I meant."

"I know, child. I understood the question. You want to know whether or not I foresaw the complete collapse."

"Yes, that is what I want to know," I said.

"I imagined it no more than I imagined suddenly growing a new head upon my body. That is not to say I was ignorant of history. I did envision a time when our empire would be in rubble like all of the other empires had themselves become rubble. I imagined that two or three hundred years from now a schoolboy from another race, another nation, would be reading about our demise. I imagined that it would be somewhat similar to my teachings. The book that he held in his hands would be thick, but of it, only three or four pages would tell of our story. He would skim through this terse and distorted version, and then give his own summary of that summary. After that, it would leave his mind, and he would have forgotten all about us. That I imagined. What I did not imagine was the utter swiftness on which wings it arrived. That was a bird I'm sure none but the insane saw in their dreams. So, to answer your question, I did see a future demise based on my knowledge of how empires were succeeded. However, I did not foresee a catastrophic failure such as the one that took place."

7

"Do you think there was anything that could have been done to prevent it?"

"No more than a mind could give you an answer to the equation infinity plus one."

"I don't understand," I said. "Infinity plus one is infinity. That is the answer."

"Today, child, that answer is correct. But tomorrow, it will be wrong," the man replied.

"I still don't understand."

"Exactly. Our minds do not stretch that far yet. But I assure you, in time man's mind will advance far enough to properly solve that equation. Just as it has already been understood that some infinities are larger than others. Infinity, my child, for the moment it is just a placeholder until a better mind arrives."

"There must have been signs, though? There must have been some warnings?"

"Of course, there are always signs and warnings. Ask any historian."

23rd Day of Rabi al–Thani

It is near the end of the month of Rabi al-Thani. I have a new handler. For the last few days we have been training for a mission. His Arabic is perfect, but he is weak with fear. I can see it in his eyes. They wander around too much. He is thinking of the ways he could die. One who searches his mind for death will surely find it. I told the man this. He said that is true. He said that even though I was being accompanied by the new handler, I should act like I am alone. He said one never follows a dead man in training.

We are being sent to the stadium. Once it was called Soldier Field. Once it was where we played our games and heard our music. Now it is where they hold their executions and spit their hatred to the attending masses. Tonight, it is to be the site of a rally in which the imam is to speak. Yesterday we were shown a video of him. Oddly, the camera work was well done. I say oddly well done because most of the time what we film is grainy and wobbly. He is an obese man with a distended belly and a dirty beard. His spits and hisses like a snake when he shouts his venom. The finger that he points with is hooked, and its nail is yellow and long. The man told me he was born from one of the devil's whores. The man said his own mother tried to kill him when he was in the womb. He said she cleansed her womb with drain cleaner, but he still would not die. He is old and he is ugly. He is a vile man with a predilection for young boys. His appetite for them is insatiable. When he is done with them, they are thrown into a dump outside the city.

In the video, the imam spoke for forty-two minutes. The crowd before him was like hungry lions. They would have ripped out the heart of their own mother and ate it if the imam had requested. We were played the video a total of eleven times. That night I recited to the man one passage from the imam that I thought he would find of interest.

> *"The prophet said, 'The Resurrection will not take place until the Muslims fight the Christians and the Jews and kill all of them.' Rejoice in it. Rejoice in Allah's victory. The Muslims will seek to kill the Christians and Jews and they will hide. The prophet said, 'The Christians and the Jews will hide behind rock and tree, and the rock and tree will say: Oh servant of Allah, Oh Muslim, there is a Christian and a Jew behind me, come kill them!' Why is there this malice, you ask? Because there are none who love the Christians and the Jews on the face of this earth. Not man, not rock, and not tree. Everything hates them. They destroy everything. They destroy the trees and they destroy the houses. Everything wants vengeance on the Christians and the Jews, on these pigs on the face of the earth. In our sewers, there are still some Christians and Jews. Seek them out and kill all of them. Bless the prophet and bless Allah."*

The man smiled. He said the imam should be careful what he wishes for. He said that without any Christians and Jews there would be little left to hate. And then what would he preach.

We exited the freight tunnels and came up near what was once the Field Museum. There was still light left in the day so we had to wait a few minutes to let our eyes adjust. Being in the tunnels, we have adapted to the low light, and this makes it quite difficult for any of us to wander around in the sun. The stadium was still only half full when we entered it. These are the most dangerous of missions. The ones where you must stand among them for an indeterminate length of time. One misstep and you are surely dead, or worse, surely captured. I kept my head straight, turning to no one, not even to my new handler. We stopped in the middle for a moment to survey the layout. Beside me was a family. I was wearing an abaya this time, and the child beside me was pulling on it to get my attention. The child was male and therefore I could not risk reprimanding him. I handed him a piece of candy, and finally, he left me alone.

The rectangular opening of my niqab is a half-inch wider on each side. It cannot be discerned. It allows me to keep my head straight while sweeping my eyes about. I was looking around when I saw a scuffle take place just off to my immediate right. They took hold of a girl and took her to one of the execution posts. They stripped her naked and tied her hands behind her back and tied her body to that post. It was then I could see she was about my age. The crowd moved nearer to watch the beating. One of them produced a whip, a cord of black leather. Between her legs and her back, he alternated the lashes. The crowd was raucous in its delight so I could not hear her wail. One hundred and five lashes. That is what I counted.

When they were done, they ordered her father over to untie her and take her away. He did as instructed. She was not more than a few feet in front of him when he kicked her in the back and sent her to the ground. He was now standing over her. She lifted up a hand. He reached behind his back, pulled out a small-caliber gun, and shot her in the head. The crowd roared, and the father walked away with a look of smugness that set me on fire. I took a few steps in his direction. My new handler quickly grabbed my hand. I was thankful that he did so. Thankful because I would have kept walking until I had caught up to him and slit his throat. For those few steps I took, I scolded myself. I know better. Here, empathy is your own executioner. The imam never showed that day. Too drunk, I was later informed.

Seven days later, we came back. Having a week to rethink our mission, this time I was eight-months pregnant. Inside my plastic belly, enough high explosives to send the imam and a good hundred of his followers to paradise. We went directly to the right of the stage where last week we had seen a roped-off area for maimed soldiers of war and women near birth. We stood by the barricades, over which was draped a long black banner. And on that black banner, in white Arabic script, were the words of the Shahada: There is no god but God. Muhammad is the messenger of God.

It was a warm night. Made even warmer by the torches lit at the sides of the stage. My handler was sweating. I could see large beads form at his temples and then make their way down the sides of his face. I remember thinking he would be dead soon, my handler, that is. If not so tonight, then some other day. He was not a man created for this work.

Beside me was a girl. She smelled of mint and thyme, from cooking, I assumed. I looked her way for a moment. She had on a hijab with dark sunglasses hiding her eyes. The shape of her face seemed similar to the girl who had been whipped and murdered a week before. I assumed she was probably the same age as that girl. She was there with a soldier on crutches, one leg on the ground and the other severed at the knee. I assumed he was her father. I thought she did not deserve to die. I thought of many things that night. I know better than to think of anything at all.

We waited through two speakers as we had before. Their speeches were the same. Our cue was to act exactly one minute after the second speaker said his last words. I arched my back and placed a hand on my belly as if a labor pain had suddenly shot through me. When I lowered myself to the ground and sat back on my heels, those around parted to give me a little more room as we had expected. By then, I had already lifted up the bottom of the plastic mold and eased the explosive pack out, where it now rested between my thighs.

My handler was then supposed to kneel in front of me. He was supposed to act as my curtain. He was supposed to put his hands on my shoulders while I moved the explosive pack under one of the barricades. He did nothing. He was paralyzed with terror. Instead, another man knelt before me and looked me in the eyes like he wanted to fuck me. I looked straight back at him, offering him hope.

Finally, my handler crouched at my side and put his hand on my belly. That infuriated the man. He pulled out a sidearm and put the barrel to my handler's head. He then started berating my handler for not coming to the immediate aid of his pregnant wife. And as he was doing so, I was listening closely for the click of the trigger. I was getting ready to send all of us to our respective resting places.

Fortunately, the man withdrew the gun and walked off. My handler breathed out a sigh of relief and helped me get to my feet. I wobbled a little as I arose, and with my right foot, pushed the explosive pack underneath one of the barricades where the Shahada was draped.

We were supposed to wait for the imam. We were supposed to have visual confirmation. I decided I could not risk it. I did not think my handler could remain there any longer without compromising our mission. Though we did not need it, I asked the girl beside me to help us. I asked her to help part the crowd. She nodded, and with her father, led us through the mass of people toward the back of the stadium. The lights on the rooftop of the stadium dimmed as we were midpoint on the field. The searchlights of the military trucks took to the sky. The roar of the crowd was deafening. The faces in front of me twisted into looks of ecstasy I have only seen on men who were above me while I lay below. I heard a voice come through the loudspeakers. I depressed the detonator.

I have a riddle for you the General told me later that night. Who is one that looks and speaks like the imam but not the imam? I felt sick after his words. Immediately I understood that they had used a double. I should have waited to see the imam take the stage. I had seen enough of his hooked and yellowed finger on the video where I would have known it was not him. I never should have left early to save one Muslim girl. I wondered about that night, though. Wondered if I still would have triggered the detonator even if I knew it was not the imam speaking. Before my eyes closed, I decided that yes I would have. All of them in the stadium were just as complicit in the atrocities that were being committed. No one is innocent in Ayla. All deserve to die.

The next morning they came through the sewers with fire throwers. While we live below the sewers, they are still used by escaped slaves from the labor camps and others who we have not been able to collect and bring into the freight tunnels. For my mistake, the General sent me into the sewers three days later to count bodies. I counted fourteen. The sewers stank of burnt flesh and burnt hair. It is hard to eat with that smell. You are nauseous when awake, you are nauseous when you think, you are nauseous when you return to bed. What you are not though is nauseous when you see their bodies. You are just elated that it was not you.

6th Day of Jumada al-Awwal

"Do you want me to set the pieces?" I asked the man. For the last six months, we had been playing one game of chess before going to sleep. He said eventually it would rewire my brain so that with every action I contemplated, I would be able to choose from three or four futures.

"I have not yet finished reading," he answered.

"It is the same book every night," I replied.

"It is the only one I need. Besides you, it was the only item I took before leaving the cellar of the shoe store," he said, taking the penlight off the page and setting it on the ground between us. A few days ago, upon his entreat, I was able to obtain it from the commissary. He was grateful like a child.

"I took food, medical supplies, warm clothing, and a knife," I said. "But a book. No, that never made my list."

"These words fill my mind so it disremembers its hunger. They make me forgot my sores when they bleed, and they bring comfort to my body when it begins to shiver. With regard to the knife, perhaps I was remiss. It now forces me to borrow yours if I ever find the need to slit my own throat."

"What is the title?" I asked the man. The front cover had been torn away so I was unable to ascertain it with a simple look.

"It is irrelevant. Like either my name or yours."

"Isn't what's inside of it also irrelevant? Like you and me."

"I will let you decide as I will read you a passage: 'Never shall I forget those moments that murdered my God and my soul and turned my dreams to ashes. Never shall I forget those things, even were I condemned to live as long as God Himself. Never.' " He then looked up

15

at me. "Do you find that irrelevant?"

"I have no God, no soul, and no dreams."

"That is why, child, they have chosen you as an assassin."

17th Day of Sha'ban

I was at the Grand Market this morning. The morning is when it is most crowded and therefore the least dangerous. I was with my third handler in four months. The last one killed himself. I found no surprise in his suicide. He ingested a gallon of kerosene. We were able to recover a good portion of it from his body. These fuels we do not come by easily.

We had been sent to terminate the military commander of Ayla, Mullah Akhtar Mohammad Osmani. The General told me that when he arrived in Ayla after the invasion, he ordered all the blue-eyed children who survived to be gathered up. He then ordered their blue eyes to be removed. Outside of his mansion in Ayla, the General said there are six replicas of peacocks. The eyes of some of those children are preserved and woven into the tail feathers of each.

Every morning we were told, he liked to walk around the market and choose his own eggs for breakfast. I was there selling eggs in a basket. In case our mission was compromised, the bottom of the basket was lined with an inch and three-quarters of C-4. In the event the mission was not compromised, I was to sell the military commander the eggs we had injected with thallium. Either outcome I accepted.

I was stopped at a fig seller when I saw him and an escort of his soldiers not more than twenty yards from where me and my handler stood. I clenched my right hand to signal to my handler that our target had been spotted. I took no more than three steps when a girl bumped into me and brought her head close to mine so that her mouth was near my ear.

"You are the one," she said in a whisper, she said in Arabic.

The man behind her was on one leg, and the scent of mint and thyme on her body were unmistakable. I started to move my hand underneath the basket to find the trigger when she spoke into my ear again.

"If you do not follow me, I will tell them right now who you are."

That time her words were delivered to me in perfect English, with no trace of an accent. It first brought a chill to me, but after another thought, I withdrew my finger from the trigger. If she were one of them, she never would have asked me to follow her. There would be no need. After identifying me, we would have been rushed right there, and the race would have been on. I either would have been able to trigger the C-4, or I would have found myself dragged off to an excruciatingly long and painful death. I nodded my head and stretched the fingers on my right hand to signal to my handler that while our mission had been compromised, the situation was for the moment not inextricable.

We were led out of the market and onto a street that was filled with both livestock and the harried morning crush of the Ayla denizens. The girl was walking fast, too fast I thought for the situation. We were the only ones at that pace, which alone can bring attention to the Hisbah and the soldiers who watch every heartbeat of the city.

Finally, we came upon a storefront that was still shuttered. The unassuming white sign above it in simple black Arabic script called it out as a café selling shawarma and falafel. The man with one leg let us in. Immediately, after closing and locking the door behind us, he drew a gun from his belt and directed my handler to sit. The girl took me through the kitchen and into another room. She lit a few candles and left. I looked around. The room was simple. On the floor, a mattress. On the wall, a framed picture of the Grand Mosque during the Hajj. The lone window was covered with a black cloth.

Upon her return, she brought in a tray and set it on the ground in front of me. On the tray were some falafel, a bowl of fruit, a few slices of lamb, along with a cup of mint tea. She also brought in a gun of her own, of which no attempt was made to conceal.

"Please, sit. And have something to eat."

I waited for her to sit and briefly took a second look at the gun. Then I sat. I did not reach for any of her offerings, even though I wanted to take all she had brought and shove it into my mouth. There were two reasons I did not. The first was that I did not want to make her think I was weak. The second because I did not want a hand to leave the basket of eggs I was holding in front of me.

"Would you rather we talk in English or Arabic?" she asked.

I said nothing.

"Since you are my guest, I will therefore speak in your tongue. You are famous up here, do you know that? They are offering great sums of money for your capture."

Again I remained silent, though I was aware of the price on my head.

"They think you are a man dressed in women's clothing. I am glad you are a woman. Women here they believe are no smarter than oxen."

"Why didn't you say something when you knew it was I who placed the explosives?" I asked.

"Because the imam deserves to die. Most of them deserve to die. They have distorted everything. This is not Islam."

"Then why were you at the rally?"

"So they think I am one of them."

"Who is the man escorting you?"

"My uncle, from my mother's side. He protects me when he can."

"Do you always wear them?" I asked, speaking of her sunglasses.

"Most of the time. I am sensitive to light. My father stuck a fork in my left eye when I was a child. He did not want to be reminded of my mother's blue eyes."

"Why not your right eye?" I asked.

She then took her sunglasses off, along with the niqab she was wearing this time. I did not expect what I saw in front of me. She was stunning. Her perfect black hair unfurled to her waist like a flag. Not a strand I saw was frayed. Her skin was radiant and luxurious. Her bottom lip was full, her top lip thin. She had an oval face, a nose perfectly set upon it. But her eyes, they were magical, and I began to wonder if I was dreaming all of this.

"They are colored differently," I said.

"Yes, the brown one is from my father. He is from the Arabian Peninsula. Yemen, to be exact. The blue one, as I have said, is from my mother. She was from Iran."

"Was?"

"Yes, she was from Iran. My father killed her. He took a large rock and smashed it against her head over and over until it caved in. She didn't even look real after that. It was like I was staring down at a cracked pottery jar."

"What was the offense?"

"She spoke back to him in front of his family. He is the first one we will kill."

"The first?" I said.

"Yes, the first. Then we will kill my husband."

"And the reason for your husband's death?"

"He beats me. One day I know he will kill me."

"I do not see any marks on your face," I said.

She then stood up and placed the gun on the sill of the window behind her. After removing her sandals, she removed her abaya with absolutely no shame whatsoever. Underneath she had on a chemise, dark blue. Satin, I assumed. Her chest stretched it taut, but the black lace trim left the cleavage to the imagination. From there, the rest of the chemise followed her skin like water until it quit mid-thigh. Her legs were pressed together, thin and adoring. I continued on to her feet with a woman's curiosity and then hurried up again with a man's lustfulness, wondering if that was all she had worn. She was intoxicating, and I found myself wanting a sip, just a sip. If she had asked, I certainly would have made love to her.

But signs of beatings, I saw none. And so in question, my eyes landed upon her eyes. She answered by removing her chemise. At that moment, her unclothed body before me, I wanted to undress and press my skin gently against hers in order to comfort her deep bruises and scars. I wanted to place my lips on hers and then roll my tongue over her flesh. I wanted to fall asleep beside her and then wake to her in the morning. For another woman, I had never felt like that before. I was mesmerized. And if I believed in either gods or devils, I would not be sure which one I was looking up at.

"Are you satisfied?" she then asked as she picked up her garments from the floor and began fitting them over her body. Afterward, she took the gun off the sill and sat again.

"Why not just kill them yourself?" I asked.

"I am not able to kill like you are able to kill."

"You are holding that gun like it is the hand of a familiar friend."

"We are all familiar with them up here. They are a part of our life. You certainly must know this."

It was at that moment the name Fatima was called. She stood up quickly and then so did I. My handler stumbled into the room, pushed in by a crutch of the man with one leg.

"They have come early to open the restaurant. The shutter is being lifted as we speak," the man with one leg said in Arabic.

"Who are they?" I asked.

"My father and my husband. It is their restaurant," she said.

"I should end your life this very second," I said as I pushed her against the wall, the knife hidden in the sleeve of my abaya now at her throat.

"I do not care if you run the blade across my neck. It would be better than living like this."

"Give your gun to him," I said to her uncle. Reluctantly, he handed it over to my handler. I then relieved her of her own gun. "Will they have weapons?"

"Most likely," she whispered in reply as we could hear their voices coming closer.

After removing the knife from her neck, I nodded to my handler to stand near me as I took a position on one side of the door. The girl and her uncle were on the other side, disarmed and spectators now. Her father and husband made one pass by the door. We could hear the moving of crates or boxes. We could hear them speak. I glanced at my handler. The gun was trembling in his hand.

It was the candles. I am almost sure of it. None of us had remembered to extinguish them. When both her father and husband quieted for an unusual length of time, I realized it had dawned upon one of them, as it had dawned upon me. The barrel of the AK-47 slowly moved across the threshold. Though I had been trained, I had never killed that close before. It wasn't as intimate as I thought it would be. The knife went through the neck of the gray-bearded man without effort as if through the skin of a fig. I expected more resistance. What I did not expect was him to still be able to fire the weapon. Her uncle fell immediately.

I was now on Fatima's side of the door. The worst possible position as I was across from my handler. I blinked twice to remind him to hold fire. You never know with these handlers. From outside the room, her husband called out, "Ali, Ali." He then sprayed eight or nine rounds into the room. My calf felt like it had been sliced open. It was from a ricochet. The noise on the street began to gather momentum as I'm sure all of them were wondering where the sound of the gunfire was emanating.

Her husband jabbed in the barrel of the weapon and quickly pulled it back. Again he repeated the maneuver. I knew he was walking in next. Everyone believes things are safe in threes. Like with her father, I went to plunge the knife into his neck. He was taller than I thought and instead it entered his shoulder. He barely twitched, and then he kicked me back a few feet. When my handler put the gun to his head, he pushed the weapon aside and knocked him with the stock of the AK-47. He took aim at my forehead. I closed my eyes.

The ring of a gunshot that close leaves you disoriented. It leaves you without a sense of where the bullet has originated. I did not feel anything, and I was wondering if this is what death is actually like. I was wondering if it had already traveled through my brain, leaving me with just these thoughts as my last.

"We must go quickly," Fatima said.

I turned to her. Her face was freckled with blood splatter. I slowly lifted up a hand and gently wiped both of her cheeks with the sleeve of my abaya. After that, she knelt to set the gun in the hand of her dead uncle. It should have occurred to me that she may have been carrying more than one weapon. It also should have occurred to me to kill her right there. I know better.

The three of us exited through the back door of the cafe and into an alley. From there, we cut through the Grand Market, and then finally found a deserted street where my handler and I could drop into the sewers.

"You cannot follow us," I said, gun pointed at her chest.

"And where am I to go after these deaths? You might as well kill me."

"If I take you with, a return would not be possible."

"I do not want to return. Ever."

17th Day of Sha'ban

I asked my handler to take Fatima to the washing area while I was being attended to by the man. He was dressing the flesh wound I had received. I told him everything. I did not leave out one second. With regard to all I had related, he had only one question for me.

"How do you know they were her father and her husband?"

"I suppose I do not know," I answered, speaking honestly.

"Then in the story, you should have said you killed one man and she killed the other."

"I will watch her," I replied.

"And when the watchman sleeps, who then?"

"You want me to kill her, don't you?"

"What are you going to tell the General?"

"If I tell him all I told you, he will kill her himself."

"Then I am grateful he is our general."

"She saved my life."

"Yes, to enter the gates unknowingly, one does not kill the gatekeeper."

The man secured the bandage around my calf and then returned to where he was sitting. He picked up his book to read again. He seemed at ease. To be at ease with one's self is all that can be asked for in this life. It is the true meaning I have now come to believe. When I was just killing, I was at ease. My mind now though is a paradox. It has shut itself down, but at the same time the synapses are firing off like a fully automatic weapon with an endless clip of ammunition at its disposal. My thoughts are radiating out in every direction so that they have only a beginning and no end. I cannot think. I cannot think at all.

When my handler returned with Fatima from the washing area, I took him aside. I told him to forget what had happened. I told him it was not necessary to file this in our report. I told him he should consider himself lucky to be alive. I told him protocol was for me to detonate the basket right there at the market. I was not lying to my handler. We should not be alive.

28th Day of Sha'ban

"You are beautiful," Fatima said as she lay beside me.

"Feral dogs you find beautiful?" I replied.

"Then if that is how you see yourself, you are the most beautiful of all the feral dogs."

I was unsure of how to respond. Finally, I found something to say. Something I had wanted to say when she first kissed me.

"Is this your first time with a girl?"

"Of course," she said. Though I remember smiling as if I believed her, I did feel her answer was untruthful. It did not bother me. Her lie, that is.

"Do you regret leaving Ayla?" I asked of her.

"No, I do not regret it," she said as she put a hand upon my cheek and started to caress my skin. I closed my eyes, her touch was like that of silk cloth. When I opened them again, I brought to her another question.

"Do you regret leaving your God?" Suddenly, she pulled back her hand from my cheek as if my cheek had become a hot stone.

"My father has been killed, but when asked if I had a father, I still must answer yes I did have a father."

"I am cold. Do you mind if I return to my clothes?" I replied as I felt a shiver run through my body.

"If you do not mind that I leave my clothes where they had fallen after you disrobed me."

I sat up and dressed. Twelve days had now passed since I had taken her into the tunnels. She blended in well. No one questioned her arrival. It meant that neither my handler nor the man had betrayed my confidence. I was grateful to them for that. And for that, I split half of my rations between them. They did not refuse. No one refuses food down here.

"I have to return to Ayla tomorrow," I told her.

"Who is it that you have to kill?" she asked.

"I am never told until the moment I go up," I lied. I was going back to the Grand Market for another attempt on the military commander's life. The General told me that my entrance back into the tunnels depended on Osmani's entrance into Jannah. Those words were not said lightly. They came like a stern warning from a father to daughter. They came with his finger pointing in my face and his spittle in my eyes as I stood against a wall in the command center.

"I will be waiting for your return," she said.

"And if I do not return?"

"Then I will go up into Ayla to find you."

"That would be a death sentence for you."

"We are already dead," said Fatima.

"Yes," I answered, "you are right. We are dead already. It is the suffering that still awaits us, though."

"Suffering is a gift. In it is hidden mercy."

"Rumi," I said, understanding that Fatima had quoted the 13th-century Sufi poet.

"You are taught well down here."

"One must know their enemy," I answered her as I knelt to give her a kiss goodbye.

As I lowered myself, she put a hand on the back of my neck and pulled me down so that I fell atop her. With her lips, she was not gentle this time. She was pressing into my teeth. For the first time, her touch was uncomfortable, and so I started to withdraw. And as I did so, she bit down upon my bottom lip. Blood she had drawn from me. I wiped it off and raised my hand to her. She did not flinch. Of course, she did not flinch. Pain and love she had already wedded long before me. I quickly stood up. She pulled a blanket over her body and rolled over.

29th Day of Sha'ban

The commander came looking for his eggs again. And I again came selling mine. On our way to the Grand Market, my handler and I came upon a gathering crowd. They were hurrying their steps from all directions. In Ayla, it meant only two things. Either it was for another speech or for another execution. As we were getting brushed and bumped by the rush of people, I tried to reroute our course around them, all the while keeping my eyes straight ahead. I wish now that I never would have stopped to see what was fascinating all of them. For when I did, I saw that three young boys were being strung up on wooden gallows. My handler grabbed my upper arm and squeezed it to the bone for me to keep moving along. It did not work. I was unable to move as if my feet were suddenly in thick mud. I broke from protocol and asked the woman in front of me what their offense was. She said they had been caught dancing. I returned my eyes to the boys who were now fifteen feet in the air with ropes around their necks. I could clearly see their faces. They did not even have the decency to cloak them. The one on the left had tears streaming down his cheeks. The one in the middle had a blank expression. It was the one on the right though that affected me the most. He was holding onto a red ball. A soldier was up there with him, trying to pry that red ball from his grasp.

A woman then ran up the steps of the gallows. One of the mothers, I presumed. She was immediately shot in the head. And then, as the soldier was finally able to unloosen the ball, the traps below their feet were released, not together but in some sort of sick sequence. The boys fell one at a time, each twisting in their own ways, each dying their own short deaths. At that moment, I swore the commander would not live another day, even if it meant that I would not live another day.

He was there, of course. The commander that is. I walked a straight path to him. When I got within ten or so feet, one of his guards held out an arm to stop my progress. I pushed past that guard and was immediately struck in the back by the butt of his rifle. The force of the blow sent me to the ground, but fortunately, I was able to keep hold of the basket. When I looked up, it was the commander himself offering me a hand. I took it, and he brought me back to my feet. His soldiers then encircled me, and he began to pick through the eggs in my basket, examining each one. And each one that did not meet his approval, he crushed in front of me and wiped the yolk on my abaya. I was not humiliated. This is war. In war, there is only survival. In the end, he chose six of my eggs, but not before lifting up my abaya and sticking two of his fingers inside of me. I gave him no reaction. He then pulled his two fingers out and wiped them on me too. The soldiers laughed and off he went.

"What would you have done if he didn't select any of your eggs?" the man asked.

"I would have taken out my knife and plunged it into his skinny neck."

The man nodded. I then looked over to Fatima.

"She has been asleep for hours," the man said.

"I told you she is harmless."

"It is day. Those who sleep in the day have dreams of the night."

"She is in my arms at night," I responded.

"Your arms have eyes?" the man replied.

19th Day of Ramadan

I woke up just as they were fitting me with a black hood. It had neither holes for my eyes nor one for my mouth. To secure it over my head, they looped a rope around my neck and tightened it so that I had to struggle for each breath I took. I was then pushed against the wall, where my hands were bound and some long garment of sorts placed on me. As we walked, I counted the footsteps and listened to their breaths. There were four soldiers escorting me. I wondered how they would kill me. I wondered if they had already killed Fatima. I wondered if the man would be there to bear witness to my death. I thought of the words to speak if they too thought the man responsible.

When I finally reached my destination of judgment, I was immediately met with such an onslaught of sound it could have been hell's battlefield they had escorted me onto. Underneath my feet, the ground shook as if hundreds of horses were galloping by. Accompanying the steeds, a thunderous pounding to urge them on. And while all this raged, I seemed to hear a fury of artillery being fired away in rapid succession that sent my head into a whirl.

"Goddamn, I don't think I missed a fucking note this time, did I, Translator," the voice said, and immediately I knew it to be that of the General.

"No, sir, you did not."

"Oh, you have no fucking idea how good that feels to finally nail that Hammett solo. Got to be up there with the best of 'em. Better than sticking my tongue in the prom queen. Better than picking off that sniper at the Mannheim Front. And even better than any shit I've ever taken. Fuck, I feel like going up there right now and shooting some fucking ragheads. All right, someone take my guitar, I've got business to attend to. Sergeant."

"Sir, we have—"

"I know who the fuck you have there, Sergeant. I'm the one who sent for her. Jesus Christ. Take that hood and abaya off of her. Keep her bound, though. She doesn't deserve the goddamn use of her arms."

As my hood was being removed, I was thinking I would have rather had them keep it on. For my offense, I did not want to meet the disapproving eyes of the General. I would rather meet a disapproving bullet from his gun. The man may have been a father to me, but the General was my mentor—a monolith of a man whom I had always looked up to ever since I had started my training. He is the one who believed that I, even at the age of fifteen, could carry out all of the missions that he had conceived. The General was now walking toward me, wiping the sweat from his face and head with a small black flag inscribed with white lettering of the enemy. He handed his towel over to a soldier, and the soldier handed him a glass that was filled with an amber liquid one quarter from the top.

"Do you even know why the fuck you're here?" he asked as he put a hand to his chin and cracked his neck from side to side.

My mouth had just opened to answer when he squeezed both my cheeks with one hand, and I had to swallow back the words I was just bringing up.

"Don't. Don't you dare. That was rhetorical. Don't say a goddamn word until I say you can say a goddamn word. You got that?"

I nodded my head.

"Good. Now, I'm going to tell you why you think you're here. And then, I am going to tell you why you really are. You think you're here because I found out you felt sorry for some Caliphate cunt and decided to bring her into our tunnels. Am I right?"

I nodded again.

"Exactly what I thought. However, the real goddamn reason is that I send you, my number one assassin, on a hit to take out Osmani. And instead of killing that motherfucker that day, you come back with their number one assassin. I mean if that isn't the perfect goddamn example of irony, I don't know what the fuck is. But, besides learning the meaning of irony tonight, we are also going to learn the meaning of the word serendipity. Anyone here want to give it a shot before I tell the whole fucking class?"

The man behind the drums raised one of his sticks in the air.

"PFC Thomas," the General said, calling upon him.

"Sir, serendipity is coming across something fortunate when you least expect it."

"Goddamn, Thomas, that was excellent. Not only have you been doing a yeomen's job on the kit lately, but it also seems you've got a fucking brain. Translator, give PFC Thomas a Kit Kat. Oh, I've got a joke for you, Thomas. What do you call a drummer who shows up at your door without a girlfriend?"

"Don't know, sir."

"Homeless. That's what the fuck you call him. All right. Where in the hell was I?"

"Serendipity, sir."

"Thank you, Translator. Yes, serendipity. Coming upon something in your favor when you least fucking expect it. So, not four hours ago, our reconnaissance team is returning from a mission. And lo and behold, as they are about to descend into one of our entrances, they are met by your new friend, who just happens to be leaving with a little souvenir she's taken from our tunnels. You want to take a guess at what she

34

decided to bring back with her to Shariaville after vacationing down here with us?"

I shook my head.

"Well, she decided to take back a Jew. Your Jew, to be specific. She had him bound and gagged and ready for delivery. I mean that's fucking beautiful. Not only do you infiltrate the enemy's stronghold, but you decide to return with a souvenir. All right. I'm done with this shit. Let's get on with it. I've got one more surprise for you. And believe me, sweetie, I've saved the goddamn best for last. Sergeant Martin, bring that Caliphate bitch in."

"Yes, sir," the sergeant replied.

Fatima was led in. Over her head, in disrespect, they had tied tight a plastic bag. Only a few pinholes they must have poked because I could see her working hard. The bag expanded little when she exhaled but was sucked deep into her mouth as she drew breath. Covering her body, the black and white flag of Ayla.

"Sergeant, unveil," the General said.

From arms to torso to feet, Fatima was covered in what at first glance appeared to be an elaborate design of black lines. I was thinking back to when I saw her body unclothed. But like a chameleon, she had changed her skin. It then struck me that for the last week she had never taken off her clothes. She had said the dampness and cold were starting to bother her.

"Take a good goddamn look," the General said as he dragged me by the hair and brought me before her. "Pretty fucking elaborate, isn't it? I mean when I first set eyes on that shit I thought this is the best fucking tattooed chick I've ever seen. I mean I got to admit I had a pretty big hard-on looking at her. But then, when I got closer, I realized it was a black marker, not ink. And at first, I thought, yeah, that's just too fucking cool, she's tatted herself in marker because up there in the Land of Allah there aren't too many goddamn tattoo parlors. That was until it dawned on me that what she fucking drew on herself isn't some fancy Arabic shit, it is actually . . . Anyone, anyone. Go ahead, Translator, you got your hand raised."

"It's a map, sir."

"Fucking right it's a map, Translator. A perfect rendering of our tunnel system. Go grab yourself a Kit Kat from the desk. Oh, and not any of the ones with white chocolate. Those are a bitch to come by lately. Goddamn towelheads seem to have a predilection for them."

He was absolutely right. Fatima had mapped out our entire tunnel system on her body. All night while the man and I slept, she must have been walking around.

"Corporal, grab that board in the corner and have a few of your men strap our guest to it. PFC Thomas, behind Translator I have some cleaning materials. Bring some rubber gloves, a few sponges, and that ammo box. Don't tilt the fucking box, though. It's filled with masonry cleaner. Which, if you don't know, is basically a mix of muriatic acid and water. So don't be spilling any of that shit. I breathe in enough crap around here as it is."

Fatima offered no resistance as they laid her supine on the board and secured her to it. When the plastic bag was removed from around her head, she searched her eyes about until they landed on mine. I expected a look of repentance. Instead, she stared back at me and turned her lips up into a smirk. Not a second later after that, she started screaming, "Allahu akbar." It was the most piercing and frightening sound I had ever heard.

"Oh Christ, I am so fucking tired of that 'Allahu akbar' shit you have no idea. It's got to be right up there with 'inshallah.' Fuck, if you didn't know better, you would think those were the only goddamn words in the Arabic language."

From his pocket, the General took out a handkerchief, dipped it in the ammunition box, and then stuffed it into Fatima's mouth. Her body writhed about as if she was being electrocuted. Then, her head slammed back down on the board she was strapped to, and her eyes rolled back into her head.

"First Sergeant Jensen."

"Yes, sir."

"When she comes to, wash that map off her body with the masonry cleaner and pour a few cups into her mouth. If she isn't dead by then, put a bullet in her head. And as for you," the General said as he looked at me, "I really don't give a rat's ass what you do. You want to stay and hold her hand while she dies, be my fucking guest. But she is going to die. Concerning the state of your future health, I'm not sure yet. But now wouldn't be the time to fucking ask. Understand?"

I nodded. And then from the corners of my eyes, I saw the man. He must have entered while Fatima was screaming. I only looked at him briefly and then quickly hurried my eyes away. At that moment, I wished for the same fate as Fatima.

2nd Day of Dhul-Qa'dah

I was placed in isolation. Complete darkness. No one was allowed to speak to me, and I was given one meal a day, if molded bread and rotten fruit can be considered such. I did not care, though. I welcomed the punishment. I would have welcomed death if my body had not fought otherwise. For the first fourteen meals or less, all I had in my head were thoughts of Fatima. Her betrayal was on me like my own skin. I wore it when I was awake, and I wore it in my dreams. Eventually, it passed. Eventually, I accepted that there was someone stronger than me, even if that someone was now dead. My fortieth meal I took through the slot. Two cooked eggs, a bowl of stewed rabbit, and a Kit Kat bar. The man let me finish eating before he spoke from the other side. He did not have to wait long. I devoured all of it within a minute or so.

"He is releasing you today," the man said as he handed me a cup.

"I do not deserve a release," I said after drinking the whiskey.

"There is a job for you."

"A suicide mission, I assume."

"They have all been suicide missions, have they not?"

"But some with more probability than others," I replied.

"Yes, that is true," he answered. "You are to kill the imam."

"I have had that mission before."

"This one is more personal. This time they want someone to sell you to him."

"He prefers boys," I said.

"They are going to make you a boy."

"Who is it that will sell me?" I asked.

"I will be the one."

"You are going to be my handler?"

"I volunteered."

"There was no one else, was there?"

"Yes, there were no others who wanted to go."

"No others who wanted to go with me you should have said."

"Someone will be here within the hour to clean you up."

"I am sorry."

He said nothing in return. I did not expect him to say anything in return.

5th Day of Dhul-Qa'dah

The man was playing a game of chess by himself when I awoke. My body was still cold from sleep, and so I threw on another sweater. I watched him for a little bit before finally deciding to have a few words with him. Since I had been released from isolation, we had barely spoken to each other. That was three days ago.

"I have decided to go alone. As a boy, I would not be in need of a handler. The Hisbah will not question it," I said to him. He moved a white knight into position but still kept the horse's head pinched between his fingers. After a minute of contemplation, he let it go and then spoke to me.

"And how you do plan on selling yourself. As a prostitute? They would execute you on the spot."

"And you, a Jew, whose Arabic is pitiful, how do you plan on offering me for sale?" The words had just left my mouth when I realized he had no intention of offering me for sale to the imam. "You do not plan on selling me, do you?"

"Arrangements have been made."

"I do not want your arrangements. I have brought this death upon myself."

"No one brings death upon themselves unless they hold their own knife."

"Fatima was my knife."

"You could not have known," he said in my defense.

"But you knew. That is the reason she was able to take you captive. You followed her, didn't you?"

"It was my own misstep. I did not realize she was aware of my presence."

"I will not have you sacrifice your life for mine," I said.

"It is not in my plan to trade my life for yours. It is in my plan to deliver you to someone who can then deliver you somewhere else."

"And you do not think the General will find out?"

"My lies and deceits I have always kept to myself. That way, there is no one else to spread the truth."

There was no point in continuing any further. I unclasped the cross and chain around my neck and set it on the ground between us. Before every mission, I always gave it to him for safekeeping. It was a not so subtle act to let him know my decision was final. Alone I was going up into Ayla to assassinate the imam.

"Where you have set it will be its final resting place," the man said after glancing at the cross and chain.

"It was but a trinket to me."

"Perhaps, but you have worn it like a wedding ring," the man replied.

"I have worn it in deference to the priest who gave it to me. And I have always found it odd that after handing me over to you, he removed it from his own neck and placed it around mine. It was just as odd as when my mother handed me over to him just after the invasion. We had never even set foot in a church before that."

"Neither was odd. Both were sensible actions considering the situation at the moment of each decision. Your mother thought you would be safer in the basement of a church, just as later on, the priest realized you would be safer in the cellar of my shoe store."

"How was it that you even became friends with him?"

"As you know, his church was only a block from my shoe store. Sometimes he would be there to buy shoes. Other times he would be there to just talk."

"And so why didn't he remain in the cellar with us?"

"Because he wanted to find your mother and bring her back with him."

"For what reason? They didn't even know each other."

"Of course they knew each other, child. Lives are not randomly saved."

"And why didn't you tell me this before?" I asked, a little surprised that the man had not mentioned it to me.

"Until now, the question was not asked."

"So if I were hungry, you would not offer me food until I requested it?" I asked him.

"Yes, that is correct. I would keep eating until famine became victorious over your silence. It is then I would offer you food. It is then I would know you are truly in need."

"How? How did he know her?"

"Certainly, at this point, you must have already deduced the answer to your own inquiry."

His words did not seem real. They came to my ears like a dream. How was it possible that I was the daughter of a priest? I asked the man a few more questions. He said for all he knew my father had confided in no one else but him. He said perhaps it was because they had become friends. He said perhaps it was because my father thought a Jew would understand. He said he had never told me because the past should never influence one's future. I didn't need to ask him why he had told me now. The answer to both of us was obvious.

I picked up the cross and walked out of there. As I wandered about the tunnels, a storm of thoughts raged inside my head. Should I now believe in God and renounce my sins? And would it even matter being the bastard child of a priest? Should I accept the man's offer and abort the mission? Or should I disremember the past and continue forward? I was moving fast, my head down. My shoulder struck something, and I was taken hold of and pushed up against a tunnel wall.

"Watch where you walk, boy. Next time I'll break one of your legs. Or both, maybe."

He finished by pressing the palm of his hand into my forehead and knocking the back of my skull against the wall. On any other day, I would have run after him and slit the back of both his legs. However, as he walked off, I couldn't seem to move. I could only watch the vestment he was wearing scrape the ground, continuing to add to the inch or so of sludge that was already there.

11th Day of Dhul-Qa'dah

A new imam has been appointed. The General allowed me to see her body. I will not forget her. For to forget her would be akin to having her die a second time.

2   THE GENERAL AND THE TRANSLATOR

I was deep down in a dream. My mind was replaying the day the drones came. I knew it was a dream even though I was asleep. I knew it because my mind plays it frequently.

I awoke that Chicago Christmas morning to a loud assembly of voices coming through the window of my Rogers Park apartment. I rushed out of bed to see what all the commotion was about. There on my neighborhood street, it seemed everyone was out except for me. They all were looking at the sky, but from my view, I couldn't see what was capturing their interest. I didn't bother to get dressed. I only bothered to throw on my purple and white Northwestern hoodie. As I stepped outside, I looked up to see hundreds of drones flying by. Some had a trailing banner that read "PEACE ON EARTH." The other drones were dropping fake snow from their underbellies. People are so easily amused I thought and walked back inside.

That was the real part of that complex dream. That was the part my mind recreated so accurately. The imaginary part is where I start running down the street screaming at them to get back inside. I yell at them that it is a ruse. I yell at them that soon they are all going to die. I am tearing my lungs out saying how half-witted can everyone possibly be. I was deep down in that dream when I awoke gasping for air. A hood had been placed over my head. I began to flail my arms and legs about, but my body was rudely turned over, and my hands were fastened behind my back.

I was lifted to my feet and led out of my quarters. I guessed it was probably about two or three in the morning. This was my guess because my circadian rhythms haven't varied much from when I was living above, and also because my body was still in need of sleep. I wasn't frightened, though. What I figured is that this must have something to do with my recent graduation.

Three weeks prior, I had completed the Sector 4 class on Arabic and Islamic Studies. By all standards, the three-month course was intense and exhausting. Twelve of us in total. Classroom instruction was taught by four different teachers, 16-hour days, seven days a week. We ate, slept, and did our mandatory calisthenics in there. The only time we were allowed out was for bathroom breaks. Each of us there had some prior background. Mine had come from college, where I had minored in Arabic, majored in economics. At the time, I thought it would prepare me for a world that was just coming to terms with the new Caliphate. Like the rest of us, I believed they had finally abandoned their doctrine of terror and were ready to assimilate into a world of global trade and peaceful coexistence. We were all fools. And I, now as I write this, even more of one for graduating first from the Sector 4 class. A girl that I had befriended there finished the class dead last, and she was given a position in the Department of Excavation. Right now, I would have gladly taken that assignment.

We walked along. It was obvious I was not going to be spoken to. It was also obvious I was not to speak to them. We passed through a series of checkpoints. At each, my two guards spoke their names and then when asked for the code, answered with "Ride the Lightning." Finally, after about fifteen minutes, I heard the code uttered once more and then the opening of what I think to be a door. I find that strange and believe my mind is playing a trick on me. I haven't heard the opening of a door since before I descended into the sewers.

The hood was removed, and I found myself staring into a large room. It is our command center I can only assume, but not one I would have imagined if told beforehand that it was my destination. It is neatly divided into five separate areas. At the far wall as I look straight ahead, it is a garage band setup of musical equipment with a foot-high stage. To my right, it is a philosopher's hideout with shelving of books and a long tattered couch. Off to the left, it's a voyeur's nest of computers and video screens. Behind me, as I glance over a shoulder, a devil's bunker of weapons and ammunition. And finally, in its geographic center, there is a large table made up of long wooden planks that are supported underneath by wooden construction horses. On it, a map laid out with plastic army men, plastic tanks, and plastic military vehicles grouped together and spread all about. It would have brought a smile to my face if not for the interrogation that was taking place off to my immediate right.

There, I see an Ayla man unclothed, perhaps in his late twenties, strapped to a chair. There are streaks of blood down the left side of his neck, the side where an ear had once been. His eyes are squinted, not from the light, but from the swelling around his sockets. It is then I notice beneath his legs, which are shackled, a bank of car batteries.

While there are two probes clipped to his genitals, only one of the probes is attached to a terminal. So, he is temporarily disconnected from the circuit. There, on the floor, I also see his missing ear and a few teeth scattered about. The rush of last night's meager fare begins its journey from my stomach to my esophagus. I taste the decay but somehow manage to force it back down. I do not want to look weak.

"I'm just not buying it. You manage your way into our sewers, strapped with thirty pounds of explosives, and you say it was of your own volition. You must think I'm a complete fucking idiot. Now, who sent you?"

It is the general speaking in Arabic, though while not perfect, it could be understood on the streets. It is the general I know because he fits the legend that everyone speaks of. He is everything I have heard of him and more. He is a few inches over six feet. From the deep parenthetical lines on his face and white hair of his crew cut, I put him in his mid-sixties. But his body belies his age. It is a massive build that looks as menacing as an Abrams tank. Even unloaded, his biceps stretch the short sleeves of his camouflage uniform well beyond their capacity. His arms are decorated in full-sleeve tats. An angel on his left forearm is the most prominent. Above it is a single eye, below it two cupped hands. Then higher up on that same arm, the Latin words for "Gift from God." Though he is standing still, I can only imagine that when he walks the earth beneath him begins to shake.

"There is only one God and Muhammad is his prophet," the prisoner spits out.

"Oh Christ, will somebody please cut off his other goddamn ear," the general says, obviously now becoming exasperated with the prisoner's declaration of faith that I can only assume has been a constant refrain throughout the interrogation.

Though the prisoner is bound to a chair, one of the other soldiers walked behind him and took hold of his shoulders. Another one then fit an already bloodied bandana across his mouth and tied it tight at the back of his head. A third soldier then began a sawing of his remaining ear. It is an act of duty by the soldier as I did not see any emotion whatsoever from him. The prisoner rattled about as if he was being jolted by a current of electricity. It was over in thirty seconds or so, and the last of his hearing apparatuses was summarily tossed to the ground. The general, in the corner of the room, his back to the prisoner, started shaking his head before speaking in Arabic again.

"I have to say, I am curious as to your thoughts right before this uneasy death I am about to serve upon you. Do you actually believe there are seventy-two virgins waiting upon your arrival?"

The general then walked over to him and took to a knee.

"I mean you don't look like an asshole to me. In fact, I see a lot of similarities between us. I see the resolve, the valor, the warrior. But there is one major difference. And it's not religion. It's just plain goddamn horse sense. Because I sure the fuck know if someone promised me seventy-two virgins if I blew myself up, the first thing I would have asked for is photos. Not that I haven't hogged it a few times. But seriously, what if you get to paradise and find that all these girls are eighty years old and just the ugliest fucking hags you have ever seen. So ugly that no one wanted to fuck them and that's the reason they're still virgins. Did that ever cross your mind? Cause I don't think it ever did. And do you know what I think that makes you then?" The general then took his hands and squeezed the cheeks of the prisoner. "It makes you a fucking . . . Translator. What is the Arabic word for dickhead?"

It was the first time since I had entered the room that the general had acknowledged me. I turned to the soldier by my side and quietly told him I did not know the Arabic word for dickhead.

"Sir, he doesn't know the word for dickhead."

"Then tell him to just give me the fucking word for dick and I'll use that."

I gave the word to the soldier, and he relayed it to the general. After the general spoke it, the prisoner managed a smile. Two ears missing, face bruised and bloodied, testicles one connection from a painful end, and still, he puts forth a smile. I found it incredibly hard to believe. The general promptly reciprocated with a smile of his own. Then, he walked behind the prisoner and started to rub the bearded area of his face, as if he was prepping him for a shave. Before I knew it though, the general had unsheathed a long-bladed knife from his belt clip and slit the man across the throat. The blood jetting out from his carotid arteries caused me to wretch and leave last night's meal on the floor in front of me.

"Jesus Christ!" the general shouted as he looked at me over the dying prisoner. "Someone get him something to wipe that fucking mess up."

While I was waiting for one of the soldiers to find me some cleaning materials, I watched as the general returned to a position in front of the prisoner. Now he was crouching before him. He was watching him die, but not in a sadistic manner at all. It was as if he was saying to all of us, if you're going to kill someone like that, then have respect for it, embrace it, and understand that by all of heaven's justice it is in all likelihood that you will meet the same fate. The last exhalation from the prisoner finally came, and the general stood up.

"Get him the fuck out of here. Bathe him and send him to the Lime Line before sundown, whenever the fuck that is."

The guards unfettered the prisoner from the chair, placed him into what looked like a laundry bag, and were starting to haul him out of the command center when the general shouted.

"Set the goddamn bag down and remove the body!" The two soldiers did as ordered, and the general spoke again. "Corporal James!"

"Yes, sir."

"I want you to take a look in the bag and tell me how many ears you see in there." The corporal got on his knees and began inspecting the inside of the bag. "You only got one in there, don't you?"

"Yes, sir. Only one."

"And do you know how the fuck I know there's only one in there, Corporal James."

"No, sir, I do not."

"Because the other one is still lying on the floor by the leg of the fucking chair we tied him to. Now go over there, pick it up, and place it in the bag. Goddammit, Corporal. Show death some respect. It was earned."

I was out of my head at that moment. I couldn't grasp onto anything of that which I had just witnessed. Fortunately, a soldier came over and handed me a bucket and a couple of rags. I was grateful for the cleaning duty. It gave me something else to occupy my thoughts with.

After I finished wiping up my vomit, I decided to keep going and started in on the blood and urine near the prisoner's chair. The general had gone over to a metal storage cabinet in the back of the command center and took out a bottle of Scotch, from which he poured himself a drink into a Manhattan glass. He then sat down on the couch, which was to the right of me. It was almost like he had entered another room. And it reminded me of when I was a child, sitting on the floor in the living room while my father was having his nightcap.

I had already used up my quota of stealing looks in the direction of the general, so I put my head down and hurried to clean the last few square feet that I had left. I was perspiring profusely now, and my eyes were blurry from the sweat. I raised my sleeve to wipe away the film so I could see more clearly. And after doing so, I noticed that on the wall to my left hung a framed painting of Picasso's "The Old Guitarist." I had seen it many times as a child and teenager, on field trips to the Art Institute. It always struck me as the most poignant of the collected pieces. To me, there was nothing in the world that captured the loneliness of life more than that painting. I remember it made me want to die young. It evoked feelings inside of me that I never knew existed. I was so locked onto its magnetism and transcendence that I didn't even realize the general was now speaking to me.

"It's fucking real in case you're wondering," he said.

"How did you—" I started to ask.

"I went there my goddamn self and retrieved it. About two years ago. Only had to kill three of those fucking sand monkeys to bring it back. It was the one piece I didn't want to see destroyed. The rest of the shit in there I couldn't have given a fuck about. Doesn't even come close to this masterpiece. You know anything about Picasso?"

"A little. I—"

"That goddamn Spaniard was around twenty-two when he did that. Who the fuck knows that much about death and suffering at that goddamn age. At twenty-two, the only thing I was thinking about was banging chicks and drinking beer. This guy was looking into fucking souls and God was noticing. He took hold of Picasso's little hands and laid down the brush strokes for him. He said listen, motherfucker, you want to live this, this is the note that life resolves itself onto. You're alone and you don't have a fucking chance. And whether you like it or not, this is how I set this world up."

I didn't know what to say. I wasn't even sure if the man before me was real. If he had said he was the Archangel Michael himself, I would have half-believed it. I did know though that while I wanted no part of being his personal translator, at the same time, I felt no safer in these freight tunnels than at any other time. This was God's son of the Old Testament. This was Moses with an M4 in one hand and a grenade launcher in the other. This was the man who would ensure all of our deaths would not be in vain.

"Get on your goddamn feet. And no more of that pussy shit. You hear me. I can get by speaking their fucking language, but unfortunately, I can't read it. So, I need someone to replace the last motherfucker I had here."

I nodded and stood. I had no intention of inquiring as to what had happened to the last motherfucker who held the position. He then set his glass down and walked over to where I was standing. My cheeks he took between his forefinger and thumb, squeezing so hard that I found my tongue being pinched. I fixed my eyes on his eyes, knowing that's what he wanted from me. I expected black but was surprised to find the irises the color of blue lace agate. Like everything about him, it was another contradiction.

"Good, because you're mine now," he said and let go of my cheeks. "Lance Corporal Bates," he then called out.

"Sir," the soldier replied as he hurried over and stood beside the general.

"Put that hood back on him and escort him home. After that, go get him a uniform from the storage area. PFC Thomas will be waiting for you with further instructions."

"Yes, sir."

"Translator," the general said as he turned to me. "Start packing up when you get there. You'll be moving tomorrow."

"Yes, sir," I said.

"Oh, and welcome to the United States Marine Corps of Sector 4, son," he then said to me. "You're one of us now."

I didn't want to be one of us now. I didn't even want to be me now. But what choice did I have? I nodded my fidelity and then was promptly hooded before being led away.

∞ ∞ ∞

After arriving at my quarters, the lance corporal left to find me a uniform. I sat down on the floor and put my head to the wall. I would have started to bang it against the clay if not for the other four people who were asleep there. I was still nauseous and I was still shaking. I felt as if I had just returned from a slaughterhouse, not of animal but of man. My thoughts had become my own enemy and to retain my sanity, I knew I needed to quickly befriend them. I certainly didn't want to be a part of this, but now I no longer had a choice.

Whether it be naiveté or self-deception, I was unaware that our tactics were just as brutal as theirs. Were we no better? Perhaps it is just mankind I began to think. This is what we have always been and forever will be. We are cruel and inherently we are beasts. It would be hard to flip a page of history and argue to the contrary. But pacifism I understood isn't a choice in a war such as this war. It would bring about our extinction. And maybe, really, that is all this life is about—survival. If one must fight savagery with savagery, then so be it. And we were already standing on the cliff of extinction. The general understood this. I was still having trouble with it.

I began to gather up my things. It didn't take more than a few minutes. My two sets of clothes were already in a black shoulder bag, the same bag I had taken with me during the invasion. The same bag I had over my shoulder as I ran from building to building looking for sanctuary after the Mannheim Front had finally collapsed. I tossed in four books: one on the general history of Islam; another an Arabic-English dictionary; the third and most important in a plastic cover—a Neal Adams signed DC Comics' book from 1978 entitled "Superman vs. Muhammad Ali." Lastly, "The Wealth of Nations" by Adam Smith. I remember joking to a girl I was hitting on while attending a Northwestern frat party that those four books would be my desert island collection. She rolled her eyes and smartly walked away. I assume she's dead now, most likely as is everyone else who attended that bash at Sig Alpha Ep. I do hope their deaths were merciful though, unlike the prolonged and inhuman one I now envision for myself.

I glanced at my watch. It was 3:17 a.m. For some reason, I don't remember my last thoughts or my last words when I am going through a life change, but I do remember the exact time. When my father died of pancreatic cancer, my twelve-year-old eyes read the death certificate to see that the hospice RN had called the time of death at 4:25 a.m. After pinning Tommy Gagnon in eighth grade for my only first-place win, the clock on the gymnasium wall had the upset at 5:19 p.m. When my mother drove away after helping me unpack in my dorm room it was 2:14 p.m. When the girl I spoke of above broke from the conversation it was 1:17 a.m.

"They recruited you, haven't they?"

"Yes, they recruited me," I answered as I looked in the direction of the voice. From where I was sitting, I could tell the words were coming from a far corner of the room. Even with your eyes dilated, darkness down in the freight tunnels can be infinite. Though I could not see, I knew who it was. I had spoken to him on a few occasions.

"Did you meet him?" the voice said, and I understood he was

referring to the general.

"Yeah, I met him," I said softly so not to wake the family of three who also shared the same quarters.

"Is he like what they say he is like?"

"He is that and he is more," I said.

"They say he's crazy. They say he's going to get us all killed sooner than heaven has planned."

"Those who say that haven't met him then."

"Do you think you'll get to go up there?"

"I don't think so. They are using me only to translate, not to fight."

"I want to be up there again. I want to feel the sun on my face."

"I know. Me too," I said.

"When you see him again, tell him he can use me. I'm ready."

"You're needed on the line," I answered, referring to the food line where he was stationed.

"All they have to do is point me in the right direction. The first word of Arabic I hear, I'll set it off."

"Don't be ridiculous. We don't run suicide missions. You know that."

"I don't want to live like this anymore."

"None of us want to live like this anymore."

"Please," he entreated.

I didn't know what to add after that, so I didn't add anything. I kept in silence, a cowardly silence now that I think about it. But I could offer him no comfort. He was maybe nineteen or twenty years of age. I had never asked. Most of the time you don't want to keep speaking too long for fear it might turn into a relationship. This is not a place for relationships. From the few conversations we had, I could only surmise that he was already blind when he got here. Most likely during the invasion as he did speak of things he once saw.

A lantern of light appeared outside the entrance. The lance corporal had returned. He parted the curtain and entered, after which he handed me a uniform and a pair of black boots. As I took them from his hands, I noticed the camouflage shirt had a dark stain at the neckline. The lance corporal also noticed it.

"I'll find you another one tomorrow," he said to me and then lowered the light just enough so I could no longer see the dried blood.

I wondered how old he was. The one who had last worn this uniform that is. I wondered how he had died. Was he shot in the head? Did the blood drip from the corner of his mouth? Did they drag his body back from Ayla or was he found in the sewers just above us?

"Be at the commissary at 11:55 a.m. Two soldiers will be there to greet you," the lance corporal then said. "Here's an envelope. You'll be asked for the code word inside."

After he left, I looked over to the kid. I felt him looking back. We both knew I wasn't going to make a case to the general for his suicide. I probably should have though. His death was imminent. His left eye had been infected for the last two weeks. In a day or two, maybe a week, it would spread throughout his body. They would take him to the infirmary. A shot of penicillin perhaps if they happened to have some. A morphine tablet or two to hold his hand while death circled above him. I wasn't sure whether I envied him or not. The fierce pain that would visit him certainly not. But the freedom that came after that, yes, maybe. It all depended, I suppose. Depended on whether you believed that there was truly a heaven after this. And then why, why was it necessary to die so miserably just to reach a better place? If any one of us was cast as God, we certainly would have fashioned a more benevolent ending.

∞ ∞ ∞

The alarm on my watch went off at 11:00 a.m. There was now no one there with me. The two children were already at school. Their mother was also gone, now five hours into her day at the hydroponics lab. The kid, to whom I had spoken with late in the night, of his whereabouts I could only venture a guess. Depending on his will, he had either reported to work at the food line or decided that his last days on this earth would be more comfortably spent lying supine on a makeshift cot in the infirmary. I was actually glad they were all gone. I did not want to say any goodbyes. I just wanted to leave. A callousness I could start to feel forming over me. Not unlike the ones that slowly began to cover the tips of my fingers after I had decided to pick up my guitar again back when I was a college kid. Jesus, what I wouldn't give to be living once more in a time of studying and campus sin.

∞ ∞ ∞

I had already walked a half-mile or so when I heard loud voices up ahead. I wasn't close enough yet to see any faces. The voices were of two men. That I could discern. Whether it was a friendly conversation or a heated exchange, I could not tell as the acoustics down here act to amplify and exaggerate all sounds. They could have just been workers from the Department of Streets and Sanitation, discussing how miserable their existence was.

When I made the turn around the bend, I saw there were actually three people and not two. One man had his hand on the throat of a teenage girl, and the other was brandishing a knife. I dropped my bag and stood as if I was a soldier, hoping they would disperse immediately.

They did not. Although, the man holding the young girl's throat did let go of it, and the other lowered the knife to his side. I looked to the girl and watched as she eased herself down the wall, then proceeded to wrap her arms over her knees and place her chin upon her chest.

I bridged the distance slowly, inserting myself between the one near the girl and the one brandishing the knife. My eyes bounced around the three of them a few times before I finally spoke.

"I'm under the direct command of the general," I said in hope that the mention of his name alone would cause them to disperse.

"So fucking what," the man who had been holding her throat replied.

"Her offense?" I asked, then checked the man with the knife to ensure he had not moved any closer. Even a small wound here could be fatal.

"Look. Look at her goddamn belly."

"What is it with her belly?" I asked.

"Are you goddamn blind?" he said. "Don't you see it?"

I honestly did not notice it when I first came upon them. A trick of the light I presume. Or perhaps I was just focusing on their eyes. But when he proceeded to free her arms from around her knees and then stepped a foot upon them to straighten her legs out, I immediately saw that she was eight months in bloom. I could also see her ankles were bound with some bike chain of sorts and secured with a padlock.

"Which one of you put this restraint on her? My God, she's pregnant. Have you lost your minds?"

"We had nothing to do with that. She has been chained like that for months."

"Why?" I asked.

"Because the Caliphate whore keeps trying to escape."

I slowly crouched down beside her. Even though I had set a hand of comfort upon her shoulder, she still did not make her face known to me.

It was then I noticed she was fingering a black rosary in one hand and Islamic prayer beads of olive wood in the other. The contradiction I would soon come to understand.

"I am going to see the general. I will take her there. Let him decide what to do with her."

"You may take her, but it will not be while her lungs are filled with air."

I had removed my eyes for a time longer than I should have from the man with the knife. He was now behind me and the flat of the long blade across my neck.

"What will killing one Caliphate girl accomplish?" I said.

"I did not say she was from the Caliphate. I said she was a Caliphate whore, seeded by one of them above. We barely have food and water for ourselves. We are not feeding one of their mouths."

"The child to be born is unaware of which God it is to follow," I said, though I truly had no conviction of the words I had spoken.

"It will know no God. And that will be the best for it."

We all knew that would be the last line he would deliver. From his pocket, he took out a screwdriver, of which I understood was about to be plunged into her throat. I had no other choice but to gamble. I reached up to grab the wrist of the man behind me. His hand I directed toward the leg of the other. After the knife had entered his thigh, I pulled it back out and hurried to my feet. The man who was behind me fled. The other gave a look that made me believe that if an infection did not set in, he would be back for either me or her. I started to regret the decision to stop their intentions. Enemies you do not want here. Eventually, you will encounter them again.

The next few minutes I tried unsuccessfully to free her from the bike chain shackling her ankles. I could not pick the lock with the tip of the knife, and it would have been futile to try and sever a link of the chain.

"What they say is true," she said. I turned to find she had finally raised her head so that I could see her face. My God, she looked even younger than I had originally thought.

"What is true?" I asked.

"That I am a Caliphate whore. Within my belly is a Caliphate child. But I will not part with it. It is from God. Praise be to Him," she uttered in this voice that I swear came with some sort of reverb. I remained silent. "You can go now. Do not worry about me. God will protect us. He has told me."

"I am not leaving you here," I replied. "Come on, let's go. They might return."

I helped her to her feet, and we walked for a bit. However, with her ankles bound, we were not putting enough distance between us and the spot where I had found her. So, I lifted her in my arms and started to carry her. My arms weakened quickly though, and I had to put her down. I looked back from where we had come and thought I heard voices. It seemed wise to just get off the path. The next residence we came upon we entered. I ushered her to a seat on the ground. From my shoulder bag, I took out a piece of bread and offered it to her, along with a plastic bottle of water. She shook her head, then fixed her eyes on something off to my left. I followed her gaze and saw that we were not alone.

The woman met my eyes and then looked over to the girl, after which she stood up and began to walk toward us. I couldn't keep my eyes off of her. The red dress she was wearing hugged her body tight. She had the figure of a teenage girl but her face, while still beautiful, had run ahead to about forty years of age. She had red hair. The ends of it fell over her breasts, which were half exposed and still firm. I could hardly believe what I was seeing.

She knelt and placed her hand on the girl's cheek. The girl smiled. I was looking at her ivory-pained nails when my nose began to twitch. Frankincense. That is what she smelled like. I knew the scent well. After my graduation, I had traveled to Israel for a month. In the Old City, in the markets of the Jewish and Muslim quarters, it burned day and night.

"You may go to your business. I will look after her now," she said to me in an Eastern European accent that I guessed could have been either from Ukraine or from the Russian Federation.

"They want to kill her," I said.

"They will kill no one," she answered with a bit of a huff and imperiousness that dismissed my admonition.

"I'll leave you this knife."

"We do not need it," she said, using the pronoun to indicate she had already claimed possession of the girl.

"Fine then. I'll be back after my shift with something to remove that padlock."

"It will be gone by then."

I gave the girl one last look and stood up. I was about to cross the door when I turned my head over my shoulder. The girl already had placed her head against the bosom of the woman as if mother and daughter had been reunited.

As I began walking to the commissary, the unsettling words of the young girl returned to my head: "Within my belly is a Caliphate child. But I will not part with it. It is from God. Praise be to Him. You can go now. Do not worry about me. God will protect us. He has told me." When I first heard them spoken, I was still shaken from having a knife at my throat, so I didn't have the time to really think them through. Now, as I was walking alone, they became a disturbing companion. What could she have meant by saying it was from God? Did she truly believe that with a sane mind, or was it just a delusion of a frightened young pregnant girl?

I reached the commissary at 11:53 a.m. It was lunchtime, so there was a line of people waiting to make use of their work credits for items such as soap, candles, shoes, underwear, and some snack items if available. No real food though per se. Real food was distributed solely at the food line and meted out only by ration cards, which were equally distributed at the first of every week. Most of the time, that was the only way one knew that another Monday had arrived. Needless to say, there was a thriving black market for what could be eaten or drank. While illegal according to our bylaws, no one to my knowledge had ever been brought up on charges.

The line as always looked like one that was leading to an infirmary rather than for one that was leading to a store of necessities. Few spoke, and understandably so, for what really was to be said. I saw the soldiers arrive and I walked over to them. I handed them my identification papers, and after reviewing them, they asked for the password. I opened the envelope and said, "Search and Destroy." We moved on. I counted three bends along the freight tunnels when I was rudely pushed up against a wall. There I was frisked. There they bound my hands and placed a hood over my head. The general wasn't taking chances. And why should he? I could have easily been one of them.

∞ ∞ ∞

As soon as I arrived, he dismissed my escorts and shoved into my chest a stack of notebooks written in Arabic.

"Put these in English and have them on my desk by the end of the evening."

"Yes, sir," I said and then saluted him.

"You got a fucking date, Translator?"

"No, sir," I said.

"Then put that salute away and sit your ass down somewhere. This isn't a goddamn take-home assignment. I lost three men retrieving those. They're from a post just outside the city. Pretty fucking important, I'm guessing."

"Yes, sir," I answered.

I got to work immediately. The general was right. They were pretty important. The notebooks contained troop movements, a roster of new recruits for a buildup in the city they were starting, correspondence from high-ranking Ayla officials, and some information that detailed our latest attacks in the city. While I was working, I kept glancing over to him. He had taken off his uniform jacket and was on a bench lifting weights. In between reps, he sat there re-stringing a guitar. When he finished with both, he stripped out of his camouflage shirt. The silver cross and chain that had oddly been in his shirt pocket and not around his neck fell to the floor. He didn't notice, and so while he was pulling out a new shirt from a desk drawer, I went over and picked it up.

"You finished already?" he asked after turning around.

"No, sir. Your cross and chain. It fell out of your pocket while you were removing your shirt."

I held out my palm, and he swiped it into his own.

"Thanks, Translator," he replied and placed it in the pocket of his new shirt.

"You're welcome, sir."

I didn't leave at first. I was having trouble reconciling the cross and the man. They didn't seem to belong together.

"You got something else to say?"

"No, sir."

"Then why the fuck are you still standing there?"

"I was just wondering about the cross, sir. You don't seem like . . ."

"Like the type who would have a cross?"

"Well yes, sir," I answered. "Something like that."

"Since you're so goddamn inquisitive, the cross was given to me by my grandmother when I was nine. She unclasped it from around her neck in a hospital room and placed it in my palm a few hours before she died. It's a fucking gift of remembrance, nothing more. If she had handed over her fucking dentures, then that's what I would have in my goddamn pocket. Now get the fuck back where you were."

"Yes, sir."

∞ ∞ ∞

I started back in on my translating of the notebooks. The troop movements and build-up near the edge of Ayla I learned were due to a threat from another faction that was nearing the city. This faction appeared to be staking a claim to Ayla. It took me another three hours or so to complete. I then composed a summary for the general. I brought it to his desk and placed it in front of him.

"A little fucking summary. Goddamn. Good work, Translator. The last motherfucker just handed over the translated documents and left me to read through all the other shit."

"What do you think?" I asked him after he lowered my two-page synopsis from his eyes.

"I'm not in this position to think, Translator. I am in this position to know. And I know that in a week's time there's going to be a war above our goddamn heads. And that's good for us. That will keep them occupied and off our ass for at least a little while. First Sergeant Johnson."

"Yes, sir," a young man immediately replied as he stood up from his position at a long table where the computers were.

"Get your ass over here and escort Translator to his new quarters. I'm done with him for the day."

"Do you want me to bind and hood him, sir?" the first sergeant asked.

"No, I want you to take his goddamn hand into yours and whisper into his ear all of our little secrets. Of course fucking bind and hood him, Johnson. This motherfucker just translated a stack of Caliphate documents like he had been born in Saudi Arabia. The last thing I need to wake up to tomorrow morning is a thousand fucking towelheads outside my command center waiting to light me on fire."

First Sergeant Johnson walked off to the back of the command center. In the interim, I stood there by the general's desk and watched as he reached in a drawer, took out a Bible and started reading from a point where he had placed a bookmark. I suppose I didn't realize I was watching him. It was just that, as with the cross he was toting, I couldn't seem to understand the juxtaposition of a man of war reading a book of God. His eyes floated off the page and fell onto mine.

"Now I suppose you want to know why the fuck I'm reading this, don't you? Right now, I'm betting you're thinking I'm some kind of Jesus freak."

"No, sir. That's not exactly what I'm thinking."

"Then what the fuck are you exactly thinking?"

"I'm just wondering whether you actually believe in God or if you're just studying him."

"That's good, Translator. I suppose I would be pondering the same goddamn thing if I were you. To tell you the truth though, I'm not really sure. All I know is that if there is a God, He sure does like a good fucking war. Think of all the battles that have been waged in history while He's been at the helm. And He never steps in right away. He always watches and waits. Waits for the stones to be thrown, the arrows to be shot, the cannonballs to be fired, the mortar shells and rockets to be launched, the chemical weapons to explode, the atomic bombs to be dropped, and now the biological agents to be delivered. You believe in that God, Translator, you better ready yourself for heaven because it sure as hell isn't likely to be as peaceful as everyone's been saying. This guy's got a voyeur's penchant for watching destruction, and there's no sober reason to think that if He does exist, His kingdom is filled with flowing fucking rivers and endless fields of lavender. My best guess is that when we arrive there, He is going to give us a big old salute, hand us a perfectly tailored military uniform, and then proceed to tell us which fucking team we're on."

I didn't know what to say after that. The words left me dumbfounded and rattled. Not because they at first seemed so outrageous, but because they seemed so logically constructed. This couldn't have been the first time man had contemplated this. Certainly, on some tablet, in some scroll, in some text or in some e-mail, another one of us had postulated a heaven such as this. It couldn't possibly have been given birth today. First Sergeant Johnson returned. He hooded and bound me. My first full day was over.

Entry #2

The next day I awoke early. I was in my new quarters now, in which I was the only occupant. A luxury and privilege here. But an accommodation necessitated by the work I was going to be doing. I'm certain the general ordered it. If there was any translating I had to take home, he wouldn't have wanted any other eyes to fall upon the papers.

I walked over to the Department of Occupancy and Vital Records to give notice that I had moved. A requirement for those of us who changed quarters. For some reason, they had no record of me but would enter my new address. On my way back, I found an official envelope pinned to the wall. It said I was to report to the Department of Excavation until further notice. I started to give it thought but then realized if it was truly a reassignment, and the general had been displeased with my services, then I would have been evicted from my new place of residence.

The Department of Excavation was ball-busting work. It was twelve-hour days of either carving out the clay earth just on the other side of the tunnel walls or hauling it away. Rumor had it that we were trying to link up with a Sector 3, which rumor also had was situated to our south. I'm not one for rumors down here. You hear so many of them that eventually you stop believing in their validity. The girl from my course on Arabic and Islamic Studies was still there. For the first few days, we just exchanged glances. On the third day, we started to copulate. There weren't any long discussions and there wasn't any intimacy. We barely even kissed. After our long days, I would follow her back to her quarters. She would lay down, turn on her side to face the other way, and bring her pants and underwear to her knees. I would pull down my own and hold on to her at the waist. She would be in her own head, and

I would be in mine. We didn't want love. We didn't want commitment. We only wanted the mutually agreed upon touch of another human being. We only wanted that ephemeral flash of release that pushes out everything else you had been thinking about.

∞ ∞ ∞

After my tenth day at the Department of Excavation, I was awoken, hooded, bound, and taken away. It was 5:55 a.m. when I entered the command center. The place was already a hive of activity. I sat in the corner of the room at the desk where a sheet of paper had been taped to a wall that said "TRANSLATOR." My place had now been permanently assigned, as far as one could define permanent down here. The general was pacing about from one end of the room and then back to the other. He reminded me of a cougar I had seen at a zoo once, except for the knife in his hand. That my cougar didn't have. Strapped to the interrogation chair this time was an Ayla woman. Her niqab and abaya were on the floor, leaving her covered with only a very modest beige undergarment, which was embroidered at the chest. I guessed her to be mid-thirties. She was quite thin and wearing black-framed glasses. She wasn't bruised and she still had both her ears. They must have just started the interrogation I thought.

"Goddamn fucking rats. It never ends. You kill one, you kill twenty, it doesn't seem to matter. They just keep coming back again and again and fucking again. Rats with thobes, rats with uniforms, rats no older than nine, rats from Iran, rats from Yemen, and now a rat with a black abaya carrying an AK-47," the general said to all of us. "And why in the fuck do they keep coming through our sewers. None of the other sectors seem to have this much activity."

My eyes left the general for a moment as I focused on that last sentence. It was true then. There were other sectors beneath Ayla. And in that, I found some comfort. Comfort that all of us here weren't alone. A macabre comfort that we weren't the only ones being hunted and slaughtered. Then I began to think of my mother and younger sister. Perhaps plausible it was that they had found refuge in another sector. In the beginning, I had scoured Sector 4 looking for them. It was a quest of insanity that lasted for three months. Insanity because no one from the suburbs had made it in after the invasion. But if there were other sectors here, then why wasn't it possible that we had sectors everywhere. Stop, I then told myself. You know better. Hope, that's what all gods fit inside the hearts and minds of those they create to keep them obedient and faithful. It's only a ruse from above though. A Trojan horse if you will. Once inside, it may seem like a gift, but in the end it's only filled with disappointment, horror, and then death.

"Translator, come over here," I then heard from the outside world. It seemed distant and echoed. I ignored it at first. The next sound, though, was a puncturing scream that sent me down an embryonic river right back to where I was. "Goddammit, Translator, get your head out of your ass and get the fuck over here."

"Yes, sir," I said while rushing to my feet and bringing my body beside him.

"Jesus Christ, Translator. Where the fuck did you go?"

"Nowhere, sir," I replied.

"If I have to call your name more than once again I swear to fucking God I'm going to send you up there with a tattoo on your bare chest that reads: 'I Fucked the Imam's Daughter in the Ass.' You got that."

"Yes, sir."

"Good, now fucking translate this for me," the general said as he

70

reached in the front pocket of his shirt and handed me a folded piece of paper. "We found it stuffed in the panties of that cunt you see strapped to the chair."

I read it once. Then I read it again.

"Well?"

"It's a notice, sir. It says that any citizen of Ayla who captures an infidel from the sewers will be rewarded with two hundred gold coins. One thousand if the infidel is a Jew."

"Dead or alive, Translator? Do they need to bring us back breathing or with maggots crawling out of our ass?"

"It doesn't say, sir," I replied and handed him back the sheet of paper.

"So that's why the fuck they keep coming lately. They decided to turn the whole goddamn populace into bounty hunters. Holy shit, what a great fucking idea."

The general neatly folded up the notice, placed it back in his pocket, then set his hands on his hips. After a shake of his head that came with a puff of air through his nostrils, he unstrapped his side holster, and with a flick of his thumb, put the barrel of the massive silver gun to the side of her temple. Those who would be in the line of the exit wound hurried to their feet and moved to a safer location within the command center.

"You got anything to say before I blow your goddamn . . . ," the general began to say in Arabic. "Translator, give me the fucking word for 'brains.' "

"No need, sir," I answered.

"And just why the fuck is that?"

"She speaks English."

"And just how in the hell do you know that? You met her before? Went fucking falafel shopping with her and her uncle at the souk? Maybe the three of you went to afternoon prayer or something?"

"No, sir. The emotions on her face. They were in line with what you were saying. She understands."

"Is that true? You speak English?"

The woman nodded her head.

"Well goddamn, Translator. You are one observant motherfucker. First Sergeant Johnson, go in the second drawer of my desk and get a Kit Kat for our new recruit here. No, let me change that order. Get him two Kit Kats."

"Thank you, sir," I said, really the only thing I could say considering I was never one for sweets.

"All right, back to where I was. You have anything to say before I blow your goddamn brains out?"

"Please," she began in the most humble entreat I had ever heard, "may I have my children?"

The general looked around, perplexed at the request.

"And where the fuck are these children?"

"Taped to the inside of what I am wearing. You may lift it up. They are there."

"Well, thank you for the invitation."

The general lifted the undergarment. The three-by-five photo he ripped off and put it in front of her face. She looked at it for a moment and then nodded her head. The general dropped it from his hand, and as it floated to the floor, he pulled the trigger. The force of the bullet toppled both her and the chair.

I walked over and reached down. There, now in my hands, the photograph. In the picture, she was crouched wearing a hijab and a full coverage bathing suit. Behind her was nothing but a body of calm water, aquamarine in color. In her arms closely wrapped were two girls, one of maybe four years and the other no older than seven. One was holding up a plastic orange pail. The youngest had her small arms outstretched, palms up with a collection of seashells to show the person behind the lens. In the foreground to the left, the impression of three perfect sand angels. I wanted to run over to him, rip the gun out of his hand and shoot him in the chest. Instead, I knelt and fit the memory into her lifeless hand.

"You done over there?"

"Yes, sir," I answered.

"First Sergeant Johnson, get her out of here."

"You want her at the Lime Line before sunset, sir?" First Sergeant Johnson asked.

"No, bring her body to the sewers. Take this piece of paper, shove it in her mouth, and put her on display so all of the other goddam Ka'ba lickers get the message that we're not fucking around here either."

First Sergeant Johnson untied her from the chair, picked up her body, and threw it over his shoulder. He departed from the command center immediately afterward. The general was now in the back of the room. He already had the two doors to the seven-foot-high gun-metal gray steel cabinet flung open. He already had the neck of a whiskey bottle in the grip of one hand and an old-fashioned glass in the other. Both he brought with him to his desk. I waited until he started his pour. I figured what better time for my protestation.

"You didn't have to kill her," I said.

"Well, you're a little late with that request, Translator. You should have spoken up earlier," he answered, then knocked back the quarter glass he had filled.

"It wouldn't have mattered."

"You're fucking right it wouldn't have mattered," he fired off while proceeding to pour himself another round.

"She had two children."

"You're right, she did. And now if you're done pointlessly defending the dead, you can get back to the station I so graciously set aside for you and begin translating that shitload of papers stacked on it."

"You could have just imprisoned her."

"Goddamn, Translator. I hope you understand that if it wasn't happy hour on this side of the desk, I would have already had your skinny-ass neck in my hand just waiting for your eyes to somersault into the back of your head."

"I just want to know why you shot her, sir."

"Are you testing my patience, Translator?"

"No, sir. Not at all, sir," I replied.

"Okay, I'll entertain your inquiry, Translator. But this is going to be the last fucking time you're ever going to speak to me again without being prompted. Are we crystal fucking clear on that?"

"Yes, sir."

"Good, then I'll tell you why I shot her. First of all, we don't have a goddamn prison. And the reason for that is because we are the only fucking people who are supposed to be down here. Secondly, we don't have enough food for ourselves, so I find no reason to start a food pantry for all the fanatical fucks who want us inverted on a cross while their children throw stones at our fly-infested bodies. But even if we did have a prison, and we did have enough food for her, I still would have taken out my gun and bored a forty-five caliber hole through her skull. And do you know why?"

"No, sir."

"That's right, Translator. Of course, you don't know fucking why, because you have no goddamn idea why she was strapped to that chair in the first place."

"You're right, sir, I don't."

"Well, two hours ago, while you were having a wet dream, a few of my men who were cutting through the sewers on their way back from a supply raid, heard two gunshots. They followed the sound for about two hundred or so meters before coming up on that cunt. And right at her fucking feet, the bodies of a man and a teenage girl. Now I'm thinking that gives me every fucking right to execute her in the exact same manner as she did to those two escapees from Ayla."

"I didn't know, sir," I answered, my eyes lowered and embarrassed now to be standing there.

"Don't get on my shit list, Translator. I'll rip that soft heart out of your body while it's still fucking beating."

I returned with one nod of my head. I was still wondering what to do with my body when he ordered me to take a seat on the lone couch in the command center. As I was sitting, looking at the clay wall because I didn't know where else to put my eyes, he passed me by and slapped me hard on the shoulder. It rattled me, but I understood it wasn't one of animus. It was one that a father would have given his son to let him know that all had been forgiven and it was time to move on.

"Okay, boys, time to fucking play," he said while he was lifting up one of the guitars from the three that were resting on stands up against the back wall. On it, I noticed it had the words "FUK EM UP" written in white on the all-black body. As he clipped on his black leather strap and plugged the cord into an amp, I watched as three other soldiers left their posts to get behind their instruments. He raised the mic stand so that it was now teeth high, and then started to tune the guitar. Afterward, he gave the strings one strum before looking over to me.

"You ever see a guitar like this, Translator?"

"No, sir," I said.

"This here piece of machinery is an exact replica of a 1989 ESP MX220, replete with EMG 60 and 81 pickups. Besides that forty-five you saw me unload a few minutes ago and a few AR-15s, it was the only other fucking thing I took from my apartment before I left for the Mannheim Front."

"It's a good looking guitar, sir."

"You're damn right it's a good looking guitar, and it plays even fucking better than that. James Hetfield played one just like it. You know who the fuck that is?"

"No, sir," I replied.

"Yeah, that doesn't surprise me. The first time you walked in here, I had you pegged as some pansy-ass lover of top forty shit."

"I listen to all types of music, sir."

"Great, fucking great. That's something you tell some chick at two a.m. in a bar because you haven't been able to get in anyone else's pants for the last seven hours. True lovers of music put their souls into one type of music and that's it. They wake up to that shit. They live their day with that shit. And when they put their goddamn tired head down on a pillow, it's the last fucking thing they hear."

"Yes, sir."

"Now take a look at the poster on the wall over there. One of my men, God rest his soul, gave it to me last year. Best gift I ever got. That's James Fucking Hetfield. The goddamn 455 big block behind the band Metallica. Hetfield's the messiah on a concert stage. The preacher of metal. He's got long hair in that photo, but he cut it short just before they released the Load album back in ninety-six. That pissed off a lot of people. I understood it fucking completely. I mean, shit, if the Romans hadn't murdered Christ, I bet you anything He would have severed His locks too. You get old, man. Can't go around looking like that forever."

He then gave the guitar another strum and checked both the bass player and the second guitarist to see if they were ready. With the toe of his black boot, he lightly tapped one of the pedals on the floor in front of him to switch it on. "PFC Thomas."

"Yes, sir?" the soldier behind the drum kit answered.

"We're going to begin with 'Nothing Else Matters.' Now don't fuck it up like you did a few days ago. I'm going to do the intro, and then you come in right before the verse begins. And stay in time. You got three measures of twelve-eight. After that, give me another measure at six-eight, followed by one more in twelve-eight. You fucking got that?"

"Got it, sir," PFC Thomas answered as he twirled one of the drum sticks over his head.

There was no count to lead the band into the song. He just placed the pick between his teeth and closed his eyes. I suppose at that moment what I was expecting was some sort of sonic blast to come raging out at Mach speed through the amps set in the back corners of the room. Instead, what came forth was a sweet melodic dirge that sounded to me like he was playing at his mother's funeral. The notes resonated so long after being fingerpicked you could almost see them floating off in the air. When he finally began to sing, it was difficult to reconcile the steel body and chiseled face of this man with that haunting baritone of a voice. I was mesmerized. I shuttered my own eyes, and my mind drifted back to the day I dropped into the sewers.

The city was in flames, and I was walking fast down Madison Avenue toward the lake. Automatic fire was shattering storefront glass, and RPGs were opening gaping holes into the buildings all around me. It felt like I was alone, but I wasn't. The street was crowded with others just like me. You would have thought at first that we were all rushing to catch a train. Yeah, I guess that's what you would have thought if it wasn't for the unlucky ones who happened to be in the path of either the bullets or exploding ordnance. Our stampede paid no attention to either their screams or their half bodies. Finally, I stopped, realizing the futility of it all. The lake would have only been a final burial ground. I drew in a deep breath and thought of just walking back the other way until my life was quickly put to an end. That was until I glanced at the middle of the street and saw a woman and the infant in her hands being helped down a manhole.

I returned to the song. And now, it seemed like he had an entire orchestra playing behind him. He took the solo. His fingers slid down the fretboard, and the notes climbed a ladder to the heavens. It was perfectly executed and no longer than it should have been. He then leaned close to the microphone and spoke his last words: "So close no matter how far. Couldn't be much more from the heart. Forever trust in who we are . . ."

Yes, and he was right on that final line, "No, nothing else matters."

The general fingerpicked the song to its conclusion, and let the last notes fade out as if they were smoke from the last drag of a cigarette. This wasn't his swan song, but it was his prelude to an end he must have understood was near. I watched him slowly remove the guitar and set it back on its stand. The tears in my eyes I quickly wiped away and returned to my desk. The day was just beginning and my emotions were already spent. How he was able to remain rock-steady was absolutely unfathomable to me.

Entry #3

The general was wrong when he stated that within a week's time there would be a war raging over our heads. It actually started three weeks later. On some days, it was so intense that it shook us down here in the freight tunnels for hours. The general spent most of his time either working out new Metallica songs with his band or pulled up in a chair in front of the command center screens like he was watching a video game. Those screens, which were networked to clandestine cameras positioned throughout Ayla, gave us a limited front-row seat to the battle. As I write, by our best estimate, the faction trying to overthrow Ayla was occupying about a quarter of the city. For us, there was no vested interest as to who would eventually emerge as the victor. The best outcome would be a prolonged conflict that severely weakened the side that would ultimately claim the city.

As much as I hate to use the phrase "good times," as of course, it has to be taken in context, these did seem to be good times for us. The soldiers' morale was stratospheric because we were, for obvious reasons, not running any missions. For the moment, the only real dilemma we had, or should I say the general had, was a quest for a set of guitar strings. During his last jam session, he had snapped the high E string to the point where it could not be salvaged. The other two guitars he had in the back of the room had already been cannibalized to the point that neither had more than two strings running down the fretboard, obviously neither of which held the high E string. A few days earlier he had sent two soldiers in search of someone in the freight tunnels who might have some guitar strings. They had just entered the command center and were giving him their report.

"Well?" the general asked.

"Nothing, sir."

"No one? Not one fucking person down here came with a guitar."

"It doesn't seem like it, sir. And we did a pretty thorough search," one of the soldiers said. "We can try one of the music stores up in Ayla once the fighting subsides."

"There are no music stores left up there, Private. Jesus Christ, are you fighting the same goddamn battle we are."

"Yes, sir," the private answered, even though the question was rhetorical.

"Then if you are, you would have already known that one of the first things those camel-sodomizing assholes did after the invasion was to destroy every fucking music store we had up there. Which just pisses me off to no end because it just shows how ignorant these motherfuckers are of history, even their own goddamn history. Because if they weren't, they would know that the last real fucking caliph they had, Abdulmecid the Second, played the goddamn violin. And he didn't seem too worried about what the fuck either Allah or Muhammad had to say about it. Now go find me a fucking set of strings, preferably Ernie Ball RPS 10s, and don't come back here until you do. Christ, all I want is to rip out a little 'Fade to Black' and then go up there and shoot a few of those ignorant motherfuckers in the balls. You ever hear that song, Translator?"

"What, sir?" I said.

"Don't give me that 'What, sir?' shit. I know you got one ear to this conversation."

"No, sir, I haven't heard it," I confessed.

"Well, you fucking need to hear it. At 5:05, Hammett starts in on the solo and doesn't stop kicking ass until a good two minutes later. Best fucking solo in the history of rock and roll. Fuck, he just shreds that goddamn fretboard to pieces. Nothing like it. First time I heard it I was in my Camaro, Levi's just past my ass and screwing some jock's girlfriend. I think I was sixteen or something. Shit, that's America, Translator. You got someone's girlfriend in the backseat. You got a case of Budweiser chilling in the trunk. And you got Metallica blasting from your Blaupunkt speakers. Jesus, those were good fucking times."

"I'm sure they were, sir," I said, and then asked the general how he had obtained all the equipment in the command center if the Caliphate had destroyed all the music stores after the invasion.

"A raid on a warehouse last year, Translator. It was supposed to have light bulbs and a bunch of other shit we could use down here. Instead, it ended up having only musical equipment. So, the boys brought me back what you see here. As far as I'm concerned, the best goddamn mission we've ever had."

It was right after the general finished speaking that another soldier was let into the command center. She was small, no taller than five feet two. She had a black ponytail coming out the back of a camouflaged baseball cap. Mid-twenties I guessed. On the pocket of her uniform, in permanent black marker, were drawn nine tally marks.

"At ease, PFC Smith."

She dropped her salute and then reached into that pocket and pulled out a set of guitar strings.

"Nice fucking work, Smith. How in the hell did these fall into your hands?"

"Sir, from two men down in the west end."

"Good fucking job. You want a Kit Kat?"

"No, sir. One more thing, sir."

"Go on, PFC Smith."

"Our water's been shut off again."

"Those motherfuckers. For the life of me, I don't know why the hell I just don't go in there and terminate their existence. It would sure as shit save me a lot of goddamn headaches."

∞ ∞ ∞

We walked southeast through the freight tunnels for about three miles. I knew this because of the street names that were stenciled on the concrete walls. I knew this because for a year while I attended Northwestern, I had also been a bicycle courier. By my third week on the job, I had memorized the city grid. Distances were easy to calculate, one block was one-eighth of a mile. I miss those days. I miss weaving in and out of the traffic at reckless speed and then gliding around pedestrians like they were moving construction cones. It was as if the city was my own motocross course. Every delivery was a harrowing but exhilarating experience. In that job, I had only one objective, and en route to that objective, I was beholden to no one. I was free then. And if it had paid enough, I would have dropped out of college immediately and kept pedaling for the next forty years of my life.

The general and I were accompanied by a modest but heavily armed contingent of eleven soldiers. Five were at the point. Six were in the rear. All were carrying M4s and double belted with enough ammunition strapped across their chests to take on perhaps a platoon of Ayla regulars. We were headed to Tunnel X. That was the only thing I knew at the moment. Until I decided to inquire.

"If you don't mind me asking, sir, what exactly is Tunnel X?"

"It was here about 3 months before Sector 4 was discovered, Translator. They don't bother us. We don't bother them. That's the fucking agreement. That is until they break said fucking agreement by shutting off our water, and then I have to bring my ass over there. Which is highly fucking inconvenient because I'm trying to run a war over where I'm at."

"Who are they?"

"A small group of Jesus freaks led by some guy who thinks angels keep speaking to him."

"They're sitting on the main shut-off valve, aren't they?" I said.

"Yeah, it fucking runs through there. And every time the guy has a vision, he closes it until I come down there to hear what the angels had to say to him."

We walked a little farther until I had one more question to ask of the general. I wanted to know why if they were just followers of Christ, did we come loaded up with enough weapons to fight a platoon of Ayla regulars.

"Because in their goddamn version of the New Testament, Translator, Jesus seems to be not only the Son of God but also an arms dealer. They're armed to the fucking teeth."

A few minutes later, we were met with the unmistakable smell of death. While there wouldn't have been anyone there who hadn't come upon this sickeningly sweet odor before, this was different. This was the smell of an in-progress apocalypse. This was a scent I can only imagine that the curator of hell wears to the wedding of his daughter. Everyone pushed on through, though. No one wanted to look weak in the presence of the general. That was until we walked along a little farther and came to an abrupt halt as a swarm of flies put up a wall twenty feet ahead of us. The noise was so loud that you would have had to shout to hear the person next to you. None of it impressed the general.

"You pussy fucks better be stopping because someone was able to squeeze a goddamn Abrams M1A3 down here, and it's got its 120 mm smoothbore pointed right at your balls."

"No, sir. Flies. Thousands of them."

"You think I'm watching a different fucking movie than you, Private."

"No, sir."

"Then keep fucking moving. They're goddamn blowflies to be specific. Everyone's got a right to a meal."

The general was correct. They were blowflies and they were dining at the most magnificent feast of their short lives. On two overhead pipes that ran on our left and right, hung the bodies of soldiers from the Caliphate. They had been stripped of their uniforms, which were neatly folded below their feet. What was odd, though, was that they weren't hanging from their necks as one would have expected. Instead, they were held up there by some harness contraption of copper wire that ran across their chest a few turns and then was looped under their armpits. By the lack of decay, it was obvious some had just been brought to the table. Others I assumed had probably been there for a week or more. This I based not only on the extent of the decay but also on the number of maggots and carrion beetles crawling in and out of them. To keep from vomiting, I began counting bodies. I was at number fourteen on my side when I came to the last one.

Maybe I stopped because there wasn't a large swarm around him. Maybe I stopped out of some sick curiosity to see how he had met his fate. Most likely, though, it was because he couldn't have been any older than fifteen years of age. I took my flashlight off of his face and moved it down his body. I didn't have to travel very far before I saw that someone had cut perhaps a three-by-four section of skin out of his belly. There, a formation of blowflies had found his intestines a perfect perch to take rest.

I returned the beam of light to his face and began to wonder if he really believed his life had served a higher purpose. At that moment of death, did he really believe in martyrdom, or was he wishing for just a little more time to be a kid? All those thoughts were racing around my head when his eyelids rolled open like a storefront gate. It was so horrifying that my body startled back, my feet crossed, and I hit the ground. A moment or so later I found myself being lifted up.

"Stay in line, Translator. This isn't a goddamn museum tour where you're given time to ponder over the art pieces."

"He's alive, sir."

"Which one?"

"That one there, sir."

The general followed the direction I gave him and took a few steps over to the young soldier of the Caliphate. He cupped the face like a father would his son, and then gave it one quick, merciful twist.

"There. Is that fucking better?"

I didn't reply.

"I'm going to take that as a fucking yes. Now, don't you fall back unless I give a goddamn direct order. You got that?"

"Yes, sir."

The general hurried our steps until we met up with our men. Twenty meters ahead, the tunnel widened to three times its size. We were now staring at two tunnels. On the wall leading to the tunnel on the right, written in carmine lettering, the words:

God judgeth the righteous, and God is angry with the wicked every day – Psalm 7:11

On the wall to the left, written in the same blood red, the words:

For whom the Lord loveth he chasteneth, and scourgeth every son whom he receiveth– Hebrews 12:6

The general ordered the men to move into the tunnel on the right. It was twice as wide as the one we had been traversing. Instead of one set of railroad tracks, there were now two. I don't believe we had advanced more than thirty or so meters through this new tunnel when we came to another abrupt halt. Except for the general and myself, everyone dropped to their knees, and the sound of weapons being locked and loaded echoed throughout the tunnel. They shone their lights on us, and we reciprocated. It was like two cars in the middle of nowhere facing off against each other.

The general pushed away the men in front of him and began making his way toward the front of our line. I stayed back, sweeping my eyes over their position. In the middle, they had the barrels of two M240s set side by side peering over a toppled desk about three feet high. The flanks of the machine gun nest they had protected by slabs of concrete, five men to a side. I had a count of twelve until in the corner near the door, I saw a little girl standing there holding what I was soon to find out was a ram's horn. It was an impressive display of force, one that made me believe if someone had accidentally fingered a trigger, we would not have been the ones to survive the ensuing firefight.

"Tell him I'm here."

One of their soldiers glanced down at the little girl and gave her a nod of his head. Like the rest of them, dressed in a single white robe that was belted by a rope, she put one end of the ram's horn to her lips and blew out a series of notes. A few seconds later, it was answered by the sound of another ram's horn on the other side. The door was then opened, and we were invited in.

We filed into what I assumed was the welcoming room. It was illuminated in candlelight and heavily perfumed with the scent of cloves. There were skulls on the floor, and there were skulls set into small alcoves. It could have been hell's anteroom, or it could have been heaven's waiting area. A ram's horn blew again. Through the back came in two identical women with long cinnamon-colored hair falling past their waists. They couldn't have been any older than twenty-five years of age. They couldn't have been any less than six feet tall. Both had a book in their hands. They spoke in unison. They both said, "Choose." The general obliged them, and set his hand down hard on the book on his right.

"The Good Book has been chosen," they both then said. For the fourth time, the ram's horn sounded.

Six feet six. Maybe an inch over that. He was bearded. One eye patched with gauze, and like all of them, was wearing nothing but a white robe belted in rope. He gave all of us a look before setting his right eye on the general, who was starting to speak.

"Gotta fucking say, I love what you've done to the exterior since I last visited. You're going to have to give me the name of your landscaper. He does great work."

"Their deaths were ordained. But they are the last. There shall be no more."

"Yeah, well, I sure as hell hope not. Because you were taking one big motherfucking risk by hauling those Caliphate soldiers down here. We all live on the same goddamn block if you haven't noticed. They find you, that means they find me. Now, if you don't mind, I'd like to get to the reason why you shut off our water again. Because it's not only me now who wants to put a few bullets into you. There are others in my sector who are questioning why we keep putting up with this bullshit."

"Hark, before me the great Moses, the mighty warrior. By his people sent. And his people say, 'And wherefore have ye made us to come up out of Egypt, to bring us in unto this evil place? It is no place of seed, or of figs, or of vines, or of pomegranates; neither is there any water to drink.' "

"And Moses said, 'I'm not sure about the fucking figs and pomegranates, but the reason we have no water is that some asshole over in the tunnels next to us keeps shutting it off.' So, let's get on with it. What the hell did the angels tell you this time?"

"Last night, General, my name was Caleb and I was walking through the ruins of your sector searching for survivors. From those of the dead who wrote of their lives, I began collecting the pages they had written upon. Praise be to God."

On their side, they all answered, "Praise be to God."

"And last night while I was dreaming, I was sixteen and giving the high hard one to Lori Maggiano in the back of my Camaro."

"There is more, General."

"Please. Go on. Your show."

"Before I collected the writings of those in your sector, I came upon a grand room of like no other I had seen. Inside I found a man naked and inverted on a cross. The skin of the body was unbruised and untainted, but the face was blackened by flames. I neared, and there on the ground before him, was the uniform he once proudly wore and the weapon he once wielded. And just as I was about to say a prayer to deliver his soul to heaven, I came to realize that they had torched him alive."

"And just how the fuck do you know they did it while he was still breathing?"

"Because General, you spoke to me at that moment and said, 'Kill 'em all.' Your last words, General. The final ones before I picked up your weapon and ended your life."

"That's it. That's the reason you shut off our water this time? To tell me I was going to die? Fuck, we're all going to die. You, me, and even that little girl with her ram's horn. No one's getting out of here alive."

"Yes, General, what you speak is true. But those of us in Christ will rise first. Then we who are alive, we who are left, will be caught up together with them in the clouds to meet the Lord in the air. And so we will always be with the Lord."

"Well, if I were you, I would remember to bring a parachute. You may just want to come back down because it could be that His heaven is worse than his earth. Now turn on our goddamn water, or I'm going to separate your hands from your body and crank that valve with both of them."

The general made a start for the exit and was at the door when two of their men stepped in front of it to block his advance. Slowly, he turned around.

"Do you really want me to fucking shoot them?"

"There is one more thing. In the vision, I saw the girl and her child hiding in the remains. They were the only ones who survived. This I know and now you. She was wearing this though. It must be placed around her neck, for she is the deliverer."

He then produced a crucifix and laid it in the open palms of the little girl by his side. She walked it over to the general. The general gave her a glance before setting his eyes back on the man.

"And what if I don't take it and put it around her neck?"

"Then she and her child will die, as all men die."

"You're out of your fucking mind. Someone here needs to tell you that before you get them all killed."

For the first half mile or so back to the command center, the general remained silent, uncharacteristically so. I was wondering if the prophecy had found its way into his thoughts. Everything the man had said at first seemed like it could have been easily conjured up. An ending like that was not so implausible. The command center would one day be overrun. And most likely, it would be where the general made his last stand. That we all could have prophesized. What did seem though as if it arrived from the future was when the general was told his last words would be "Kill 'em all." That was the one that made all of the hairs on our bodies stand up and give more than a little credence to the tale.

"Right on fucking schedule," the general said as the pipe supports began to rattle, and water started to flow through them once again.

I certainly wasn't going to ask the general if he believed in any of what had been foretold. But I did have a few questions that I thought I could ask. Since I was unable to get a good look at the two books that the two identical women were holding, I wanted to know what they were and why he choose the book on the right.

"One was the Bible, Translator. And the other was the Koran. They present them to me every goddamn time I come."

"Which one did you choose?" I asked.

"Which fucking one would you choose?"

"The Bible," I said.

"Christ, you're about ready to take over the command, aren't you?"

"What do you think would happen if you chose the Koran, sir?"

"Well, I really don't fucking know, Translator. But if you're so goddamn curious, the next time we have to drag our ass back over here, I'll let you be the spokesperson so all of us can find out exactly what the hell happens when one chooses the Koran in a heavily armed den of Jesus freaks."

∞ ∞ ∞

I sat in my quarters late that night. There were new stacks of papers to be translated, but I was unable to set my mind on them. Instead, I was trying to pry the medieval-looking crucifix open without damaging it. Yes, trying to pry it open because it was also a locket. A locket that was hinged at Christ's right arm. It was the most unusual piece I had ever seen. And then, after abandoning my attempt to open it, I just sat there and turned it over and over again, wondering if it was real or a reproduction. In the end, I concluded that it must be a fake. I threaded a piece of thin leather rope through the loop at the top so it could be delivered and placed.

Yes, I was the last one to leave Tunnel X. Yes, I relieved the little girl of the crucifix and hurried it into my front pocket. At 4:14 a.m., I stood up and left. At 4:33 a.m., I stepped into the quarters of the girl and the prostitute. The girl was alone on a mat. She was curled in a fetal position, quite in the arms of Morpheus. I placed the crucifix around her neck. She did not stir. I was just getting up from my knees when I realized that I had not seen the prostitute. So, I aimed my flashlight to the far end of the wall and then switched it on. I only had to move the light a few feet when I saw her sitting there. She was not alone. She had her red dress unbuttoned and latched onto one of her breasts an infant. We said nothing to each other, neither in our voices nor in our eyes.

Entry #4

The war finally came to an end. The reigning rule of Ayla prevailed, and much to our dismay, it did not lessen their strength. In fact, in the end, their numbers within the city only increased as reinforcements arrived for their last and decisive battle. That was three weeks ago, and as I write again, we are no better positioned than we were when it began. I now realize that this is my eternal tomb. It is no longer a question of whether I will die here. It is just the questions of how and when I will die here. I would like to put down that I am resolved to this fate. But I am not. I want to live, and I want to believe in a God who will intervene and swoop down from above like a deus ex machina. It is a foolish belief though. Not unlike the belief I held onto when I was twelve that my father would not die of pancreatic cancer. The general was right. Our God loves a good fight, and unfortunately, I have come to the same conclusion that we are all just props on his battlefield.

∞ ∞ ∞

I was with the general late into the night. With us was Gunnery Sergeant Muncie. He was inventorying munitions and weapons. I was working on forging identity documents. The general was sitting on a stool looking at the map of Ayla and studying troop positions of the Caliphate. The door opened and a soldier walked in with a woman. She was dressed in a black abaya. In her left hand, it appeared as if she was holding a niqab. She looked no older than thirty years of age. The general briefly lifted his head and nodded to the soldier who had brought her to us. The soldier saluted and then departed. A minute or so later the general finally looked back up from the map and addressed her.

"You may speak, Lance Corporal Myers."

"Thank you, sir. My post spotted a mini school bus pulling up to a warehouse in the Ghadir Khumm area earlier this evening."

"Go ahead," the general said as he lifted a hand to his face and began feeling his fingers over the day-old growth.

"It was full of kids, sir. Both girls and boys. By their prison uniforms, from the Bihiima labor camp."

"How many?"

"We counted sixteen children, sir."

"I didn't mean how many kids, Lance Corporal. I know how many goddamn seats are on a short bus. Christ, I rode one for four years when I was on the wrestling team. I mean how many armed fucking towlies were escorting them?"

"Seven, sir."

"Now I'm just wondering, Lance Corporal Myers, since you're a soldier and not a fucking photojournalist, why in the hell didn't you just say 'Seven dead towlies, sir?' "

"They were guarding them pretty close, sir. We most likely would have shot a few of the children."

"So instead, you thought it better to just do nothing and return here to file a report?"

"We can go back, sir."

"Go back and do fucking what? How in the hell do you think you're going to free those kids now that they've all been taken inside?"

"I'm not sure yet, sir."

"Yeah, well fuck, neither am I." The general then stood up and arched his back like a cat. Even from where I was sitting, I could hear his spine crack as if every vertebra had been out of place. He paced for a moment or so. "I don't know. Every team of specialists we have is out on a mission right now. It's gonna have to wait until tomorrow night."

"Tomorrow may be too late, sir," Lance Corporal Myers said in a respectful protestation.

"Of course tomorrow is going to be too goddamn late. I'm well aware of that. Nothing turns these motherfuckers on like a good virgin rape party. Fucking pedophiles."

"I'll go, sir. I can take Corporal Doyer along with PFC Seznick. They had the night off," Staff Sergeant O'Neil said as he rose from where he was sitting.

"Fuck, O'Neil. What took you so goddamn long? I have one minute and thirty-two seconds on this watch since you stepped in. All the while I've been scratching my balls wondering when the fuck you were going to open your pie hole and offer some assistance. Jesus Christ, I trained you my fucking self. Now go get your men ready and report back immediately. Lance Corporal Myers."

"Yes, sir?"

"You're going to stay here with me—"

"I want to be a part of this operation, sir," the lance corporal said.

"You're going to be. But let me finish my fucking sentence, will you?"

"Yes, sir. I thought you were finished, sir."

"Well, I fucking wasn't. What I was going to append onto it before you rudely interrupted my ass was that I want you to get a message to the Jinn. I want him in on this one."

The general then walked over to one of the amps. After reaching in the back of it, he returned holding a King James Bible in one of his hands.

"Look in Numbers, Lance Corporal," the general said as he shoved the Bible into her chest. "If you don't know your Good Book, it's the chapter right after Leviticus. You'll find the instructions and codes there to make contact. Tell him we're planning our operation at 0700."

"It's short notice, sir. What if he doesn't respond in time?"

"He's not going to respond, Lance Corporal. That's why he's the fucking Jinn. But he'll be there. He waits for this kind of shit. And no one likes putting holes in those ragheads more than him."

The general and I were now alone in the command center. It was 0212. I was about to return to my desk and continue on with my work when the general, a glass of whiskey now in his hand, started to speak to me.

"You know what bugs the shit out of me, Translator?"

"No. What, sir?"

"These fucking pricks above us aren't even religious zealots fighting the good fight for the sake of Allah. What they are is a bunch of repressed fucking teenagers. And half of the time I don't even think it's their goddamn fault. It's the fault of the fucking culture. You forbid these kids from looking at porn and playing with their own dicks, then what the fuck do you think you're going to end up with. I mean how the fuck would you like having a hard-on for the last five years of your life and not being able to do anything with it. The only thing they ever wanted is to take what nature's been waking them up with every morning and squirting what's inside of it out. But the mullahs and imams were fucking smart. They used that repression to recruit every one of them. That's how the whole fucking jihad thing started, long before our asses ended up down here. Someone handed them a flyer with a few fucking quotes from the Koran and told them to join Team Allah. Inside, I damn well know they were thinking, 'Go fuck yourself, I'm not fighting for you. I'm sixteen fucking years old and certainly not ready to have an American drone shoot my ass up. You crazy bastards are out of your minds.' The Allah recruiter then said to them that on your way to paradise, you get to stick your little dick in as many girls as you can grab. And so the sixteen-year-old kid says 'Fuck, yeah. This has got to be better than sneaking looks at my sister's ass after she's slipped out of her jilbab.' "

"What do you think our chances of success are, sir?"

"Zero if you define success as retrieving all of those kids. But we'll bring a few back. That I'm fucking certain of. That bastard always comes through."

"You mean the Jinn, sir."

"Yes, I mean the Jinn."

"Who is he, sir?"

"Well, I really don't know who the fuck he is, Translator. And even if I did, I sure in the hell wouldn't be telling you. I'm still not convinced you're not one of them. But I can tell you that they fear him up there more than Allah. He's got a bounty on his head of more than four million in gold. The problem is that they don't have a picture of him and we don't have a picture of him, which makes it pretty goddamn difficult to find someone when you don't even know what the hell they look like."

I didn't want to press on, so I said nothing more. The next morning when I arrived at the command center at eleven hundred hours, Lance Corporal Myers and Staff Sergeant O'Neil were standing before the general. He saluted them off, and I was left wondering what had happened. That was until I departed the command center late in the night to head back to my quarters. There, coming toward me, a line of children were being escorted by four of our soldiers, two in front and two in back. I counted the children. I couldn't believe it. Whoever the Jinn was, against all odds, he was able to assist us in saving five of those kids.

∞ ∞ ∞

Two weeks later, after exhaustion had claimed the general, I walked over to the amp. If he awoke, I knew he would have shot me with no questions asked. Inside, I found not only the Bible but a plastic binder full of reports addressed to the general from the Jinn. Each one either detailed his operations within the city of Ayla or gave intel on what we should target. They were absolutely enthralling. It was as if I was reading letters from a serial killer. He was walking among them seemingly unobtrusive and, if not providing intel to Sector 4, then randomly killing them for pleasure. He certainly was not discriminating, and every death sentence he handed out seemed to be more sadistic than the last.

I came to the conclusion that he must be Muslim, otherwise, how could he operate in the city without being noticed. Most fantastic though, were the postscripts he would give the letters. They were mocking in tone. And not mocking of the other Muslims he lived among but of the general. Sometimes he would conclude with Metallica sucks, or James Hetfield licks donkey balls. I believed the general when he said that he didn't know who the Jinn was. However, it was quite apparent that the Jinn knew who the general was.

Entry #5

I was in the command center sitting on the couch. Unbeknownst to the general, I had stuffed the canals of my ears with a few pieces of merino wool snipped from a pair of socks. Even with that acoustic barrier, the music was still coming through loud and clear. Four songs into the set, the band was on its next one and the general was laying down the solo to "Fade to Black." By now, I knew most of the Metallica oeuvre by heart. I admit I never tired of it. If you had to listen to a cover band in the bowels of hell, why not this one then. And as a guitar player, he was as exceptional as he was as our general. It made me wonder where he had learned to play like that. It made me wonder what he had done prior to the invasion. There was this huge gap that he never spoke of. He would mention his teenage years to his early twenties, and he would speak of his time on the Mannheim Front. The years that connected those, however, were a mystery. I could only surmise two occupations. The first, and most logical, was that he was career military. For the second, I imagined that he spent his life training German Shepherds, all the while keeping the torch lit as he played in a variety of bands waiting for a record deal that would never come.

"Goddamn, I didn't miss a fucking note, did I, Translator."

"No, sir. I don't think you did."

"You have no fucking idea how good it feels to finally nail that Hammett solo. Got to be up there with the best of them. Better than sticking my tongue inside the prom queen's pussy. Better than picking off that sniper at the Mannheim Front. And even better than any shit I've ever taken. Fuck, I feel like going up there right now and shooting some Ahabs my fucking self. Okay, we've got business to attend to here.

Sergeant Raymonds."

"Sir, we have—"

"I know who the fuck you have there, Sergeant Raymonds. Jesus Christ, I'm the one who asked to bring the detainee here. Take the hood and abaya off but the leave the goddamn chains on."

PFC Thomas then stood up from behind his drum kit and threw a small black and white flag of the enemy to the general. The general snatched it out of the air and started to wipe the sweat from his face and hair, all the while slowly walking toward the detainee. All of us in the room knew it was The Assassin. We had been informed of the arrival. If there was another down in the freight tunnels who had the same rock-star status as the general, it was him. His kills were legendary. Like the Jinn, the city of Ayla was plastered with posters offering millions for his capture. The city here in the freight tunnels had elevated him to a Christ-like status. When the hood and abaya were removed, I thought, as I'm sure everyone else in the room did, that the general was just messing with us because we were all staring at a girl no older than seventeen. She was perhaps five feet ten, with honey-colored hair that meandered its way to her waist. She had on a black long-sleeved shirt, which she filled out like an Olympian. But it was her face that commandeered everyone's attention. It had to have been God-sculpted, for there was beauty in every feature. There wasn't anyone in the room who wouldn't have sold their soul for her.

"You have any fucking idea why you're here?"

She was just about to open her mouth when he squeezed both of her cheeks.

"Don't. Don't say a fucking thing until I give you permission." She nodded and he let go. "Okay, that's good. We have an understanding. Now first, I'm going to start out by telling you why you think you're here. And then after that, I'm going to tell you the real fucking reason I brought you here. Does that sound like a plan?"

This time she just blinked her reply.

"You think you're here because I found out you had the fucking balls to bring some Ayla cunt down here and give her shelter. Am I right on that?"

She nodded her confession.

"Yeah, exactly what I thought. However, the real goddamn reason is that I send my number one assassin to take out the military commander of Ayla. And instead of killing him that day, you return with their number one assassin. Now if that isn't the fucking perfect definition of irony, I don't know what the hell is. But I also have another word for everyone. And that's serendipity. Anyone want to tell me what the fuck that means."

"Sir," I said while raising my hand.

"Well, go on, Translator. Tell the class what the word serendipity means."

"Sir, it means coming upon something fortunate when you least expect it."

"Fucking right, that's what it means. And we just had a huge shitload of serendipity because not more than four hours ago, just as one of our reconnaissance teams was coming back, they spotted your new friend trying to leave with a souvenir from here. Any guesses on what she was taking back up to Shariaville with her?"

The Assassin removed her eyes from the general and looked to the floor.

"A Jew. That's what she decided to bring back. And to be specific, it was your Jew. All fucking packaged up and ready for delivery. I mean that's just goddamn beautiful. Not only are you able to get inside the enemy's stronghold, but you decide to return with a prize. But I've got one last surprise for you. And believe me, you're gonna love this one. Sergeant Martin, bring her in."

A moment later, Sergeant Martin returned with the prisoner. She had a plastic bag tied over her head and seemed to be struggling for each new breath. Around her body, they had wrapped her in the black and white flag of Ayla. The general then gave a nod to Sergeant Martin and he unceremoniously disrobed her.

I couldn't believe what I was looking at. From shoulders down, she was inked in this most elaborate design of black lines, almost like an architectural print of a building. I was still studying it when the general grabbed The Assassin by the hair and pulled her closer to the prisoner.

"Take a good fucking look. Pretty impressive, isn't it? I have to admit, when I took my first look, my cock was standing about a foot high. I mean here I was thinking this is the girl of my goddamn dreams. She's tatted all over the fucking place. After I got closer though, I realized it wasn't ink at all. It was goddamn black marker. And finally, it fucking dawned on me. This wasn't some fancy Arabic shit she had on her body. It was . . . Anyone? Anyone here want to venture a guess as to what the hell she's drawn all over her body?"

"A map of our tunnels, sir," I blurted out.

"Fucking right, Translator. A perfect rendering of it. Go get yourself a few Kit Kats from the desk drawer."

While I still hadn't found a taste for the candy bars, a month or so back I decided to start collecting them. Not as barter, but to bring to the girl and the prostitute. The girl absolutely loved them. Every few days or so I would drop by to see how the three of them were doing. Along with some baby food I had managed to obtain, I brought her the Kit Kats.

I was just reaching into the desk drawer for the candy bars when I saw two soldiers bring over a long wooden board, to which they began strapping the prisoner. At the same time, I heard the general ask PFC Thomas to start filling up an empty metal ammunition box with muriatic acid. I knew what they were going to do. But instead of contending this death, I just returned to where I was standing. Not because it was to become the most heinous act I had yet witnessed down here in the freight tunnels, but because I had finally begun to realize that any voice of conscientious objection would be coming from the voice of a fool. This was war, and all of us knew the consequences.

"Remove the plastic bag from the prisoner," the general said.

The prisoner took in a few deep breaths, and then slowly turned to face The Assassin. I was expecting her to ask for forgiveness. Instead, like any warrior of a higher power, she started screaming to her God, "Allahu akbar." The general took out a handkerchief from his pocket and dipped it into the ammunition box. He then walked over and put her to silence by stuffing it into her mouth. Her body shook violently, and I watched as her eyes rolled back into her head.

"First Sergeant Jensen."

"Yes, sir."

"When she comes back to life, remove that map from her skin with the muriatic acid and then pour a few cups of it down her throat. And if she isn't dead by then, shoot her in the fucking head. And as for you," the general said as he turned to The Assassin. "I really don't give a fuck whether you stay with her or not. But she's going to die. And as far as your status, I don't know yet. Sure as shit though, now isn't the time to ask me."

Entry #6

"Started today at noon, sir. There's a good size audience, too. They're fucking cheering, sir."

"Who's fucking cheering, Corporal Clarke?"

"The women and children below, sir."

"Shit, I was wondering when that idea would get into their heads," the general said after being informed that captives were being pushed from the top of Willis Tower. "How many did they throw off?"

"Five, sir. They threw off five."

"You can't snipe the motherfuckers?"

"No, sir. The closest position we have is at least eight hundred meters out of range."

"Then move eight hundred meters closer. Jesus Christ, Corporal, you have any idea how utterly goddamn terrifying it must be standing on a ledge one hundred ten stories up and waiting for someone to send you into a swan dive to a concrete street below?"

"No, sir, I don't. But we scouted around. There's nowhere for us to set up any closer. They've got heavily fortified positions all over that area."

"There is somewhere closer, Corporal Clarke. We've got a safe house not too far from that area that'll put you in range. Tonight I want you to take five men and a couple of 240s and stay the night there. In the morning, I want you and your men on that roof by 1130 hours."

"Sir, we're only going to be able to get a couple of rounds off before they unload about twenty RPGs on our position."

"They won't be there tomorrow, Corporal."

"How's that, sir?"

"Because tomorrow at 1145 I'm going to order in a few diversionary explosions about two klicks to the west of the Tower. They'll start moving out those positions to see what the fuck's going on. I've seen it hundreds of times. They always call in a five-alarm fire, even when it's just a kid lighting a match."

"That's brilliant, sir. We're going to pick off every one of those fucking towlies."

"You won't have enough rounds left, Corporal Clarke."

"I don't understand, sir."

"I'm not asking you to shoot the soldiers, Clarke. I'm ordering you to empty your rounds on the women and children."

"Excuse me, sir?"

"You heard me right, Corporal. I want you to mow every one of those people down."

"They're innocents, sir."

"They were innocents when they were cooking up kabobs and playing with their halal coloring books. When they decided to gather for an execution of our people, they became ducks at a goddamn state fair. Now, if you think you're going to have trouble unloading one of those 240s tomorrow, then I want your uniform right now and I'll give you a transfer to the Department of Excavation."

"No, sir. I'll gather up the men."

After the corporal left, the general looked at me.

"Oh shit, I suppose your fucking bleeding heart must be spilling all over the goddamn place at about this time."

"No, sir."

"I fucking doubt that, Translator. People don't change without reason. And you really haven't had a good goddamn reason to change. Fuck, I don't even know why I have to explain myself to you, but I will.

You know why I ordered the killing of those women and children?"

"No, I don't, sir."

"Because if we just kept picking off their goddamn soldiers on top of the Tower, they would just keep sending up new soldiers for us to shoot. They don't give a fuck. But if I deprive them of a crowd, well that would kind of take the fun out of it, now wouldn't it? Sort of like having the Super Bowl played with no live coverage."

"I see, sir."

"Yeah, I'm not so sure you do," the general said, and then reached into a drawer of his desk and pulled out a bottle of Wild Turkey, along with two whiskey glasses. "Tell me a little about yourself, Translator."

"Nothing much to tell, sir," I remember replying.

"You Muslim? You read Arabic like one."

"No, sir. I was born here."

"Not what I asked you."

"I'm not Muslim, sir. I'm Christian. Catholic, to be specific."

"Recite the goddamn 'Our Father' for me."

I recited it for him.

"They taught you well in that jihadist training camp, didn't they?"

"I learned it while making my First Communion, sir. St. James."

"Where the fuck did you go to college?"

"Northwestern, sir."

"Major?"

"Economics with a minor in Arabic."

"Tell me you don't believe in the prophet, Translator."

"I don't believe in him, sir."

"Who, Translator? Who the fuck don't you believe in?"

"The Prophet Muhammad, sir. I don't believe in him."

"That's good, Translator," the general said as he started to fill up the glasses, "but I'm still not fucking convinced. I mean I've never seen your face down in these tunnels before. And neither had anyone else I asked. Also had someone check with the Department of Occupancy and Vital Records and they have no prior record of you. All I got back from intelligence is that you suddenly appeared in the class on Arabic and Islamic Studies. Graduated first, too. That's a pretty good feat considering that class had a few Iraqi-born students in there. You want to tell me how in the hell you managed that?"

"I don't know, sir."

"Yeah, of course you don't fucking know. Pick up that glass, Translator."

"I'm on duty, sir."

"And you think I'm on fucking furlough at this moment. Now pick it up and finish every goddamn drop in it."

He must have seen my hand shaking. It wasn't only my hand though. My entire body was trembling. I got through about half of the glass before I had to take it away from my lips in order to recover for a moment from the slash and burn of the alcohol tearing up my esophagus. I was just about to finish it off when he reached across the desk and took it out of my hands.

"Jesus Christ, Translator, you drink like a little fucking girl, you know that."

I nodded my head and sucked in a few deep breaths. They were just enough to settle both my mind and body down. I knew the interrogation was over though. I could see it in his eyes. Whatever suspicions he had of me had at least dissipated for the moment.

"So, how the hell did you end up down here, Translator? Flee from home after watching those religious extremists rape your mother and sisters, then sodomize your father with the barrel of a Kalashnikov?"

"No, sir. Like most everyone else, I made my way downtown after hearing the Mannheim Front had collapsed. During the last assault, I jumped down a sewer hole. Hid out there for about 5 months or so until I came upon the freight tunnels."

"How old are you, Translator?"

"I'm twenty-five, sir."

"Goddamn, still a baby, aren't you."

"I feel like I'm a hundred years old, sir."

"Yeah, don't we fucking all." He then paused to pour himself another drink. "I was there, Translator."

"Where, sir?"

"The Mannheim Front. Jesus, did we put up a fucking fight. Wrapped ourselves up in garbage bags or whatever the fuck we had in order to keep that pathogen off our skin. Held that line for a good month. And they brought everything they had to break through. In the end, there were so many of those ragheads lying around dead that they were using them as sandbags. Eventually, though, we began to run out of men and ammunition."

"How did you get out, sir?"

"Drove, Translator. When they started to overrun the position, I hopped in a car and headed off to my parents' bungalow. It was only about nine miles northeast of where I was. Before I left for the front, I told them to stay in the basement and wait until I returned."

"Did you get there in time, sir?"

"To save them, no. To exact a little retribution, yes. They were on the front steps when I arrived. The Caliphate that is. Four of them, smoking cigarettes and sharing a bottle of my father's whiskey. I had a grenade launcher in the backseat, but I didn't want to use it. That would have been too goddamn easy and they wouldn't have felt a fucking thing. Instead, I threw my AR-15s out the window, got out of the car with my hands over my head, and started walking toward them. The Abba-Dabba on the far left started laughing, and I knew he would be the last. I won't go into all the details, but I fucked them all. And I mean fucked them. Like a queer in heat. Afterward, I gutted them, like deer. Not enough to kill them though. Just enough to where their intestines were hanging outside their bodies. My mother was a bleach freak so there was enough of that Clorox shit lying around our basement that I could use to pour over them. The body can be a slow kill, Translator, if you just know how to treat it right. I think I was with them for a few days. Can't give an exact time of death. But I can tell you that there wasn't one of them that wouldn't have prayed it came two days earlier." He paused to finish what he had poured. "Vengeance is mine said the Lord, Translator. But in His fucking absence, I came to the conclusion that I'm the understudy."

It was then I understood this man. Before I had thought he was just someone who had lost their mind in the midst of all this insanity. But they had created him. He had come off their assembly line, and they would have to deal with him. For men like him, I understood, there is a moment in life where something so profound occurs that it shatters you. And the pieces when reassembled, if ever reassembled, bear no likeness whatsoever to the person you were before. It's an amnesic blow to your past. You forget who you were, and from then on and forever after, you are just an actor.

"We're going to die, Translator. You are aware of that, correct?"

"I am, sir."

"Good, because those are the kind of people I want around me. The realists are always the stronger of the breed. We're going to inflict some damage. And don't get me wrong. I'm not on a goddamn suicide mission here. I want to keep breathing like most every other motherfucker here. Well, perhaps I'm being overly optimistic. Like half of the motherfuckers here. But to think that in the end, we're all going to walk away from this waving a goddamn victory flag is just complete idiocy. When they come, and they will come, Translator, we are going to mow down so many of those camel jockeys that it's going to take Allah a fucking supercomputer to figure out just how many virgins he'll need for those shitheads. Now get the hell out of here. I got some drinking to do. And I want to do it alone."

"Yes, sir," I replied, thinking I was going to get a reprieve from finishing my glass. I saluted and started for the door.

"Translator."

"Yes, sir?"

"Don't waste my fucking whiskey."

Those were his last words. I regrettably rushed the liquor into my throat. He walked over to where an old turntable was. After turning it on, he gently lowered the needle down onto the spinning thirty-three and a third. Immediately from the speakers came forth this electric sound of automatic fire accompanied by a barrage of mortar shells. Then, after a slight reprieve, a new riff galloped on until it rode up to Hetfield's cord-tearing vocals. Everything in the command center was now shaking, and the empty glass I had just laid on the desk was tapping precariously close to the edge. I had no other choice but to wait out the attack, for to leave in the middle would have been an affront to the general that in his eyes would have been tantamount to desertion. Finally, the song came to an abrupt end. The general said nothing, and I returned to my quarters. I tried to lay my head down and get some sleep. However, it was to no avail as the rage of the battlefield was still going off in my head at some 180 or so beats per minute.

Entry #7

"What the fuck is that, Translator?"

"What is what, sir?"

"You don't hear fucking bells?"

"No, sir."

"Everyone quiet in here for a goddamn second," the general ordered, stretching an arm out with his hand up and fingers spread apart.

When the talking in the command center was muted, I was now able to clearly hear that indeed it was the ringing of bells, almost like distant wind chimes at first. At first, I should say, because they began to get progressively louder.

"You hear it now?"

"Yes, sir," I said. "From the church, perhaps? Maybe they added them to the mass."

"First Sergeant Jensen, open the command center door."

After Jensen opened it, the sound hadn't changed a decibel. We both looked at each other, a little perplexed.

"It's not from us," the general said.

"Doesn't seem like it, sir," I replied.

"Close that door, Jensen. And then get Sergeant Allen on the line. I want to see if it's coming from the sewers. Translator, start uncrating the ammo and weapons. Gunnery Sergeant Muncie, get your thumb out of your ass and lend him a hand."

Our silence kept in the command center, even though we had not been asked to remain quiet. As I said, the sound of the bells started to get louder. We were now all on edge. All of us I know were thinking the same thing. The Caliphate was descending on our position, mocking us by arriving with the ringing of church bells. Gunnery Sergeant Muncie and I were periodically glancing over our shoulders at the phone on the general's desk. Finally, the light lit and the general answered.

"Yeah, we hear it too. Sounds louder where you're at. You certain it's not coming from the sewers? All right, keep me fucking posted."

The general had just set the phone down when it lighted again. For a minute or so after answering, he didn't say a word, just listened.

"Jesus Christ, those foolish bastards."

"Who was it, sir?" I asked after the general had hung up.

"One of our intel units up there. The bells of the churches are ringing all over the goddamn place. I could barely hear him."

"Who's doing it, sir?"

"They're not sure. They think it's being orchestrated from some labor camp escapees. Goddamn, how beautiful is that though, huh. I wish I was up there my fucking self right now. I'd love to see the look on the faces of those ragheads. Fuck you all. We've still got some fight left in us, and we're not going fucking anywhere."

The general then walked over to the storage cabinet to grab himself a celebratory drink. With his back to us, I could see that he had quickly signed the cross. It was something I had never seen him do before. I wasn't certain though whether the gesture was for the sounding of the bells or for the souls of those from the labor camp who surely in a few minutes would be coming to the end of their lives.

The ringing did fade out as I had expected. Bell by bell you could almost discern was being taken offline. When it finally ceased altogether, the command center returned to its normal activity. I alone was re-crating the boxes of ammunition and weapons when the general stepped up to me.

"You know what the strangest thing is, Translator?"

"What, sir?"

"Have you ever heard a fucking thing down here? I'm mean when the war was on up there, we could feel the rumbling of the earth if an explosion was close enough. But the call of the muezzin, the sounds of automatic weapons, their car horns and megaphones during rallies, never. So why the fuck do we hear bells?"

"Maybe it's their frequency, sir."

"Yeah, maybe, Translator. Maybe it is the frequency. I'm just not so certain it's the frequency of the bells."

"Then the frequency of what, sir?"

"Of God, Translator. The frequency of God," he replied with a fade out of his voice.

Entry #8

I had finished translating the last of the documents that were taken from a police station we had hit a few days back. One, in particular, seemed important enough for me to run it immediately to the general, even though it was quite late. The guards outside the entrance to his sleeping quarters inside the command center shook their heads upon my arrival.

"Is he sleeping?" I asked, questioning why I wouldn't be allowed in.

"No visitors tonight."

"There's something here he'll want to see," I said, holding up the documents.

The two of them looked at each other before one took the documents from my hand and entered the room. About five minutes later, the guard returned and held the door open for me. The general was sitting on a chair, a bottle of whiskey on the floor to the right of him and to the left a fishbowl full of Kit Kats. The fishbowl was a new addition, and I briefly turned the corners of my lips up. I say briefly because no sooner was I breaking into a smile that I noticed he was holding a silver chain, onto which a dog tag was looped.

"So he's leaving in four weeks." The general was referring to the imam. He had been called to Saudi Arabia and wouldn't be back for a few months.

"Appears so, sir," I said.

"You got anything else for me tonight?"

"No, sir."

"Then you're dismissed," the general then said, not even bothering to stand up and salute me off. I made a turn to the door, then turned back.

"The dog tag, sir?"

"PFC Mahan, Translator. Against all my better fucking judgment, I sent him out last night on a raid. Took a grenade for the three soldiers next to him. And all the king's men couldn't put him back together again."

It was then I realized why the general didn't want to take any visitors. Besides the loss of another young soldier, PFC Mahan was the other guitar player for the general's band. To him, I knew that band represented family. And I knew that once you became a part of that family, you also became a part of his soul.

"I'm sorry, sir. I'll say a prayer for him tonight."

"Who the fuck you going to pray to, Translator?" the general asked of me as he rose up. "Huh, who? You really think He gives a fuck what you have to say? Or any of us for that matter. Christ, Translator, isn't it goddamn obvious, He stopped listening a long time ago."

I had no reply. Instead, I just stood there and watched as he walked by me and out into the command center, where he continued on to where PFC Mahan's guitar rested. There, he draped Mahan's chain and tag over an arm of the guitar stand.

"Why the fuck are you still here?" he said with his back still to me.

"I'm leaving right now, sir."

Entry # 9

"Goddammit!" the general yelled. He had just finished reading a message that had come in from the Jinn. "Those motherfuckers."

I then watched as he walked over to the map of Ayla and fixed his eyes on the middle of it.

"Translator. Get me a tank out of my desk and ten goddamn army men."

I handed him the plastic men first and he arranged them on Al-Hayat Plaza, right next to the other ten army men that were already there. After handing him the tank, he fit it in between the two machine gunmen that had also been placed there. A minute or so went by before he nodded his head and spoke aloud.

"It's doable."

"What's doable, sir?" I asked.

"Retrieving the bodies of those two soldiers that a unit of ours left behind last night."

"I thought they hid them, sir."

"Yeah, they hid them alright, Translator. In two fucking garbage cans. But they've been found and are now hanging like an art exhibit in the middle of Al-Hayat Plaza. First Sergeant Johnson."

"Yes, sir," the first sergeant said after hurrying over to the general.

"Gather the men in that unit up and bring them here at 1400. Tell them I'm serving lunch in their honor."

"You're going to reward them, sir?" I asked.

"Goddamn right I am, Translator. Not only did that unit hit the police station, but they also took on two squads of Caliphate regulars. That takes balls of steel. So, I'm going to cook them the best rabbit anyone's ever had. Then, I'm going to tell them to get their asses ready because we're going back out there early tomorrow to bring back those soldiers."

"You're going too, sir?"

"Goddamn right, I'm going."

"What if—"

"What if I don't come back, Translator? Is that what the fuck you were going to ask?"

"I didn't mean that you weren't—"

"Of course that's what the hell you meant. But if I don't, then I guess you're in charge, Translator."

"Sir, I . . ." I stuttered.

"I'm fucking with you, Translator. Jesus Christ, of course you wouldn't be in goddamn charge. I wouldn't worry your pretty little head about it though because I am coming back. And with those boys swung over my goddamn shoulders. Now set a table for six. I've got a few more things I need to work out before I start deboning the rabbit Gunnery Sergeant Muncie brought in last night."

Entry #10

The general was at the back of the command center primping the ACU coat and trousers he had just donned. A few minutes before he had nodded for me to dismiss the two soldiers who had escorted her in. It was almost six weeks since I had last seen her. Then, she was watching her lover being bathed in muriatic acid but showing no emotion. Then, she had blonde hair flowing down her back. Now, she was thinner. Perhaps ten or fifteen pounds so. Her hair was dyed black, cut short, and parted at the side. She had on a brown thobe, perfectly tailored. She would have no problem passing for a thirteen- or fourteen-year-old boy up there in Ayla.

"How was your vacation?" the general asked.

She said nothing.

"Consider yourself lucky," he started to say while straightening out his mandarin collar. "At least you got to eat and drink. Fuck, Moses got 40 days on Mount Sinai with no water or food. And shit, Christ got forty in the Judaean desert, all the while accompanied by the goddamn devil. You try getting some rest with that motherfucker whispering sweet temptations in your ear."

He looked immaculate when he started moving toward her. He looked like he was getting ready to meet the enemy head-on. Then, he saluted her like the soldier she was, and in return, she saluted him back.

"At ease, Grace."

She clasped her hands behind her back, and he walked over to his desk to pour himself a glass of Scotch. I don't think it was the drink that brought him there though. It was as if he wanted some space between his next words and the girl he was about to deliver them to.

"You were like a daughter to me, Grace. I believed in you. And I trusted you. More than anyone else under my command. But goddamn, you really fucked up. Compromised every person down here. It was only by fucking luck that we're not all dead. And I hate having to be goddamn lucky. There's only so much of that shit you have before it runs out."

The general finally took a sip, swirling the Scotch around in his mouth first before swallowing it, as if it was an antiseptic to disinfect her past sin.

"Okay, enough of that. You did your time. And I need you on this one. I'm assuming your Jew already told you where I'm sending you."

She nodded.

"I just want you to know this isn't a suicide mission. I got the Jinn in on this one. Your Jew is going to get you in, and then the Jinn is going to get you out. I want that motherfucker, Grace. We've both wanted him for a long time. You have any questions?"

She shook her head.

"Okay, good. Go get some rest. I'll give you the briefing tomorrow at 0700."

He saluted her and she in return. As I was holding the command center door for her to leave, he called her back.

"Oh, and Grace. I'm sorry about Fatima. I had no other choice. You know that, right?"

"I know," she said, the only words she had said the entire time.

Entry #11

"You may approach, Corporal Langton," the general said and the soldier stepped to his desk.

"Sir, the imam's been assassinated."

"We put eyes on the body?"

"We did, sir," the corporal answered. "Two different units. Both put him into scope as they were carrying him through the streets."

"Goddamn, I knew she'd get him."

The general then got up from his desk and walked over to the wall that on it had our tree of faces of the most important Caliphate figures. After ripping down the photo of the imam and crumpling it in his hands, he turned back to the corporal.

"What's it like up there, Corporal Langton?"

"Pretty chaotic, sir. Everyone's in the streets right now and the Caliphate soldiers are doing building-to-building searches."

"Did you order everyone back in?"

"Yes, sir."

"Good job, Corporal. We're going to lay low for a while. Tell the men to enjoy a few days of R & R until this blows over."

"There's one more thing, sir."

"Go ahead, Corporal."

"There's been an incident, sir."

"Of course, there has. Because lately, I can never get a good report without it being followed by one that's completely fucked up."

"A suicide bomber has hit Mosque #4."

"We don't have any suicide bombers, Corporal."

"Yes, sir, we don't. We believe it was the man we sent to take out an ammunition depot. We think he took a wrong turn."

"A wrong turn, Corporal? Is that your euphemism for someone going completely off the fucking rails?"

The corporal didn't return an answer.

"All right, Corporal, refresh my memory, just where the fuck is this Mosque #4?"

"In the old River West area, sir. It used to be Our Lady of the Angels. They were also using it as a madrassa."

"How many?"

"Their papers say forty-seven children were killed. We think it's probably pretty accurate."

"Jesus Christ, what a fucking mess. The imam they would have forgiven us for. This, though. This is going to set them on fucking fire. Any word from the labor camps?"

"They've already started executing prisoners, sir."

"First Sergeant Jensen, get a message to the other sectors. Tell them what's going on. And Translator, go find Lance Corporal Myers and tell her to make an inquiry to the Jinn. I want to know where The Assassin's at right now, and if I need to send some men up there to help him bring her back in."

The imam's death we had orchestrated. As we had tried on two other occasions, it was of no surprise to anyone we had finally succeeded. Death, when expected, can be overlooked. With the madrassa, we were not aware of the lone wolf. That I am certain. The general, while ruthless to those who came through the sewer system looking for infidels, would never have ordered the killing of forty-seven school children, even if they were being trained to exterminate what remnants of other religions their forefathers had failed to fumigate.

Our best guest placed the assassination of the imam and the bombing of the madrassa only hours or so apart. Three months, four months perhaps between the events and most likely they would have thought nothing more of the incidents than ordinary attacks in the linear course of the war. Instead, because of the proximity, they in Ayla married the two into one funeral parade. The city mourned for a week. And now it wasn't just the mission of the Caliphate to seek our eradication, it was also the mission of all its citizens.

Entry #12

It was seven minutes past eight in the evening when the three soldiers walked in. The body that two of them were carrying was neatly wrapped in white linen. I rushed my eyes over to the general, who at that moment was standing over the map of Ayla with his arms spread out and hands gripping tight to the southern edge of the city. All of us knew who it was. And in respect, we pulled our stares away and immediately returned to what we were doing, though none of us made a sound. It was the longest silence I think I ever had to endure.

"Have your men lay her on the couch," the general ordered before walking over to his desk.

The sergeant nodded to his men, and they carried the body over.

"I'm sorry, sir," the sergeant then said.

The general nodded to the words of condolence and set his eyes on the floor to the left of him, where they remained as if he was paralyzed in sorrow. I wasn't sure what to do. I'm not even sure he knew what to do. Finally, I decided it was probably best to relieve him of that decision, and so I asked if he wanted everyone to leave. If anything, it gave him another chance to make an order, to resume being our general.

"Yeah, everyone get the fuck out of here."

I waited until the command center cleared and then began to make a start for the door when he called me back.

"Not you, Translator."

I stopped and watched as he started to pace. At first, I expected him to go directly to the storage cabinet and bring out a bottle of whiskey. Then, I realized he wanted this pain to come with clarity. He would not drink to her death. To him, I am almost certain it would have been irreverent to her life.

"You know what I feel like, Translator?"

"I can't imagine, sir."

"I feel like God. I feel like what a dumb fucking idea it was to send my child to the slaughterhouse. And now, just as He must have, come to the realization in the aftermath that the sacrifice didn't mean a goddamn thing. But at least I understand now, Translator."

"Understand what, sir?"

"Understand why He never intervenes down here on this fucking earth. I know what He's thinking now. He's thinking to hell with all of them. No mercy, no heaven. For anyone."

I had no words for that. He was probably right. He then walked over to the couch where she lay. He took to a knee, and after pulling down the linen to reveal her face, I heard him talking softly. It could have been to her, or it could have been to God. He finished by signing the cross over her body and looking at me over his shoulder.

"Go find First Sergeant Johnson. Tell him to send for the Jew. He should have one last look at her."

I left to find Johnson. After that, I returned to my quarters and lay awake for what was probably hours. I imagined the last moments of The Assassin's life as that Caliphate unit closed in on her. I imagined the horrors that now lay ahead. I imagined my death but still could not imagine the pain that would accompany it.

Entry #13

The attacks on the madrassa and killing of the imam were followed eight days later by the issuance of a decree banning women from wearing niqabs and burqas. Now they could only pair hijabs or khimars with their abayas or jilbabs. The effect on us was devastating and our body count was rising. We could no longer walk among them under the camouflage of their own theocratic law. It greatly limited the intelligence we could collect, as our cameras up there had limited viewing. No longer could we do our daytime reconnaissance in their busy markets and streets, strolling unobtrusive in the midst of them. No longer could we pinpoint raids on stores that carried necessities we needed like bags of flour, stationery, toiletries, medicine, medical supplies, batteries, light bulbs, and fertilizer for our hydroponic gardens. And, no longer could we orchestrate those grand missions on their police and military units or those assassinations we carried out to let them know that none were truly safe.

Now, we had to feel our way blindly through a nighttime city that had always been under curfew. When all your targets are through serendipity, it makes you nothing but a gambler. And if you play long enough, all gamblers eventually run out of money, as we were starting to run out of soldiers. This was not something the general was ignorant of. A resistance could not afford a war of attrition, in either supplies for its people or targets of its occupiers. It had to fight a war of survival and a war that let the enemy know it could still kill. It had to hang on until reinforcements or a miracle arrived, neither of which we understood would be coming our way. The end was nearing and I was readying my head for it.

∞ ∞ ∞

I couldn't sleep and arrived at the command center early. The only soldiers there were the ones at the surveillance cameras. The general was sitting on a chair practicing on his guitar, which was not plugged in. I stood at attention and listened.

"At ease, Translator," he said after finishing.

"Thank you, sir. I see they were able to find you some picks," I said. A week ago he had misplaced his last one and had to resort to using a quarter. That twangy sound he was getting pissed him off to no end.

"No, I found a set in a pocket of my guitar case. Fucking forgot I had them there. Not like me to be forgetful."

"It's understandable, sir. Considering the situation."

"That's no goddamn excuse. I'm here to lead. Not to forget. You know what I'd do if I wasn't in command of this sector?"

"No, sir."

"I'd go find him."

"Who, sir?" I asked.

"Hetfield. I'd bet you my left fucking nut that right after the invasion he moved his ass back to Lucas Valley. Probably not too far from the ranch he has there. I got him living in the woods, writing new material, bowhunting for food and picking off the Ahab stragglers that happen onto his turf. I don't see him as part of some militia. I see him with his family, going about his duties to make sure they're safe and sound." He then paused for a second. "You know what I would ask him, Translator?"

"No, sir, I don't," I said.

"I'd ask him if he's finally written off God for good now. The first time was when his mother died when he was sixteen. His parents were

Christian Scientists. And when his mother got cancer, she didn't seek any treatment because according to her faith, one is healed by God's hands alone. The problem is that God has no hands. He's just got eyes, Translator, just eyes."

"I'm sure he'd be glad to have you up there with him, sir."

"Maybe he would. Maybe he wouldn't. But I'd fucking show up there anyway."

The general then stood up. As he was returning the guitar to its stand, he looked over to me.

"All right, Translator. We got shit to do. I want that list on my desk in an hour. Goddamn, I feel like a 1945 Adolph Hitler getting ready to pinch the cheeks of children I know are too young to even give a decent wipe of their ass. This just fucking sickens me."

The general was referring to the list of new inductees I was compiling. He had been forced to lower our conscription age from eighteen to fifteen in order to replenish the ranks. Prior to that, we had no problem pulling in new soldiers from the sewers. Those were the escapees from either the labor camps or wanderers who had managed to survive the nearly three and a half years since the invasion. Now though, in this last month, there wasn't one soul who came through the sewers of Ayla. It had become a dead zone. I no longer feel safe. And in this uneasy state of fear, I now feel the cold and hunger again. And I now hear the silence. And in that silence, I imagine the sounds of footsteps of Caliphate soldiers scurrying into position in our freight tunnels. I imagine I am unable to pull the trigger and put a bullet into my head when the exact time calls for it. I imagine they are dragging my body away. I imagine my body nailed to an inverted cross. And there, I am wondering why it is taking death so long to free me from this pain.

Entry #14

The door to the command center opened and another soldier entered.

"Jesus Christ, even when I have explicit fucking orders I can't get a fucking minute of peace. Excuse me, Translator."

I stepped aside and the sergeant took my place.

"Sir, the post is set up across from his quarters, and we got eyes on him as we speak."

"Good work, Sergeant Raymonds. Keep those shifts in fours. I don't want anyone fucking falling asleep."

"Yes, sir," the sergeant replied, saluted the general off and then left the command center.

"Something wrong, sir?" I asked.

"Yeah, there's a lot fucking wrong, Translator. We got a spy in the house."

"You think they know where we're at?"

"If they knew where we were at, Translator, we wouldn't be having this conversation. We'd be waist high in dead fucking bodies, both theirs and ours."

"Do you know how he got in?"

"My best guess is that he came through the sewers a while back and was picked up by one of our patrols. Right now, he knows one of the entrances but has no way of getting that intel back up into Ayla unless he escapes. And since we got all of the egresses guarded, I'm pretty fucking certain he's not getting up there with his Caliphate heart still beating."

"Why not bring him in?"

"Because the best spies in a war to have are the ones who don't even know they've been discovered. I want a little more time to see just what the fuck he's up to before hollowing out his skull with my Bowie knife."

"How did you find out?"

"Went to mass last Sunday to see how the new priest was doing."

"Didn't know you attended Service, sir?"

"I don't, Translator. I was there out of curiosity. Last priest we had, as you know, we found strung up in the tunnels. Apparent suicide. Found that a little fucking odd. So, I wanted to have a look around to see if maybe it was someone in the crowd who had a problem with the clergy."

"What gave it away, sir?"

"Two things. First, he was reading the Mass from fucking cue cards. Then, at the Eucharist, he lifted up the chalice but never tilted it enough to actually take a drink from it. Now to me, that's either a priest on the wagon or a good Muslim. And since I've never heard of a priest on the wagon, I'm pretty sure we got a good Muslim. A soon to be dead one. But a good one nonetheless."

Entry #15

I worked until 2201 hours. Afterward, as I had now been doing with some regularity, I brought myself to the quarters of the prostitute and the girl. As I was about to enter, I encountered one of our soldiers exiting. He gave me an indignant push in the chest and then went about his way. I entered. The prostitute was sitting on the floor. She had a pocket mirror held near to her face. By candlelight, she was applying a new line of lipstick to her lips. I gave her a stern look, one of reprimand. She knew what I meant.

"Those eyes remind me of father's," she said, briefly turning my way.

"And what if the girl awoke?" I asked.

"Then she would have woke alone," she answered after smacking her lips so that they were now crimson. "We in room just down way. He walk me back like gentleman."

"There's some meat here today," I said, referring to the loin of rabbit I had been able to obtain.

"What do you eat if your food now our food?" the prostitute said to me after I had unfolded the food from within the blanket I had been carrying. Along with the rabbit, I had brought along a loaf of bread and three Kit Kats I had earned. I set it all on the ground.

"I require less than what I am given," I replied.

"Your body says you are liar."

She was right. Since I had started bringing them the lion's share of my rations, my weight had dropped noticeably.

"How are they doing?" I said, glancing over to the girl and infant, who were both in their dreams.

"They sleep better than us. That I am certain."

"Is there anything else that you need? Candles, perhaps?" I said as I looked at the candles situated about the room. All of which seemed to be at a quarter mast.

"No, they now burn as if no need for wax."

"You don't find that odd?"

"I find it more odd I am soon to die in freight tunnel directly below city I once live in for only seven days."

"And how do you know your death is imminent?"

"Soldier you just see tell me he love me like one tell wife. It always sign end of something nearing beginning."

"Has she said anything to you about the infant?" I asked with a momentary glance at the girl.

"She say many things about infant."

"Do you believe her?"

"I believe in nothing, so I am not one to ask."

"I'll be back tomorrow," I said and then made a start to leave.

"Wait."

"Yes?" I asked.

"I tell you one more thing. I tell you sometimes there more voices here than people."

I left. I did not inquire any further as to the nature of those voices. She wouldn't have told me anyway. But I believed her. I suppose I needed to believe her. Needed to believe that there indeed was some divine providence looking over at least two of us down here in hell's waiting room. Perhaps it was an agreement reached between the god of Islam and the god of Christianity. A holy concord whereby the god of Islam allowed free passage to the Christian girl and her half-Muslim infant in exchange for a warrant to invade the freight tunnels.

Entry #16

Without warning, the hand of the general shot out like the tongue strike of a cobra and took hold of the sergeant's neck. For a good five feet or so he carried him off with that chokehold until he had the sergeant pinned against the wall. In all of my time here, I had never seen him so inflamed with any of his men.

"Escaped! How the fuck could he have escaped? We had him under twenty-four-hour surveillance. To me, that means we got eyes on him every goddam second. To you and those clowns underneath you though, it means a little fucking catnap here and there is all right," the general continued screaming, all the while spitting his words onto the face of the sergeant. "Jesus Christ, Sergeant Raymonds, you just signed our fucking death warrant."

My best estimate was probably sixty seconds now that the sergeant hadn't been able to take in a breath. Like all of us in the command center, I feared the general wasn't going to let go until the sergeant expired right there. I looked at the other soldiers. No one seemed as if they were going to intervene. I therefore found myself with no other choice but to hurry over and lay a hand of reason on the shoulder of the general. As I did so, I tensed my body, readying it for a blow from the general. However, he pulled his hand away and the sergeant collapsed to his knees, gasping for the breaths he had missed.

"Get him the fuck out of here," the general said before turning around and heading toward the cabinet where his bottles of whiskey were stored. He momentarily veered off course to swing his arm like a machete at the drum kit. The hi-hat and snare he leveled to the ground. The sergeant took to his feet and left. I stayed where I was, afraid to leave but certainly not wanting to remain. The bottle uncapped, the general put his back to the cabinet and tilted that square chin of his up. He had a long drink in him before looking my way.

"After I finish this, you're taking a walk with me, Translator. First Sergeant Jensen."

"Yes, sir," Jensen answered.

"Get a message off to Major Adams in Sector 3. Tell him we've gone code red over here and need to dock."

The priest had escaped. The Assassin was dead. I imagined us now a sub finally detected by the enemy. Our time left on earth had now been pronounced in heaven. All of us in the command center knew it. The escape of the priest meant that the Caliphate now knew we were operating out of a level below the sewers. They would soon be arriving in Sector 4. But as with all things in heaven, that time was unknown. It could be hours, or it could be days. Since I had been with the general, not executing the spy was the first mistake I had seen him make. Unfortunately, it happened to be a mortal mistake. And he, more than anyone, knew he should have killed the priest immediately after discovering he was one of the Caliphate. Perhaps, that is why he spared the life of the sergeant. We arrived two miles to the south from where we began our walk from the command center. It reminded me of a construction site. The whole crew stopped their work and stood at attention to salute the general.

"At ease, men. You can get back to work. I'm here for First Sergeant Crowe," the general said.

They dropped their salutes and continued about their digging. We waited a moment before a soldier came up to us, wiped the sweat off of his brow, and then shook the hand of the general. He was a few inches taller than the general and could have passed for a college lineman, except that at the moment he looked more like a coal miner with the smudges of dirt on his hands, uniform, and face.

"General," he said while saluting.

"I put you in charge and yet you still dig with them."

"I lend them a hand now and then, sir."

"How much longer you got here, First Sergeant?"

"Two weeks, sir. Worst case. Two and a half. And that's assuming Sector 3 is still digging at the same rate we are."

"What if I tripled the men you have down here?"

"Maybe buy us a few days. That's it. There's only one tunnel to dig. Can only fit so many men in that space at one time. Did you contact Sector 3?"

"I will as soon as I get back to the command center. I'll tell them they need to pick it up on their end also."

"So now we're down to about 10 days," the first sergeant said.

"Still a long fucking time before we link up."

"They know where we're at, sir, don't they?"

"Yeah, they know, First Sergeant. All right, I'll send those men down here. They should arrive in about thirty minutes. In the meantime, you should probably set up a defensive position. If you need them, I can send down another 240 and some M32s."

"I'll take what you can spare, sir."

Entry #17

I picked up my first guitar at fifteen. A Glarry ST3 Fender Strat rip-off that I bought online for about sixty dollars. Played it through high school a bit and then through my four years at Northwestern to give me a break from studying. I was never a great player. But I could play by ear if given enough time to listen to the music. I had even joined in with a few friends at a few open mics around the city.

The first song took me about three and a half weeks to learn. The next three, maybe two weeks apiece. I practiced on an acoustic guitar I had picked up at the commissary. It was an old Washburn that had a nice full-bodied sound. The action was pretty high, so it helped to form some pretty good callouses on my fingertips. It took a while that day to get my courage up. But somewhere toward the end of the night, I walked over to the general and handed him a sheet of paper.

"What the fuck's this?" the general said after he took a glance at my setlist of four Metallica songs.

"I can play Hetfield's parts on these, sir?" I said.

"Play it on fucking what, Translator?"

"Guitar, sir. I've been learning them."

"Bullshit."

"No, sir. I can."

The general put his eyes back on the setlist I had given him, and then called over to the first sergeant.

"First Sergeant Jensen, plug in one of those guitars over there and bring it to me."

"Yes, sir."

The general fit the guitar over my head as if he was awarding me a medal, helped me to adjust the strap, and then took a step back.

"It's umm . . . It's going to be 'Fade to Black,' " I said as I took a coin out of my pocket.

"You just play, Translator. I'll tell you what the fuck it is."

I put two fingers on the fretboard and could feel the general staring at the formation. After my first run-through of the intro, I saw him give First Sergeant Jensen a thumbs up to raise the volume. I was now into the first verse strumming an Am, C, G, Em chord progression when the general grabbed the neck of my guitar and muted the strings.

"Well, fuck. That's good enough for me. First Sergeant Jensen, grab your bass. PFC Thomas, get your ass behind that kit. We've got some playing to do."

I didn't think my audition would be followed by an immediate performance. Mentally I wasn't prepared. And neither was I physically. As I stood off to the left of the general, my left hand was shaking and my legs were beginning to notice the heavy burden of my body. They were waiting for me though and so I began the intro again. The general started in on the solo not long after and his notes seemed to float off the strings like they were balloons being set free. PFC Thomas and First Sergeant Jensen followed right behind and now, for the first time, I felt as if I was truly part of the United States Marine Corps of Sector 4.

The next two songs were sonic attacks. And then, somewhere through the middle of the general's ferocious solo on the fourth song, I noticed that the red bulb off to my immediate right was lit. I had to do a few double takes to make sure it wasn't my imagination. I thought about pulling the plug out of my guitar to get everyone else's attention. That thought I interrupted with one that said what in the hell does it matter now. Just enjoy this moment because it will be the last one you will ever have. You knew it was coming.

The general held that last note until he got every last bit of sustain out of it and then walked over to the amp so that the feedback was like a screaming siren. After it was all over, he returned his guitar to its stand as if he was laying an infant back into its cradle. He then took a towel to his face and headed over to the security screens. His eyes were darting from image to image when finally he started heading for his desk. On his way, he gave a solid pat on the shoulder of Jensen, who was standing there like a mannequin.

"First Sergeant Jensen. If I were you, I'd pawn that fucking bass you have in your hands for something that might just do a little more damage."

"Yes, sir," the first sergeant said, finally coming out of his trance.

The general picked up the phone. We were all silent. We were waiting on his words like Abraham at the rock.

"Lance Corporal Wells, you ready to do some killin' today? That's good. Cause in about five fucking minutes you're going to get your chance. They've broken through and are heading your way. Well, I'm glad you asked, but no, it's not a goddamn drill. I'm looking at about thirty infantry that in about a few more minutes are going to be right up on your ass. Set up a position a block down and give 'em everything you have. And, Wells, if that unit of yours falls, I don't care if you're missing your goddamn arms and legs, you better find a way to use your tongue to move a few coal cars into position to block their advance. We need to slow those motherfuckers down until I can get some more men your way."

"What do you want me to do, sir?" I asked after he set the phone back on its hook.

"Get the ammo and all those weapons out of the crates. I want them all lined up when the men start arriving."

"Are you going to sound an alarm?"

"What fucking alarm, Translator? There's no goddamn alarm here. Alarms bring panic and panic brings confusion. We'd be running into ourselves."

"Shouldn't they know?" I asked, referring to the people of Sector 4.

"That's a philosophical question, Translator. Is it better to have time to think about your death, or is it better to just be informed at that fucking instant?"

"I'm not sure, sir."

"Neither was I, Translator. But the question had to be answered, and so I gave it one."

Entry #18

Seventy hours since it started. We ran out of amphetamines a day back, and now we're chewing qat leaves in order to keep our bodies in motion. The general ordered me back to my quarters to get a few hours of rest. I'm so wired though, and my head is pounding so hard that I can't seem to get the sleep both my mind and body need. And since I can do neither, I have decided to make what I understand will probably be my last entry in this diary.

What's left of us, has pulled back to a perimeter that leaves only 1000 or so meters to the command center. They're everywhere now. I was hoping for gas, but it's become obvious that they want him alive. He understands that. And if it meant his surrendering would save a single one of our lives, I know he would have already walked himself out there wearing only his Metallica T-shirt and the words "Fuck the Caliphate" inscribed in black marker on his forehead. But he knows his surrender wouldn't matter. He knows they would still torture every one of us before escorting him away.

I'm terrified. God, I'm absolutely terrified. When death is inevitable, each sip of breath is a joy that you're still alive, and each exhalation is a regret of what you could have done. I have a picture in my head and I have a sound in my ears. They are gathered outside the command center indenting the door with a battering ram. They are screaming "Allahu akbar," and they are screaming "La ilaha illallah, Muhammadur Rasulullah." The door falls forward. I empty my M4 into the first wave. I reload and empty it again. They do not care and I am out of ammunition. I have my Glock 19 out of its holster. I have the barrel indenting my temple. I have a finger tapping lightly on the trigger. They rush me. One forks my neck with his hand, and another relieves me of the gun I have at my head. I see myself being led away. I am thankful to my creator when my lungs expand. I am desperate for death when they deflate.

Entry #19

It is 10:39 p.m. Directly above me is a manhole that I have read is about two miles from the entrance to Sector 5. Directly behind me is the passageway I have traveled. It was known to no one except for the general. Unfortunately, on my climb up to the manhole, my hands slipped off the ladder and I fell back down, breaking my leg.

I have been here for almost five days. For my thirst, I lick the moisture that slides down now and then from the concrete. It is just enough to allow me the strength to move this pen across the page. For sustenance, I have nothing anymore. My last Kit Kat I consumed a day ago I believe. Sooner or later, they are going to find this passageway. Or, sooner or later, my body will give up its fight.

In my lap, I have my Glock 19. I stare at it frequently. However, neither the hunger nor the pain in my leg has yet to persuade me to put it up to my head. And so, to keep my mind off my own death, I think about the crystal balls of Sector 4. I think about whether the girl was able to escape with her half-Muslim child. I think about the general inverted on a cross and burnt alive. And then, I think about my last moments in the command center.

When I returned there, the door was wide open, and ammunition was being passed out to returning soldiers who needed to rearm. I took the place of someone whose commander had called him away, and as I stood there with four others, it reminded me of an old-time fire brigade passing out buckets of water down the line. Unfortunately, we were running out of "water" to kill the fire.

During a break in which there were no soldiers waiting on us, the five of us would turn to the security screens. The images from the video feeds were absolutely terrifying, and in horror, we watched as they decimated our defenses. When they tired of firing their RPGs and automatic weapons into our lines, they sent in suicide bombers. I saw soldiers with only fractions of their limbs left continuing on with the fight. I saw women and young girls being punched in the face by the stocks of AK-47s and then being dragged off by their hair. The old they came upon were either having their throats quickly slit or necks quickly snapped. Babies and children were being ripped from the holds of their mothers and stomped on underneath the boots of the invaders until the heads spilled open. Since our cameras gave only a visual display of the carnage, you had to put your own soundtrack to the screams and cries that were emanating from their wide-open mouths.

The general calmly ordered retreats from area after area as if he was matter-of-factly switching off circuit breakers to a house in which he was trying to conserve energy. We were running out of areas, and although it didn't show on his face, he was well aware that we didn't have more than a quarter day left until they reached us.

"It's time for you to leave, Translator. I'm ordering the command center door closed in about five minutes," the general said as he put an arm around my shoulder and ushered me over to a corner of the room.

"To where, sir?" I said.

"To exactly where this fucking piece of paper tells you," he replied and then stuffed it into the front pocket of my uniform.

"I'm staying here with you, sir."

"The hell you are."

"I'm not leaving, sir."

"I'm not asking you, Translator. It's a goddam fucking order."

"No, sir."

He then stepped back, pulled out his forty-five, and pressed the barrel into my forehead so hard that I had no other choice but to lean into it in order to keep from toppling over.

"We're going to die here soon, Translator. And my order to all the soldiers in this room is going to be to fire every bullet they have except for one. And that one, I want them to empty into their own fucking skull. But with you, Translator, I don't see that happening. I see you hesitating just long enough for one of those goat fuckers to grab you and rip the gun right out of your hand."

"I'll do it, sir."

"No, you fucking won't. So I'm giving you ten seconds to exit this position before I euthanize you."

He would have put that bullet into my head. Of that, I have no doubt. I could see it in his eyes. He was right, and he would have done what I couldn't have done. When I exited the command center, I opened the folded sheet of paper. On it was a crude sketch of a map. It led me to an area unknown. It led me to here. God, just take him into heaven. I know he's already dead by now and I know he's standing there at your gates. He may not have been a warrior of your words, but he was a warrior for those you had born. He'll fight for you there. And there is no better man that you would want by your side.

∞ ∞ ∞

It is 5:17 a.m. Dawn is readying her carriage for another journey across the earth sky. How beautiful that will be. How I wish I could be there for her arrival. I have only one last entry. And God, it is for you. Please, when I die and my soul is to take, I ask that you not put a uniform on it and ask me to fight. As you can see, I am only a translator and not a soldier.

3 THE NURSE

Nurse's Entry Log, Patient #12

Time: <u>12:19:00</u>   Day: <u>6</u>   Month: <u>Dhul-Qa'dah</u>
Gender: <u>Male</u>   Height: <u>5'11"</u>   Chest: <u>41"</u>   Arm Length: <u>35 1/4"</u>
Weight: <u>129 lbs.</u>   Shoe Size: <u>12</u>

<u>Notes: Measurements arrived yesterday and recorded. By photo taken,
he is bearded. Trim is short. He is Caucasian with an olive tone. Color
of hair is brown, worn without a part. There is no sign of recession at
either the temples or the crown. The patient appears healthy. I am in the
company of Private Scott. The private arrived here at 12:10:00 hours.</u>

Nurse's Exit Log, Patient #12

Time: <u>12:51:00</u>   Pulse Rate: <u>77 bpm</u>   Blood Pressure: <u>121/75</u>

<u>Notes: The patient exited at 12:46:00 hours. His demeanor was calm.
He spoke little during the course of treatment and showed no signs of
anxiety. He requires no follow-up.</u>

Patient #12

I was arranging the rolls of tape and washcloths on a table when the access code was rapped on the door. It startled both me and Private Scott, who was acting as my sentry. I looked at my watch to see it was a half hour earlier than the assigned time. The next sound I heard was the click of the safety on his weapon. As I looked at Private Scott, I could see that his finger was now on the trigger and his eyes locked onto mine. I reached down to my ankle and pulled out my weapon. After also flipping my safety to the off position, I gave him a nod. Private Scott unlocked the bolt to the door and stepped aside. The man behind it entered with the barrel of Private Scott's M4 pointed to the side of his head, and the sight of my Ruger American 9mm aimed directly between his eyes. At first, I did not see his uniformed escorts. Then, they entered the room and stood beside the man. According to the protocol, I looked down at the table to ensure the picture on the cell phone screen matched the patient. When it did, I told the two soldiers they could take leave.

The door was bolted shut again, and the man stood there waiting to be instructed. Though he was as thin as the rest of us, he wore it differently. He wore it like he had the strength of a hundred men. I looked at his eyes to see if they held the same resolve as his body. They were even more determined. More determined than any of the other patients I had previously serviced. And that worried me.

"You may have a seat over here," I said to him, patting a hand atop the examination table that was situated in the middle of the room where I was standing.

He walked over and seated himself, folding his hands together and setting them between his knees. And while his demeanor seemed quite placid and he had purposely placed his hands in plain sight, I moved my working table back a few feet. One can never be certain down here. This is not a place to trust. It is a place to thank God every day. And it is a place to curse Him every night. But it is not a place to trust.

"You're early," I said.

"They dismiss at 1745. There would be no one there if I arrived here any later," he replied.

It was an answer he should not have given and words I should not have been privy to. And I was angry that I had been told. I was to be ignorant of any facts, like those of a firing squad are ignorant as to which one carries the actual bullet.

"Then you should have told your commander," I said.

He did not have a reply to that, which seemed a little strange to me. I turned from him and continued with the prepping of the items on my table.

"You're the nurse?" he then asked.

"Yes," I said.

"I expected a man."

"I am sorry to disappoint you."

"I am not disappointed. It is just what I expected."

I hoped that those were the last words he would speak. However, he continued on as if idle talk was the norm for an appointment such as this. I had no other choice but to engage him, though. Not doing so could agitate him. And that could have dire consequences. I wanted him to remain quiet like all the rest. I did not want to enter into any prolonged conversation. I did not want to get to know him. I never wanted to get to know any of them.

"Please remove your shirt," I then asked of him.

He unbuttoned it with haste. Most who come here are hesitant. I gave a good look at his chest. The wounds were obvious. Gunshots, large caliber. Four I counted. From their location, I was surprised he was still alive. He set his shirt aside. I reached over to the table and dipped the cloth in my hand into a basin of water. When I turned back to him, he was pulling out a lighter and a rolled cigarette from his pocket. I dropped the cloth on the ground and quickly confiscated both. He rushed to grab my wrist. Not as if he was going to twist it in order to set the objects free, just to let me know he disapproved. Private Scott rushed over and jabbed him hard in the shoulder with the butt of his M4. It must have hurt like hell, but he didn't show any of the pain. He just unfurled his fingers and withdrew his hand slowly, like that of a retreating cobra who had been warned by his handler.

"If it was that important, you should have had one before you came," I said to him sternly though I did not raise my voice.

I took another cloth from the table, dipped it into the basin of water, and began cleansing his chest. The four bullet entries I washed over were like large countersunk holes and it made me squirm a bit. I felt like a mortician, a coroner, which if anything went wrong after he left, I suppose I was. I had begun washing his back when he spoke again.

"Is this necessary?" he asked of me.

"It is not. But it is part of the protocol," I said truthfully.

"How long have you been doing this?" he asked.

"Almost as long as I have been here," I answered.

"And that has been how long?"

"I am not certain. I do not count the days like the others." It was the truth. I saw no reason at all to tally my misfortune. I took a towel and dried him off. He lowered his arms down. "Please leave them up. There is a garment I need to put on you first."

Over his head, I slipped the garment I had sewn myself the night before. It was crudely fashioned out of a rice sack. The hessian was a good first layer, resistant to moisture in case he started to sweat. This man though I could not envision perspiring.

"I had a daughter," he said as I was smoothing out the wrinkles. "Lily. Her name was Lily. What was your daughter's name?"

I froze for a moment in the question. I could feel my body wanting to shake. I could feel my hand wanting to reach out and slap him. Instead, I turned my back to him and began the final preparations at the table. He went on speaking.

"We were in the foyer by the front door of our house. My wife had just finished fitting Lily's little arm through the sleeve of her coat. She kissed Lily on top of the head and I then kissed her, my wife that is. You remember minutiae like that. You remember it after the fact. As if there was something in the details that could have been changed to change the outcome. But in all actuality, there was probably no sequence of events that could have changed anything that night. I could have been the one who fit Lily's arm through the sleeve of her coat and kissed her on top of the head and the end result would have been the same. But an addled mind does not believe that events prior have no effect on the outcome. An addled mind holds on for years to the belief that if just something had been different, some small disturbance in the sequence, then the final outcome would have been different, much different than the one that occurred."

I wanted him to stop. I did not want to get to know him. I wanted him to remain anonymous to me like all of the others.

"I was there with my daughter for a dance," he continued. "It was a dance for only fathers and daughters. She had on her favorite princess dress, powder blue with white frills. Atop her head, she had on a silver tiara set with rhinestones. On her feet, shoes like slippers with a jewel on the front and a heel that lit up with every step she took. Over her hands, to her elbows, she wore long white gloves. I gave her permission to line her lips red, but just for that night. For that concession, she gave me a kiss on the cheek, and in turn I smiled so wide that into my mouth one could have fit the entire universe."

I lifted up the first vest from the table and turned back to face him. He already had his arms raised for me. The top four leather pockets were fitted with two TATP tubes apiece. On the back, the batteries, timer, and detonator were placed at the bottom. Above that, two pouches that I had filled with screws and ball bearings. I told him he would have to be careful now. I told him these are not as stable as we would like them to be. I told him if he bumped hard into something it could go off. He nodded and continued on.

"Lily and I walked to the dance that night. We lived only eight blocks from the Catholic school she attended. It was a cold night. Bitterly cold, in fact. But beautiful. A light snow that could easily have been mistaken for confectionary sugar was falling all around us. There was no wind to speak of, but the clouds were moving fast through the sky, like a caravan of ghosts in a mad rush to a destination they only knew. The moon was a thief, so bright and full it seemed as if it had stolen all of the sun's light once and for all. It was all so perfect. So perfect in fact that it must have pricked hell's jealous rage."

I had just finished tying the straps at the sides of the vest into large bows. How ridiculous that I always tied large bows I thought when it wasn't at all necessary. I was now performing a check of all the wired connections.

"During our walk, Lily would intermittently release my hand and break out into a sprint. When she got far enough away, she would stop and look back. It was then I would come running up to her. And each time that I did, I would take her into my arms and lift her high up into the air, twirling her around and around. I remember thinking why does it have to be a dance. Why can't I just leave work early every night and take her out for a walk? Why have I become a slave to a job that I do not even enjoy? My life. It is right here before me. It is right here in my arms."

I returned to the table and picked up the belt that I would strap around his midsection. In those leather pockets, I had packed nails. Some were three inches in length, others were five.

"When we finally got to the school, I held the door open for her to enter. I always held the door open for Lily. I wanted her to know how she should be treated when she became a young woman. That she should not expect less from the man she was to love and marry. She did not walk right through this time. Instead, she pulled my hand away and closed the door. There she gave me instructions in the most gentle of ways, by bringing them forth in questions. She asked if it was okay if we did not dance together that night. She asked if it was possible that I did not come up to her while she was playing with her friends. I agreed to both requests and then opened the door for her again. She ran through it. I stood outside for a moment and looked over to the church that is connected to her school. It is a magnificent structure. A brick façade from the year 1910 with twin bell towers and a grand dome of white, modeled after St. Peter's Basilica in Rome. A church that makes you believe in God. Atop stand twenty-six angels. At night, they are flooded in the brightest of light. I remember signing the cross. I remember thinking there must be a heaven. I remember thanking God for Lily."

"Too tight?" I asked. He shook his head like I knew he would. I could have tied it like a tourniquet and he still would have shaken his head.

"The dance was in the basement gymnasium of the school. It was well decorated. Her mother had lent a hand that morning. Streamers and balloons adorned the side walls. Silver stars, snowflakes, and icicles hung from above. The floor was covered in glitter. It was magical. Magical not only for the children but also for the fathers who attended. As Lily had requested, I stood on a side of the gymnasium and kept out of her way. But I never let my eyes leave her. I was amazed at the way her other classmates were attracted to her as if she was some opposite pole of a magnet. She gathered all of her friends into a circle where they all began to dance. She directed everything. My little Lily, how little I really knew about her I thought."

"I have garments for you now," I said to him. "You will need to remove your pants and shoes."

"Socks?" he asked.

"It is up to you. Sometimes they wear them, sometimes they do not."

I walked off to another part of the room to where I had set the white pants, thobe, and sandals. He waited until I returned to undress. I know he waited so I wouldn't miss a word.

"I stood there for let's say twenty minutes before one of the other fathers made an introduction. What we talked of I do not remember. His name was Uwe. That I do remember. It's an easy name not to forget. I was wondering if he was German. He looked German. As he was talking, I heard the sound of the doors closing to the entrance. It was faint over the music playing but quite unmistakable as they are large and heavy doors. When I turned my head, I could see five or six of them. I knew immediately who they were. They were all in black with their signature scarves around their necks and balaclavas hiding their faces. This had not been their first event. They had already struck in a few cities during the year. Isolated incidents we were told so as not to alarm us.

"They screamed 'Allahu akbar' and then began firing randomly with their automatic weapons. Uwe was one of the first. The bullet buried itself into his head mid-sentence. Strangely though, he was able to finish his thought. I found that odd. Odd, but I suppose logical. The brain has already released the words and the mouth is still forming them when the bullet pierces the skull, enters the cerebral cortex, and then exits. So, why shouldn't his last words have been completed? 'Who are those people?' he had asked. It was a fortunate shot. Fortunate for both. Fortunate for the gunman that his random aim immediately found a victim and fortunate for Uwe that he did not see his daughter cut down in mid-stride as she came running over. Anyway, I ran for my Lily as Uwe expired. In the mayhem, I was pushing aside other children as they screamed, some of who fell to the floor. I am not proud of that. It haunts me to this day. But what other option was left for me."

He paused for a moment, looking into my eyes. I suppose he was looking for forgiveness. I'm not sure I gave it to him. I am not sure what my eyes returned. He continued.

"When I reached Lily, she had already dropped to the floor and was curled into a ball, her little white-gloved hands over her ears. I covered her with my body and then put a hand over her mouth. If asked, I could not say how long we lay there in terror. A minute, two minutes, eternity. All are the same interval of time in a moment such as that. The bullets now were being fired in short intervals. I knew they were executing people. No longer was it random. The footsteps. That is what you are tuned into at that moment. You are waiting for your turn. You are wondering if you can cheat death. You are praying to God, promising Him your soul and selling all future options on your life. One of them was over us now. Though my eyes were closed, I could hear him breathing, the exhalations of a beast. Lily squirmed for a moment, unaware. I had no other choice. I hurried myself up to reach for his weapon. He fired four times into my body. All of them felt like I had been struck with a sledgehammer. I was instantly propelled backward. I could feel the squeeze on one of my lungs and each breath I took after was excruciating. I was face up, staring at the ceiling when what seemed to be a white cloud quickly erased all that I was looking at."

I saw him teeter a bit as if those shots had entered his body again. I reached out and steadied his body, afterward easing him back to a sitting position on the edge of the examination table. I could not have him fall. I was soon enough though to find out that it was not the bullets that had caused him to falter.

"I awoke in a hospital bed one week later. It was the dead of night. The morphine drip into my vein belied the corporeal damage that had been inflicted. Immediately I unplugged myself from the machines and made it into the hall before collapsing. Two days later, I awoke again. My father was to the side of me in a chair. At the door, my wife's father. One knows instantly when deaths are about to be announced. My father-in-law told me my wife had died. I asked how. He said she had taken a bottle of vodka along with a bottle of drain opener. An agonizing end that I know she wanted it to be. When he left, I turned to my father to ask of Lily. He said she had passed in the gymnasium."

He then reached out and grabbed my hand so hard that I could hear the bones of my fingers crack.

"You understand, it is not that I was weaker than her mother. It is not that I wanted to keep on living. It is just that I craved revenge more than I craved death. And vengeance, above even love and hate, is the most powerful of all desires. It is the opiate for the body and mind when they have lost all will to keep moving forward. And that revenge I only partially satiated. A few weeks after the attack, four of them were killed in a street battle in the middle of Lake Shore Drive. The other one they captured and put on trial. He did not make it that far. I shot him as he entered the court. I was tried and convicted. Two years I spent in jail before the invasion. When chaos reigned, the jail was abandoned and I fled. Now, I am here before you."

"I am sorry," I said. It was a trite condolence, I know. It was unsatisfactory in every way. But I had my own horrors. And they had already hardened me to stone.

"Is there anything else?" he asked.

"Yes," I said. "I will need to connect the pocket trigger to the detonator. Please lift the thobe to your neck."

I walked around to the back of him. It is a connection I always make after they don their garments. However, with him, I wanted to make sure he was in the right frame of mind after concluding his story. In the end, he seemed calm enough and not at all agitated. I ran the wires to the front and clipped the pocket trigger to the belt I had put on him.

"It is not a light trigger. For obvious reasons. You will have to depress it with more than a modest amount of force."

He nodded and pulled back down the thobe so that once again it fell to the length of his ankles. I looked him over. He was a good choice, I thought. The tone of his Mediterranean skin would blend in well up there.

"We are done?" he then asked.

"With the fitting, yes, we are done. I still need to go over the operational instructions."

"I have had training."

"I understand. But I am required."

I told him that after carefully removing the belt and vest, he was to place them on the ground. I told him to wrap the belt around the vest containing the explosives. I said there is a prayer mat near the door. I said to use it to disguise the belt and vest. I said that after delivering his package to the target, he would have exactly two minutes to leave the area after depressing the trigger. He asked for the blast range. I answered by saying it had an approximate radius of one hundred and ten feet."

He pushed off the examination table and put his feet on the floor. I nodded over to Private Scott and he unbolted the door.

"Private Scott will be your escort to your next location."

He nodded and shook my hand. I was exhausted from his story, and I was glad he was leaving. He was a step out the door when it occurred to me that he did not reach down for the prayer mat. It then also occurred to me that he had no such intention of removing the vest and belt from his person.

"Private Scott, please bring him back into the room."

The private did as I had ordered, and I then instructed him to leave us alone for a minute.

"It was not forgetfulness, was it?" I asked, sliding my eyes to where the prayer mat lay.

"I have no need for it."

"If I report this, you will go nowhere."

He did not give a reply.

"Where are you going?" I asked.

"I have been ordered to an ammunition depot on the edge of Ayla."

"Your orders, but not your destination. You are returning to her school, aren't you?" I said, now understanding what he meant when he said they dismiss at 1745.

"They have turned it into a madrassa."

"So their children. That's your target?"

"An eye for an eye, so the God of the Old Testament says."

"And what do you think your Lily would say?"

"I do not think dead children say anything at all."

"No, you are right. They do not say anything at all. May heaven then welcome you."

"If it does, I will refuse the invitation."

"You must take the prayer mat, though. It will help you as you are walking around Ayla. They will think you are returning from prayer, or going to it."

"Then I will take it."

I opened the door for him. He had just begun to turn when I spoke my final words to him.

"Elizabeth. My daughter's name was Elizabeth." I felt weak after uttering it as I had not spoken her name since they had raped, tortured, and then disemboweled her before my eyes.

"Then this is for Elizabeth and Lily."

To his face, I brought my hands and then kissed him as if we were husband and wife. He understood. He knew that kiss was for our children. It did not matter whether we had conceived them together or not. He left, and I said a prayer for both our souls. It was the first time I had spoken to God since I felt my Elizabeth being ripped from my arms.

4 THE LOVERS

The Old Man and Us

The sounds of the last crying soul faded to silence. It had been what we were waiting for. We weren't alone. No one's ever alone here. But at least for all I knew, those who slept with us were not awake. My body I moved nearer to her and threw a soiled blanket over the two of us. Blankets down in these tunnels are life jackets for children and lovers. We were side by side like lazy dogs too tired to stand. I reached an arm across her body and placed a hand upon her cheek. Down here that touch of skin on skin is the only thing that makes you feel alive and somewhat human again.

"Perfume," she said.

I slid a hand into the pocket of my jeans and sprayed us both with what was left in the bottle. You stink constantly down here. Showers are by tickets and tickets are given out once every two weeks. I gave her one kiss on the back of the neck. She asked for a mint even though we were taking breaths from the same direction.

"It's the last one we have left. And it's not even a mint. It's an orange-flavored aspirin," I replied.

"I don't care. I'll take half," she said.

I broke it in two between my teeth. She stuck out her tongue and I placed it there.

"The old man is still awake," she said in a whisper.

"How do you know?" I asked.

"I saw him move his head toward us."

"What the fuck?" I replied, pulling back the hand I was just about to slip under her sweater.

"It's okay," she said.

"It's not okay. It's fucking weird. I can wait."

"No, don't. Anyway, he always watches us."

"How come you never told me that?"

"I don't know. It's not like it's a leer. It's just more like a remembrance of things past."

"Proust?"

"I guess. I wasn't thinking about it. But yeah. That's probably where I got it."

"Do you stare back at him?"

"Yeah."

"Jesus Christ. So while we've been making love, you've been gazing into the eyes of someone else."

"It's not someone else. It's just the old man."

She then reached behind her and squeezed my hand gently. That always made me want to fuck her. That always made me bury whatever we had been arguing about. I threaded the button of her jeans through the loop and eased down the zipper. I never needed any foreplay with her. Even when we were kids up there, I was always rock hard after that zipper had reached the end of its journey. I continued on, pulling her jeans and underwear down to her calves. Down here you stay half-

157

dressed. Down here you remain like kids in the backseat of your parents' car.

I slid my hand under her sweater and clamped it hard onto one of her breasts. I was in her not a moment later. I was breathing heavily. She was not. I couldn't help myself. I had to edge my head up and over her shoulder. The old man checked me with a glance as if I was just a bystander and then resumed staring at her. If I wasn't thinking about cumming in her, I would have been thinking about how much more fucked up could this get. She was right though. It wasn't a leer. And it wasn't her face he was staring at. He was just remembering what it was like to have someone that near.

Gilly's in the Tunnels

"How was your day?" I asked her after I had entered our quarters and began stripping out of my clothes. It was always such a lame start to our conversations but one that I always gave. It was fucked up to tell you the truth. It was like we were still living back in our Lincoln Park apartment. But if you didn't do it that way, you would lose your mind. The saying down here is that you have to fake it to make it. And since we weren't doing so well in the beginning, we decided to just go along with that maxim.

"Sad," she began, "we took in four soldiers and two of the elderly. None of them made it."

"I'm sorry," I replied in a tone devoid of any emotion whatsoever. A part of me wanted to yell "Cut" so I could have one more go at the line. The other part, which I let stand, told me to print it because sometimes you get so sick of pretending that you haven't become immune to all of this death.

"How about yours?"

"Just another day of digging. Wish they would tell us where the fuck we were digging to."

"Oh, I heard something interesting today at the infirmary."

"What was that?" I asked while I was slipping my University of Illinois sweatshirt over my head. I thought I would get another month or two out of it. However, after I pulled it to my waist, I widened another hole and realized it wouldn't last much longer. That sucked royally. I had already used up all my work credits on a pair of woolen socks and boots two sizes too large. I would now have to continue looking like an asshole for a little longer. Not that it mattered to me. But sometimes it did matter to me.

"It seems we have a very famous rock star in our presence."

"Who?"

"Gilly."

"Whoever told you that was lying," I said quickly to invalidate. "What the hell would he be doing here? He's from England. Well, from wherever those motherfuckers call England nowadays."

"Yeah, I was pretty skeptical at first until I remembered that he was here for a retrospective of his work at the MCA a week or so before the invasion. It's possible he never got out."

"Shit. You're right. He just might have still been here. I remember reading an article in the Chicago Reader about that show. Did they say where he was?"

"No."

"Did you ask?" I said.

"Of course, I asked."

"Hey, how about on Sunday we take a walk around the tunnels and do a little search for him. Sound like a date?"

"Sure."

"Fuck, that's what I miss most. I don't think there was a weekend that we weren't at the Bottle, Metro or Hideout listening to a band."

"Yeah, I miss that too."

Story of Our Lives

We were lovers before all of this began. We were lovers back then in our freshman year. Fifteen's such a great time to start fucking. Everywhere you do it is different and an impromptu affair. You walk around at night for hours just looking for another spot to fulfill your lust. You hit the woods. You hit the fifty-yard line of your high school. You hit the park and squeeze your bodies into the rocket ship. Now and then you get lucky when one or the other's house has been emptied of all inhabitants. It's like the first time every time. You kiss with your eyes closed and screw with them open. You talk for hours afterward. You say things you wouldn't dare tell your best friend. A walk back to where your parents live. A walk back hand-in-hand because you're not yet old enough for a post-coitus flip to the edge of the bed. A long kiss behind an elm or maple. You both enter through a window because you both blew curfew by a mile. In bed you lie awake for another hour because once again, it's been the best fucking day you've ever had.

That was our first year. Fuck, that's where I would set the time machine. After that, it didn't go as planned. We had our problems. Her infidelity or mine usually the crime. But we were kids, and how can you blame either of us for wanting a new face, a new storyline. We would break up. We would hook up again. A seemingly endless cycle of hating and then loving each other. High school ended, college came. We got stronger. We stayed together through those four years like we were married. Again, the time of our lives, pretty fucking close to when we were fifteen I was thinking. I loved her with all that my small heart could give. I think she felt the same. Who knows though? You never know. You'd be a complete idiot if you thought you did.

Eventually, we both graduated and took jobs in the city. We found an apartment in Lincoln Park over on Cleveland Avenue. We had our 8 to 6 jobs. We had our 9:30 shows, and we had our time in an endless array of dive bars. We had our parties and our friends had theirs. A perfect life for me. Perfect for her too I can only surmise. It seemed like it anyway. Six months in and I was guessing maybe another four or five years before we started talking kids.

We never saw it coming. No one saw it fucking coming. There were a few attacks in the city before that. I remember we went to the candlelight memorial for those children slaughtered in the Our Lady of the Angels' massacre. All isolated incidents, so we were told. We were just packing up our things to head back home when the drones came. We were way up north in Door County on a Christmas break from our families. On the drive back, we started to get alarmed as reports started to come in about the dead in the streets. Outbound, the roads were jam-packed. Inbound, we had a little bit of room. I drove at top speed when I could, and used the shoulder as an alternative. She took my hand across the center console. I squeezed it tight. We both knew something was seriously wrong. And that was confirmed as we finally exited the highway. The streets looked like the zombie apocalypse had come. Some walking erratically and covered in blood. Some writhing about on the ground. Some already obviously dead. We pulled up to our apartment, ran inside, and jammed chairs under the door handles. I grabbed a baseball bat and handed her a bunch of kitchen knives.

For twenty-nine days we binge-watched the reports from all over the fucking place. We kept thinking this couldn't be fucking real. We kept thinking the Mannheim Front would certainly hold off those fanatic assholes. We kept thinking then if not us, then certainly the Russians or Chinese will put an end to all of this fucking madness. On day thirty, the explosions got louder, and our television became an emergency broadcast screen saver. I told her we need to get the fuck out of here. She said we should just stay and hide. I won the argument, I guess. We grabbed what we could and stuffed it into our backpacks. More mortar shells and now the sound of automatic gunfire. We went east because everyone else was heading fucking east. We got as far as Clark and Lincoln Park West when I saw someone open a manhole cover and lower themselves in. I nodded over to her. She agreed.

And that was it, the story of our lives before our descent into hell. Five small paragraphs and it's all told. Except of course, for the time we spent getting here. But that's not something we even talk about, so I'm content with leaving it at that. I want to say that we were one of the lucky ones not to be captured or killed on that first day after the Mannheim Front fell, but now I must admit I wish two of their bullets had found our heads. Now all I want is to go first. I can't imagine her death before mine. I can't imagine staring into the lifeless eyes of the girl who showed me how to be both lovers and best friends.

A Sunday in the Tunnels of Sector 4

The tunnels were crowded on Sundays. Most of us had the day off. People were either going or coming from an aimless walk. People were either heading to or returning from the commissary. Those working the black market were standing around every hundred feet or so, making out like kings selling things you never imagined you could get in this living catacomb. Others were just out of their quarters to get away from staring down four walls until another Monday came. I was actually looking forward to this day. I didn't think we would find Gilly. But that wasn't the point. The point was that we had something to look forward to. That was something we never had before since being down here.

"Are you ready?" she asked me.

"Almost. I'm having trouble here. I don't have enough lace to get to the second loop."

"We have an extra one."

"Really?"

"Yeah. But you'll have to block."

I got to my feet and stood in front of her while she went to our hiding place. I looked around. No one in our quarters was paying attention. I did a count of the faces. Five. We still had five.

"Aren't you a little excited?"

"I suppose," I said.

"Are you going to ask for his autograph?"

"No. And you're assuming we're actually going to find him."

"Oh, we'll find him," she said confidently.

She was bouncing on her toes, the way she used to do while waiting for me to get ready for a show. Might as well, I thought. Might as well pretend. It's the only fucking thing you could do here to get through another day. A few days before we had talked about how we were actually going to conduct the search. She said we should just stick our heads into every room we passed. I couldn't disagree. It was probably the only way we would find him, if he was actually here to be found.

That though I understood would also ruin our day within no time. Down here, it would be like ducking your head into the rooms of either an insane asylum or an oncology ward looking for a fucking rainbow unicorn. So, I sold my next eight weeks of breakfast ration tickets to get us something that could muddle the reality a little bit.

"Where in the . . ." she started to say as I lifted the 375-milliliter bottle of peppermint schnapps to my lips and took a swig.

"What?" I asked.

"Give it here."

"Give what. I don't have anything," I said and put it back where I was originally hiding it.

"You want me to reach in and take it?"

"I was hoping."

She played along and reached down the front of my pants. She took the bottle out, and as she was taking her drink, put her other hand down my pants. I wanted to turn around and go right back to our quarters and make love to her.

"Where did you get this?" she asked after taking her drink.

"Found it."

"Liar."

"Maybe," I said.

"Oh, I don't care. Just give me a kiss."

That taste of alcohol on her lips brought back so many memories. It was a kiss from the past, a kiss when nothing mattered at all. We continued on. We finished off the bottle in no time, which didn't surprise me because both of us always drank like fish. We had a good buzz on. We talked about days long gone. It was one of those walks where if I had a ring I would have asked her to marry me. Ten minutes later she stopped at another room and said this was going to be the one.

I rolled my eyes and watched as she popped her head in.

"Oh my God," she said after pulling it back out.

"What?"

"It's him."

"Yeah, okay," I said, thinking she was just messing with me.

"No, it is. I'm not kidding. When I shined the flashlight in, he turned around for a second. Anybody would recognize that face."

"What was he doing?" I asked.

"It looked like he was painting."

"In the middle of hell?"

"Yeah, I don't know. What did you expect him to be doing?"

"I'm not sure. But painting certainly wasn't one of them."

"Come on, we'll just say hello and then go."

I gave her a look that said I was still thinking it over when she suggested that I should at least have a peek for myself. I agreed to it and took the flashlight out of her hand. He was standing with his back to me. He had on yellow parachute pants and a matching suit coat. He was painting on the clay wall with oil pastels I think. From what I could see, he already had drawn a moon, earth, and sun. I was just about to pull my head back out when he turned to the side and spoke to me.

"One flash of light means you might have been mistaken. Two flashes now makes me think you meant it all along. Please go get the one who is your other half and stay for a while."

We had no other choice now but to become interlopers. He was lighting more candles when we entered. He pointed to an arrangement of Moroccan-styled throw pillows for us to sit on. Hell knows where he had gotten them from. Two teacups were placed in front of us, and then he poured. It was like we had wandered into a restaurant and the proprietor himself was tending to us. When all had settled, and he had taken a seat across from us, she spoke.

"I'm sorry, Mr. Gilly," she began, "we didn't mean to take you away from your painting."

"It is I who should be sorry," he answered. "The earth has fallen on hard times and I have no rocket ship to offer you a way out of here."

She glanced at me with a smile. I smiled back. It was exactly what anyone would have wanted to hear from this iconic rock star. We stayed there for about two hours or so I think. He was hospitable and gracious. He was humble but still larger than life. We said little and just listened to him. He spoke on Japanese fashion and German art. He talked a little on the mysticism of Aleister Crowley and then went straight on to astral travel. He gave us a primer on Homer's "Iliad" and the flaws of religion. The only thing he didn't speak about was what he had been made most famous for.

When we left, he said for me to take her hand in mine and keep it there while walking back. He said to make the best of every moment. He said you understand we're not evolving and we're not going anywhere. We didn't speak a word to each other, neither on the trip back nor when we returned. We kissed to the taste of peppermint schnapps. We made love facing each other. We just had our best day since being sentenced here. So, both of us understood, why fuck that up by rehashing the past when we could just keep moving forward.

Mad, Mad World

If I had to guess, I would say that a good third of our population here have completely lost their minds. How could you blame any one of them? Insanity I am guessing can be a wonderful retreat. After being here, it's actually probably the sanest thing someone can do. There's this woman, one of the pacers, I see her all the time on the way to the excavation site. Her face tells me she's somewhere in her mid-forties. Her hair though has run all the way on to eighty. It is snow-white, thin, and frayed in every place. She walks up and down the tunnels with a briefcase in her hand and a cell phone to her ear. A lawyer or executive at one time I am assuming. She is constantly on that phone barking out orders or arguing with the dead airwaves. Her mannerisms are still condescending, and her walk still cocksure. Sometimes I wish I was her. Sometimes I wish I could dial up the past and keep it on the line. Then there are the wall talkers. These are mostly comprised of the elderly. Day and night they stand in the same position, whispering to the concrete tunnel walls. When they speak their hands are animated, gesturing all about. When they are not, they are catatonic head to toe. They piss and defecate at will, so it is necessary to have dog walkers. Those are what we call the people who volunteer to watch after them. I don't have that in me. I can't see spending my free time looking after the undead.

This is just fucking insane. This is like being placed on hold waiting for death to get back on the line. They'll find us. That I'm certain of. They'll dig us up from our living graves. We'll die twice. We'll die in a fashion worse than the first. All I want before that is one walk outside, her hand threaded through mine. Just one stroll in the sun. The heat on my face. The sunbeams on hers. For that, I would sell my soul if just somebody was buying. Nowadays, it doesn't seem like anyone is buying. That makes me a seller with no takers, a fool without any listeners. Sometimes my entire body is paralyzed with fear. Sometimes it's only my lips so that I can't seem to speak. All I know is that if I didn't have her, I would have found an easy way to check out a long time ago.

I'm An Asshole Most of the Time

"I need to talk to you," she said after I had come back from my work at the south excavation area. It had been another 12-hour day, and I just wanted to lay myself down. When she closed the bible in her hands, I knew it was serious.

"Yeah, sure. Let's talk."

"Private."

"Okay," I said and sat down cross-legged across from her. We both leaned in and put our cheeks side-by-side the way giraffes embrace. It was the way everyone here communicated when they wanted their exchange of words not to reach those of the others around.

"Please don't be mad."

"I won't be mad. Just tell me."

"I think I'm pregnant."

"Fuck," I said and pulled away from her.

"I knew you would be mad."

"I'm not mad. How could I be? It's half my fault."

"It's not a fault. It's a gift. I know it is."

"These gifts are death sentences," I said.

"For us?"

"No, for the child."

"I want to keep it."

"Do we have another choice?"

"Yeah. There's another choice. I've seen them do it in the infirmary."

"You never told me that."

"Wasn't something I wanted to talk about. It kind of twists your stomach when you see it up close. Makes you rethink what you thought before."

"How far along are you?"

"I think about three months."

"Shit. This was the last thing I was expecting. I mean we must have done it about five fucking thousand times without any protection and nothing."

"I know. It's odd, isn't it?"

"Yeah, it's odd, alright."

"I think I want a boy."

"I think I want a drink."

"See, you're not excited."

"I am excited. I really am. It's just so much to think about and my head already has no room to spare."

"Isn't that a lyric from Gilly?"

"I guess. I wasn't thinking about it. But yeah. That's probably where I got it. I know. Most of the time I'm so unoriginal. Everything I say is stolen off a lyric sheet. How pathetic, huh?"

"I love that guy, though. Always have. He makes me feel like home. I loved him since he was just a boy and God I love him even more now."

"Same," I said and wrapped my arms around her.

She was holding me tighter than I was holding her. I knew she had already closed her eyes and was thinking far ahead. I had mine open and was staring at the clay wall in front of me. It had a heart on it, and inside our initials she had drawn. I was thinking about the rocket ship in the park, and the first time I watched her draw the very same heart in black permanent marker. I was wondering if it was still there or had they repurposed our love for another one of their war machines. I concluded most likely it was gone as so would be this one when we were found.

Entry From Her Diary

Nothing to write today. Can't get my thoughts together in any coherent way. They all seem to be radiating out so fast that I can't seem to collect any one of them. Normally I would just stare at the top of the page and wait for another day. However, she was late for the infirmary this morning. It caused her to rush and forget to put away that lined notebook she had started writing in last night before I drifted off. So I thought, why not. Why not just copy from hers and place it into mine. I had plagiarized enough of her papers when we were in high school and in college so really what the fuck would it matter now.

He lies beside me asleep. I can hardly breathe much less close my eyes. I am so tired of watching everyone around me die. Death here is indiscriminate, not a soul exempt. The dead they are children whose blue bodies and blue faces make me want to scream. The dead they are old women and old men in which I see my grandmother's and grandfather's faces. The dead they're soldiers, bodies bullet-ridden and missing limbs. Then there are the suicides who are brought in here in an assortment of ages. They just ran out of hope and how can you really blame them. Hope certainly isn't an infinite well. It can run dry when you're constantly drinking from it. I tremble day and night. My teeth I find chattering even when I'm not cold.

I really shouldn't complain though. I have it better than most. I've been given two extra hearts to keep me alive. That's certainly more than most of those around me can say. I have the one that just started beating inside of me and the one that

170

seems as if it has always been there for me. I'll take that any time. I'll take that any place even here. It's funny, I didn't realize until tonight that you can be blessed even in the worst of times and circumstances.

She's Sick

She's been sick for the last two weeks. A cough that she tried to dismiss, but I started to have my concerns about. I was thinking pneumonia, and she was thinking just a cold. I told her as a precaution she should grab some antibiotics from the infirmary. She said they were bone-dry at the moment. I thought of trying the black market. However, down here antibiotics are gold, and we have nothing at all to barter with. I started planning on going above ground to perhaps steal a few things for which we could trade. One of the soldiers I had become friends with said he could let me follow him up on their next reconnaissance mission. He said he could get me a weapon and possibly point out a place to hit. After that, he said I would be on my own. What the fuck would that do? I've never shot a gun before, could never even get myself back to start in a corn maze, and in all probability, the only feat I would accomplish would be to leave my child fatherless.

I just want to hit rewind. I'd even back it up fourteen days when she was asking me what I thought of the names Michael and Jacob. She looked so radiant and alive when she said that. Motherhood I'm starting to realize begins well before the delivery. I'm fucking worried, though. I've seen this plenty of times before. I've seen death sentences handed down for the stupidest of fucking things. I've seen sepsis from scratches, raging fevers from body lice, and anaphylactic shocks from ant bites. Fuck, I can't believe any of this. I just want to yell up I quit, you win.

Panic and Dread

As had been the case for the last five days, I got permission to work only a half shift at the excavation site. As had been the case for the last five days, I skipped the lunchtime food line and went straight to the infirmary. My hunger had already been fed by panic and dread. She was on the makeshift cot by the wall. I switched places with the nurse who was sitting by the head of her bed. She patted me on the shoulder and nodded over to a table where a bowl of water and cloth rag lay. A blanket was pulled up to her neck. She was asleep, and in the middle of her body, the blanket was slowly rising and falling with every labored breath she took. I put my palm on her forehead. It felt like I had just set it down on the hood of a running car. Then I reached for the cloth rag, dipped it in, squeezed it out, and placed it on her forehead. She opened her eyes like it was a kiss from Snow White's prince.

"Hey," she said in a strained and whispered voice.

"Hey," I replied.

"I've been missing you."

"Me too. How are you feeling today?"

"I'm okay," she said, and afterward tried hard to stretch her face into that infectious smile she always gave.

"That's great," I replied, trying hard myself to give her back a smile of my own.

"Can you do me a favor?"

"Sure. Anything."

"When you come back after school today, can you grab my geometry book from our locker?"

"Yeah, of course."

"Thanks, I think we have a test tomorrow."

"Yeah, you're right. Thanks for reminding me," I said.

"You know what I was thinking about before you came?"

"No, what?"

"The rocket ship we ended up in last Saturday night."

"Yeah, that was pretty cool."

"It was more than pretty cool. It was our first time, and I'll remember the way you loved me my entire life."

She just had time to finish that last sentence before she went into a coughing fit. I lifted her up and laid her head on my shoulder. When it finally stopped, I set her back down. And at the corner of her lip, I could see that a small trickle of blood had started to run down her chin. It looked so bright and full of life, sort of like a melted rose petal. I wiped it away with the sleeve of my U of I sweatshirt, and now it was colored white, orange, blue and red.

"You should probably close your eyes and get some rest."

"You're right. I feel so tired. I don't know what's gotten into me."

"Just a cold," I said, "you'll be back at school in no time."

She closed her eyes, and I had just started to dip the cloth rag back into the water when she opened them again.

"Oh, I almost forgot."

"What?"

"I wrote you another love letter."

"Thanks."

"It's not here, though. It's in our secret hiding place. I'll give it to you when you come back over after school."

"Okay, I can't wait."

And then just like a switch had been thrown, she was back in the same state I had found her when I walked in. I was glad for that. I didn't want her to see all my tears falling out. It was actually the first time I had cried since all of this shit had happened. I don't think I held back because I didn't want to seem weak. I think it was more because I was just so fucking angry at all of this. Now though, it was easy to break down. Finally, I had come to understand that I was near to losing a love that could never be replaced. And like she had already known, it didn't matter where that love was. As long as we had each other, that place was always the best place.

Float On

I took her home from the infirmary after they said there was nothing more they could do for her. They said maybe another twenty-four hours. I told them they didn't know what the hell they were talking about. I said what a fucking waste of a space that only knows how to care for the dead. I lifted her into my arms and told them in a few days she's going to be walking back in here on her own two feet.

I screamed at everyone in our quarters when I returned with her. I told them to give me all their blankets so she could have somewhere soft to land. She was fading by then, like Christmas tree lights with a loose connection. Sometimes she would be off and sometimes on. The last thing she said, she said, "Don't be sad. You know I loved you here and I'll love you again. Our love, it just repeats no matter where." Those are the shittiest final words to leave someone with. No one should give those lines on their way out. I sure the fuck wouldn't. I would be more goddamn considerate. I would have said and half-plagiarized, "I guess I'm going to float on now. I sure hope you understand."

The old man was there beside me. He had that leather mitt of a hand up to his face. A thumb in one eye and his index finger in the other. Neither were large enough to plug those water holes. Sometimes they dripped. Sometimes they ran like a full-open tap. When she drew in that last breath, a part of me wanted to hold him for his loss. The other part, which I let stand, just asked if he minded leaving us alone because after all, I knew her a lot fucking longer than you.

Her head was in my lap when she died. I fell on top of her like someone had just blown a hole in my back with a shotgun. My tears were wetting her face when I realized that I was mourning for one when it should really be for two. I immediately slipped my hand under her sweater and placed it on her belly. It then dawned on me that he was probably still alive. It wasn't possible that the child inside dies at the same time the mother expires. There must be a few minutes of lag time so I decided to say just a few words.

I told him I was so fucking sorry for all of this. I said I wish there was just some way I could get you out of there. But right now, I feel like I'm standing over a well and you've fallen two hundred feet down. Listen, anyway, the situation isn't as desperate as I'm making it out to be. Your mother is only a few moments away. She's going to reach down with arms longer than mine and rescue you. And let me just tell you, don't shed a tear for this place because there's nowhere else you would want to be than where she's taking you. And there's no one else you would want to be with other than your mother. She's got a love greater than the universe. She's got hearts to place yours and her initials in. She's got this way of making you feel that even sometimes sadness can be a friend. Oh, and just one last thing. When in bed she tucks you in, you'll still be lying awake for another hour because once again, it'll be the best day you've ever had. I love you. Tell her I love her too.

Love Letters Make Me Want to Die

Two men came for her body yesterday. They were from the group that we call the Lime Line. It's a group that buries the dead in an extended tunnel that's on the far northwest side of the sector. A priest was waiting when I arrived there. He said a few lines to me and then to them. I wasn't really listening. To me, it was just all background noise. They'll go where they're going and not because they had been blessed. I had already condemned all religions after the invasion had hit.

They say when someone you love dies it feels like half of you is gone. I don't know what the fuck they think they're talking about. When you love someone that much, it feels like all of you has been ripped out. It makes you feel like you're standing on the edge of a cliff, and the only thing that will erase the pain is if you jump. Unfortunately, down here, there is no cliff and my breaths I can't stop because they're involuntary.

I returned to our quarters right after that. Everyone gave me a glance, but that was it. I understood. No one wants to think about those kinds of deaths. I dropped my eyes for a stare into my lap. It was the loneliest time I had ever had inside of my own head, and I knew I needed to get the fuck out of there. So, I turned around and from our secret hiding place pulled out all we had buried there. It didn't take long to find it. She had mentioned it back in the infirmary, but I just dismissed it because she had seemed to be in such a lost state. The love letter, though, she did actually write. And now I think why not. Why not just copy it and leave it as my last words. She always had a better future in her head than I did in mine, and those are the stories people want to read anyway.

Hello, my love. When I find the right time I will give you this. Telling you I was pregnant a few nights ago probably struck you blindside, and I should have had a better introduction. I really didn't think about it and I kind of just blurted it out. I know it's an addition to our love you didn't expect. I understand it might make you feel like you're headed for second place. But I want you to know that I've got enough room inside of my heart to fit both of you in and give it a first-place tie. I've always loved you, you must know that. I loved you when I first saw you, and then when you sealed it with that chocolate–chip cookie kiss. God, how my heart still beats double-time when you're near. Don't you know, we've got a story that's a lottery winner. We've got a rocket ship, and we've got stars we named from a fifty-yard line. We've got walks in the woods and all those endless talks. We've got hearts that still beat wild from our high school days and college years and we've got those late nights listening to bands and closing down those dive bars. And now, now we've got a little boy who is soon to come. What more, my love? What more could make us more complete than this?

It could have all come at a better time and it could have all happened in a better place. But things, as we know, don't always work out like that. So let's just pretend, huh? Let's just imagine, okay? It's the only world we've got and we can turn it into anything we want for him. We can draw stars on the ceiling and we can draw trees and animals on the walls. We can take walks with him through the tunnels and say they are ancient and magical caves. And every time he looks up at us and smiles, we'll be reminded of just what our amazing love could create. So please don't worry, my love, this is just another beginning for us. You know we've had so many and they've always turned out just fine. I love you. God, I love you so much.

5 THE JINN

REPORT #65:

Slow on the intel the last few weeks. But since I know you miss me so fucking much, thought I'd write anyway. Exterminated two jihadist bitches last night. Not sure what their problem was. Stopped me late at night in Masjid Park and asked me what the hell I was doing. Told them I was a fucking spy, and they should mind their own goddam business. Unfortunately, one reached for her radio. That one I plunged my knife into her eye. The other one. Well, let's say, didn't turn out so well for her either. Snagged another few boxes of Kit Kats for your candy-loving ass. You know where to pick them up. Not sure why I do this shit for you. Come up here and get your own goddamn candy bars. Oh, and Metallica still sucks. Their fucking music makes me want to put you in a hole and pour the blood of Lars Ulrich right over it.

REPORT #69:

See the photo. Guy looks like he's straight out of some Arabian GQ mag. This is a motherfucker you want. Heads up interrogation at the Fawzan labor camp. Does shit to people there even I would think twice about. Been watching him for a few months now. Likes walking around Souk #2 with his little daughter on his days off. Friday and Tuesday. Before leaving, picks up some baklava for her. And, ALWAYS, from the same stall. The seller is a leathered-faced old woman, two fingers on her left hand. Would love to take him down myself but you're better suited for the hit. Left you a case of Yamazaki 12 at House 3. Consider the blood splatter on the crate gift wrapping. And yeah, I did ask politely first before putting the cat's paw into the back of his black-market skull.

REPORT #70:

Nice job taking out the imam's double. Don't know what the fuck your obsession with him is? Same homoerotic fantasy I'm guessing you have with that shit band you worship. LEAVE HIM THE FUCK ALONE. We have a thousand more important targets.

REPORT #71:

Peace talks collapsed. Posters and handbills going up around city to join the new jihad. From what I've heard the al-Aqsa Brigade is already on the march. Really thought they were going to settle this one. The power-sharing deal though called for the imam to step down. He knew he'd be a dead man if he did so he said for them to go fuck themselves. Drones from the Brigade have started to drop leaflets saying the imam is really a half-Jew and that's the reason they're coming in. That's fucking masterful propaganda. Say he's all Jew and no one is going to believe you. Say he's half-Jew and everyone starts to wonder. It's all bullshit though. The real story is that the imam raped a twelve-year-old nephew of one of the Brigade's commanders and now they want revenge. Four suicide bombers in the last three days. Two at the Grand Market, one right outside their headquarters, and one at a rally. I give it a couple of days before the fireworks.

REPORT #72:

Al-Aqsa Brigade broke the front yesterday. They occupy about a quarter of Ayla now. City won't fall though. Last night took a scope out my window and saw all these small crafts starting to arrive. Seems the imam was able to call in a few favors. A counter is coming. Jesus, I love a good fucking fight. Stay inside. No reason to come up for air when they're slaughtering themselves. Which of course means you can go back to pulling your pud to that wallet-sized photo of the young James Hetfield.

REPORT #73:

Things here back to normal. Lot of Caliphate soldiers on R&R after the victory over al-Aqsa Brigade. You need supplies I got a store for you. Salaheddine bakery. One klick west of what was Old St. Pat's church. Some rogues selling leftovers from the war with the Brigade to the outer tribes. Lots of goodies I'm hearing. Anti-tank systems, mortars, AKs, grenade launchers and all that other feel good shit.

REPORT #74:

Joined the Hisbah last week. Guess they'll let anyone in. Assigned to the downtown area. Started out on patrol with two others. Down to one now until they find a replacement for Badeen. I know. I just get a new toy and immediately end up murdering it. Anyway, really didn't like Badeen too much. Small man who had the habit of clubbing women for the most minor of infractions. Just really pissed me off. He also liked to smoke a lot. Another goddamn thing that pisses me off. So, went to his apartment a few nights ago and waited until he stepped out to have a smoke. I have to say. It was quite enjoyable to see his little hands twitch in an epileptic manner as I continued to bash his head in. The other one is a wealth of information. Boasts a lot, revealing more than he should. He is a nephew to the right-hand man of the imam. Total fucking pedophile. Seems like hourly he's showing me naked pictures on his phone of these prepubescent girls that are sent to him by soldiers. I'll eventually cut off his dick and scrotum and shove them down his throat until he suffocates. I'm looking forward to that. For now though, he is still worth more alive to me.

REPORT #75:

Hisbah prick I work with took me to a dinner party last night. Held at the house of field general Abu Abdulrahman al-Shishani. One tall motherfucker. Sized him up at about six feet six. Long black hair. Red bushy beard, nose like an eagle. Can't really miss him. House is at 475 Umayyad. Large gray stone. Gold Coast area if you remember. Heavily guarded. Party would have made Caligula proud. Pre-festivities included a woman being raped by a white horse. Liquor in abundance. Two full bars. Imported Saudi girls walking around in nothing but black studded collars and serving up qat leaves on silver platters. Dinner was a feast to behold. No pork, though. That's the one thing they adhere to. You can rape, drink yourself to unconsciousness, and kill anyone you please as long as you keep the pig off the plate. Afterward, they flambéed a man. Put him on an inverted cross, lit him with a candle. One of us, unfortunately. Tomorrow I'll waste a few of them for that. Anyway, I didn't leave until the sun came up. When I took one last look at the house I saw al-Shishani up there on the roof. Facing toward Mecca and doing his prayers. Everyone's a creature of habit. He'll be there tomorrow. The day after that and then again. Easy fucking duck so take him out with a long range. An M24 should pop his head off like a dandelion. Oh yeah, almost forgot. James Hetfield licks donkey balls for inspiration.

REPORT #76:

No longer with the Hisbah. Prick had it coming though. Gave him a replica of the Grand Mosque for taking me to the dinner party. Granted it was a cheap piece of shit from the marketplace but he should have said thank you. Instead, tells me to get a file for him. I leave, wander behind him and then slam his fucking face into it. Unfortunately, had his head mispositioned so only 8 of 9 minarets went through. Reminded me of being a kid and not being able to blow out all the birthday candles.

REPORT #77:

What kind of shit show are you running over there? Soon as that bus pulled up with those kids your men should have unloaded on them. Not call me in and expect a goddamn miracle. You have any idea what it's like to see eleven kids get fucking blown up all at once. Jesus Christ, I got hit in the head with a tiny wrist. I'm out of my mind right now and that ain't any fucking good for anyone. Gonna get a few hours sleep and then go out hunting. Everyone deserves to die right now, which includes your dumb ass.

REPORT #78:

Got something for you. Was down at the Grand Market looking for a new tea kettle. Smashed my last one onto the head of the delivery boy a few nights ago. Long story. Anyway, saw Osmani and his entourage walking around. Guy's like a fucking rock star up here. Everybody snapping pictures of him and trying to get his autograph. You know what the hell he was doing there? Buying eggs. Motherfucker loves eggs, fresh fucking eggs. Wants to pick them out himself. So, got me to thinking. You're going to sell him some eggs. And those eggs you're going to inject with the thallium I included with this epistle. Any idea what that odorless and tasteless shit does to a human body? The first day he's going to start complaining of a little tummy ache. Next morning, he'll be vomiting all over the place and thinking he caught the flu. Around day 4 or 5, his major organs will begin slowly failing and his skin'll become so sensitive it'll feel like everything he touches is a live wire. This shit is just getting started though. During the second week, he's going to be a psychotic mess and his hair is going to be all over the fucking floor. Finally, around day 15, the convulsions will start arriving and soon after he'll drop into a coma, never to fuck with anyone ever again. Now if that isn't a perfect poison, I really don't know what the hell is.

REPORT #79:

Saw some kids hanged a few days ago for dancing. Three Caliphate soldiers on a joy kill strung them up. One kid's standing up there with a red ball in his hand. Wants to hold it on his way through the trap. They don't even give him that. They pry it away and it rolls off the gallows into the crowd. I push through all the sick motherfuckers watching and grab the ball like it's a garter toss. The kids drop, little legs twisting in the air, and inside I'm lit up like a bonfire. The hangmen leave and I follow them for about 12 blocks until they head into a garden apartment. Now, you want to know how to kill people, this is how you kill people.

I knock. Door opens. Got my barrel pressed to a head before a word is said. I walk him in. The other two are on a couch. Order all three to their knees. Bound and gag 'em. I then start bouncing the red ball until it starts getting into their heads just how fucking miserable it's going to get. Drop the drawers of one and start making love to him with my 6-inch serrated knife. In my final thrust, I push the blade so far in that the handle is flush with his anus. It takes a while to die like that. And it's not an easy death. The heart beats hard from the excruciating pain. And every time it does, more blood squirts out the body. Second one I break the C5 vertebrae. He's now got no use of his legs, torso, and hands. I then drag his limp body to the tub in the bathroom and give the faucet a quarter turn. For the third hangman, I spin the death wheel inside my head and it lands on fire. So, I empty the kerosene lamp on the corner table down his throat. Put a lighter to his tongue and the flame shoots down his fucking throat. He's puffing thick black smoke from his mouth like a dragon and running into walls trying to escape. Goddamn, I'm going to sleep good tonight.

REPORT #80:

Lot of chatter up here. Seems that Caliphate assassin who took down Sector 6 has gone AWOL. They're looking all over for her. Yes, it's a she. Now isn't that just ironic? Possible she defected but I doubt it. My best bet is she hitched a ride underground. Check your house. Soldiers get lonely. Intel already sent to the other sectors. You know the difference between Hammett and a one-armed man? Not a goddamn thing because neither can fucking play guitar.

REPORT #81:

Got your little love note. Kisses on the execution of their numero uno assassin. The muriatic acid bath was a nice touch. I'd wager my left nut it wasn't your idea. You're about as unoriginal as a Metallica song. Go easy on Grace. We all fuck up now and then. Not me, of course, but every other motherfucker.

REPORT #82:

Message received about having another go about on the imam. I would revisit that decision. I think it's a fucking stupid idea. Not only that, I think it's a fucking stupid idea. We know this guy. We know his response to everything we do. You take him out and they just replace him with another imam. The goddamn problem now is that we don't know shit about how the new imam is going to react. The 6th century Chinese general Sun Tzu knew what the hell he was talking about when he said: Know your enemy and know yourself, and you will always be victorious. And in case your reading comprehension sucks, which I assume it does, this means leave him alone. Which I know you won't because you're one pig-headed son-of-a-bitch who also happens to have the absolute worst fucking taste in music.

REPORT #83:

You got two of your boys hanging like St. Peter in Al-Hayat Plaza. Got a scope on it right now. Crosses about 8 meters up. I don't see your sackless ass coming up here and cutting them down. But just in case you do find your balls, there are 2 nests flanking an M1A2 and about 20 Revolutionary Guard on the perimeter behind sandbags. Nothing but AKs in their hands. Can't see them but I'm figuring there's probably some RPG-7s lying around somewhere. Guessing most of these soldiers have been fasting so they should be a little weaker. They need 6 days in Shawwal and most wait until the end of the month to fulfill the requirement.

REPORT #84:

Bravo. Fucking bravo. The Fourth of July display you put on warmed my cold fucking heart. Pulled up a chair and caught every second. It was definitely better than watching that douchebag channel Al-Jazeera. That late at night, all they have on are Riefenstahl rip-offs.

REPORT #85:

Nothing like sticking your dick in a beehive, huh? And not only once, you had to come back and do it twice. Just what the hell are you doing down there? That madrassa you hit was a big-time fuck-up. Not that I give a shit but everyone else up here is pissed off. Photos of the mangled bodies of those kids are plastered all over this city. I can't even wear my Halloween costume around here anymore. And do you have any fucking idea how many kills I collected dressed up like a bitch in a burqa? Oh, I'm not even going to get into you completely disregarding my advice on the imam. Great job killing that asshole. Now what?

REPORT #86:

Nothing I could do, John. Know you loved her like a daughter. Caliphate unit came up on her just before I got to her position. She put up one hell of a fight. Only had a few left to kill when I arrived. In the end though, when you got only one bullet left, you make it easy on yourself. You know that. Got her body out of there though. She'll be at House 3. Bring her home.

REPORT #88:

Jesus Christ, you fucked up with that priest. Told you to exterminate that rat immediately. Everyone up here wants in on the invasion of your sector. They all want their goddamn promotions. My guess is you got about 7 days before they start coming. Suggest to use escape tunnel to get your ass out of there. Reroute to Sector 5. Already let them know of your imminent arrival. They can take 20 of you. Listen, you stubborn asshole, you've got no fucking chance and your death isn't going to be pretty. My God, John, you had the perfect bunker and you fucked it all up.

REPORT #89:

Get the hell out of there. Dead men have no revenge. You've got two Caliphate companies outside your door and a battalion on its way.

REPORT #1:

Welcome, John. Let me introduce myself. I am the devil's father. I am the angel of death and I am the Jinn. I am the executioner that walks the streets of Ayla. That is all you will ever know. Of you though, I know everything. We're going to be great friends. You're going to kill where I cannot. You're going to rise up to be the House of Hell. You're going to be the surgeon of their pain.

6 TRAVIS

Dear Travis,

I miss you. I miss everything you gave. I miss that sweet kiss when I wasn't expecting it. Those bouquets of flowers you drew. Those heart-shaped pancakes you made. Love notes in Easter eggs and chocolate cupcakes every half birthday. Brushing my hair before bed. Reading me to sleep. Mixtapes under my pillow. Painting my nails for me. Giving me your side of the covers when I was cold and your hand when I needed something to hold on to. A stupid joke when I couldn't laugh and tears on your face because I had them on mine. You were always like that. Never a moment did you make me feel like I wasn't at all loved.

* * *

Dear Travis,

I miss so much of us. And so much of what I miss is just the simplest of things. Movies on your phone. Playing cards at the laundry mat. Dinner dates over mac 'n' cheese and all our thrift store shopping trips. Making love in the living room forts we would build. Christmas decorations that never came down and wearing each other's clothes. Midnight talks lying head to head. Candlelit bubble baths and fights with our Happy Meal toys. Maybe once, perhaps twice did I ever think of what we didn't have. Most of the time just thought it was a stroke of luck that neither of us really had that much to spend.

* * *

Dear Travis,

I'm so sorry. The biggest sorry I've ever had. I'm sorry I pulled my hand out of yours and started to run. But everyone else was running too, and I guess I just got caught up in the undertow. I swear I waited at the corner of Grand and Orleans just like we said. But those explosions and those bullets were getting closer and I had to continue on. I'm so sorry, Travis. I swear, I kicked and screamed. I swear it took three of them to pull me down into the sewers. I never wanted to go. You must know that. Not without you. Every day I still wish I left my hand in yours. Every day it's the biggest regret I have. Every day it's a sorrow that grows and grows.

* * *

Dear Travis,

Hey, you know I still look for you down here. Yeah, I know, it's been three years but you can't blame a girl for still trying. You always said I never give up and I certainly don't want to make you into a liar. There have even been a few times I thought I saw you. Same walk, same height. Same style of hair and same face at a profile. And each time, my legs got weak like they were licorice sticks and my heart started punching my chest. Yeah, those few times. Afterward, I could never decide if that one moment of hope was worth the utter torture of disappointment and despair. But anyway, I won't give up and I won't stop believing. I mean it just wouldn't make sense for us never to see each other again. Really, what God and his universe would be that cruel to keep true love like ours apart?

* * *

Dear Travis,

Okay, I don't want you to worry but I've been a little sick. Nothing much ya know just a bit of a fever I can't seem to shake. I even went to the infirmary on your long-distance advice. Forgive me, can you please. The line was long and I just didn't have it in me to wait. Besides, they all looked worse than me, so I thought I was probably okay. Do you remember the day when I fell in the shower and broke my wrist? You bicycled me all the way to the ER and told them I was pregnant just to get me to the front of the line. Afterward, I always wondered if you truly wished that I was. I always wished that I was.

* * *

Dear Travis,

All right, just hear me out. I don't want you to be sad, and I don't want you to be scared. My body seems to be ravaged with something. They said they have nothing at the moment to fight it and I said that's okay. I said I have this boy who's coming for me soon and he'll take care of everything. So, when you come and if I won't wake, don't despair and don't cry because of course, I'll just be in a Juliet sleep. You know I wouldn't leave without you. I wouldn't dare. At least without one last look into your hazel green eyes and a tender kiss. Hey Travis, God only knows how I love you so.

* * *

Dear Travis,

Yes, the handwriting's changed but I promise it's still me. It's just that my fingers can no longer hold a pen and so I needed someone to write all of this down for me. Hey, perchance, would you happen to know what day it is? I swear delirium has set in. I swear I'm on Bus 66 and you're sitting right beside me. It seems like a summer day outside, but for some reason, I have my stupid hat and gloves on. I think I asked two stops back where we are going. I think you said don't worry baby, this one takes us to somewhere only we know. Anyway, I'm glad you finally came. Because actually, to tell you the truth, I was getting tired and not sure how much longer I could have held on.

7 TUNNEL X

YEAR ONE

After all, I should not be angry with him, and perhaps neither should they. He was the one who discovered our tunnels and gave us life. He could have just stayed and lived out his days with the few of us that were with him. No one would have known. But for that first year, he risked his life day and night trawling the sewers for runaway slaves from the labor camps and those who had still been able to evade the Caliphate. In one short trip of the earth around the sun, our numbers had increased twentyfold. We were happy, I suppose. Happy in the sense we had found a home free of subjugation and free of a god whom we did not call our own. It is not that we weren't fearful of them finding us, it is just that our minds and bodies were mostly occupied building a new world. We were Israelites in a new land, pilgrims on a new shore. Now that I reflect back, it was a wonderful and glorious time.

YEAR TWO

Not more than a month into the beginning of our second year, he had gone on his daily search of the sewers. This time though he did not return and I feared the worst. I thus assembled a search party of three men. A mile or so into the sewers we came upon the bodies of five children, two Caliphate soldiers, and there also my brother. He was lying on his stomach, his long body stretched out, his gashed head turned sideways and the lips of his mouth at the fetid waterline. It was then I saw something move. At first, I thought perhaps a water spider. On closer look, I could see he was raising up a finger. We immediately rolled him over, and I lifted up his head. His left eye had been gouged to the point where it wasn't even recognizable and in his body five holes. I thought that at least we could bring him back to the tunnels where he could die among us.

For the first week, I prayed by his side day and night. The bullets that were still within him we removed. Every hour I thought would be his last. In and out of consciousness he would slip. When awake, I would feed him like an infant. When asleep, I would lay my body near to him to provide more warmth. It was obvious that if somehow he did survive, neither the use of his left eye nor the use of his legs would he have as not even a twitch came from them. Another month passed without any sign of recovery. I wondered why God was keeping him alive. Then suddenly, in the depth of the night, I awoke to him sitting beside me. I myself immediately sat up to join him.

"Angels have visited me and given words to speak," he said.

"It was just a dream," I replied, and then lay a hand upon his cheek. "Be thankful, John. Be thankful that your cheeks are once again flush with life, and your legs have been restored. It is a miracle. And whether by God or His angels, say not of it nor of anything else you may have been told while your eyes were closed."

FIRST REVELATION

The next morning I called an assembly as he had asked. I sat off to the side. A little girl came up to me with a notebook and pen. She said, "You are the scribe. Write down all you are to hear." He entered shortly after, dressed in a white robe with a belt of rope. They quieted in his presence. They all stared upon him in utter disbelief as by now it was common knowledge that he had lost the use of his legs. Arms raised, a patch of gauze over the eye that had been ruined, he began to speak and I began to write:

> *Last night, two Angels came to my bed, and this they did speak: "Verily I say unto you, that after the crucifixion of His son, God raged about the heavens and the heavens quaked. And as it did so tremble, the New Earth that He hath prepared for Man came into ruin. The streets of gold rose, buckled, and then shards of glass became. The walls of jasper crumbled into pieces as fine as sand and scorpions the size of small ships raced over to infest the once promised land. The twelve gates of pearl became ash, and the light from the glory of God was withdrawn so that only utter darkness dwelled.*

> *"And then upon heaven itself, God unleashed His fury and wrath. For the very first time it rained, and this rain was of molten metal, which sent all those in heaven to shelter. And as the angels huddled in fear, for the very first time God brought disease, which rotted the power of the angels so that none could float about anymore. And Gabriel and Michael crawled to God saying, 'Why hast thou condemned us? It was not we who crucified thy son.' And to Gabriel God spoke saying, 'Has thou not eyes to see his suffering upon the cross.' And to Michael, he spoke saying, 'And have thee no ears to hear his cries?'*

"Upon hearing this, both Gabriel and Michael fell prostrate before God weeping 'Lord, grant us forgiveness. Alleluia, salvation, and glory, and honor, and power, unto the Lord our God.' And to this God spoke saying, 'Neither heaven nor hell shall rest until my vengeance hath been fulfilled. If the Son of God they believeth not, then unto them I shall send a legion of destroyers whose flag is one color black and one color white. And this legion shall be like a stone. And this stone shall gather followers until one day it is spread across the earth to rise up against those who have crucified my son. And those below the earth, they shall hide and be fearful night and day. And those on the earth, they shall be made slaves and tormented greatly." This is the word of the Angels. Blessed are those who receive it.*

He left right after that, and I looked around at all the faces he had just spoken to. None seemed bewildered as I had expected. All were quiet, and not one I heard asking their neighbor for affirmation. It was then I realized they all believed him. Believed that God had sent the armies of the Caliphate as retribution for the crucifixion of His Son. And how could you blame any one of them? It seemed as plain as day. It was a balm to their ears. It was a reason to believe why they been sentenced here. But more than anything, they believed in his abrupt transformation from leader to diviner. A transformation that, while most may have thought was complete, was in all actuality still inchoate as this was just the beginning of the beginning.

The words he delivered in his first revelation did not surprise me. I did not think, as they must have believed, that the words had come from God. Years before all of this, years before the invasion, he had already and unwittingly been preparing for this role. As a young astrophysicist would aim a small telescope to the stars, or a child chemist would begin mixing liquids from their mother's household items, he was curious about religion. Early on he taught himself the Bible in our language, the Quran in theirs. By the time he was thirteen, he was already a scholar of both. He would pace our bedroom day and night, alternating verses from each book. When walking in one direction, he would utter verses from King James. When he turned to walk in the other direction, he spoke lines in Arabic from the Quran. It was as if he was walking in judgment, trying to decide which book was truth and which book was lie. It was strange, but our parents did not discourage him. They thought he would just eventually grow out of it, which he eventually did. That is, until the Caliphate soldiers had made the decision for him by murdering those children in front of him and taking sight from one of his eyes.

SECOND REVELATION

His second revelation to us came seven days later. Again I sat off to the side. And again, the little girl came up to me with a notebook and pen. "You are the scribe. Write down all you are to hear."

Verily, I say unto you, once more the two Angels came to my side. By the hands, they lifted me from my sleep and told me to come with them. And not a moment later, where I was standing I was not. And where I was then was at the top of Mount Ararat. The air was neither thin nor cold. The clouds were below me like fields of cotton and the sky above me the color of rust. And though their mouths moved not, they began to speak.

"Because you did not serve the Lord your God with joyfulness and gladness of heart, because of the abundance of all things, therefore He hath not put a yoke of iron around your enemies, so that now you serve them in hunger and thirst, in nakedness, and lacking everything.

"And because you were dead in the trespasses and sins in which you once walked, and all lived in the desires of the body and of the mind, He did not intercede when they took your widows as wives, your daughters as prize, slaughtered your sons and drove you into the earth like locusts.

"But God, being rich in mercy, and of great love, even as you are dead, hath sent us with a message. He sayeth, 'Prepare. For the time is nigh. Where once you were lambs of God, now you are soldiers. Make thy house a fortress. And to each within strap a sword.' Alleluia, salvation, and glory, and honor, and power, unto the Lord our God." These are the words of the Angels. Blessed are those who receive them.

ARMING OF THE TUNNELS

The units of men he assembled quickly. And though he was still too weak to join them, he directed all of the raids. With only two weapons to our name, he started slow. Most in Ayla who walked the streets in the darkest of the night carried guns. So those were the ones who were targeted first. Small arms were the reward. Later, when enough weapons had been amassed for all to carry, he began to orchestrate ambushes on Caliphate patrols. Our casualties began to pile up quickly.

"How is he?" my brother asked of me.

"I gave him something for the pain. But there's nothing more I can do for him. This candle has more life left in it," I said.

"He served God well."

"He served you well. How long does this continue? You were once a collector of men. Now you are a collector of Satan's toys."

"Make thy house a fortress. And to each within strap a sword," he said, quoting himself.

"And I say, how certain are you of your Angels? For he is the great deceiver, the father of lies. To his den, he may just be leading us so that our death is achieved."

My words of admonition did not stop him. The raids continued, and the number of our dead multiplied. The weapons and ammunition we stored like one would store grain for the winter. He had become well enough to join in the raids and appeared almost giddy that he could partake. Only I seemed to fear that one day the Caliphate would eventually become aware of our tunnels. Then, as quickly as it began, it suddenly ceased.

THIRD REVELATION

The next revelation came replete with theatrics. The assembly area, where once bare, was now filled with candles and crosses. Writings of scripture were chalked onto the clay walls, and weapons stood in wooden racks all around the room. This time, instead of walking up to the dais unannounced, he had a little girl with a ram's horn introduce his arrival. They adored it all and fell prostrate like dominoes.

And the Angels brought me with them to the farthest depths of the earth and there we walked along a bridge, which I understood to be directly over the pit of Hell. And I knew fear as I had never known fear. For below me rolled and splashed the molten earth like waves of a raging sea. And there I could smell the stench of brimstone and there I could hear the wailing of the eternally condemned. And as the Angels raised their eyes, they pointed down and spoke.

"Behold, the unbelieving, the abominable and the murderers. Behold, the liars, the sorcerers, and the idolaters. Day and

night all are tormented forever and ever. He alone hath judged them. He alone hath cast them here. Yea, we say unto you, fear Him and all His power. Glory to God in the highest."

And I fell to my knees and wept. And as I did so, the earth rumbled and the bridge began to violently twist and undulate. I swear at that moment I thought I was to join them, but the Angels took hold of me and spoke again.

"Stand and fear no more. He knows thy works, thy charity, thy service, thy patience, thy faith. He knows thy tribulations and thy despair. Of these words take heed, mark those in your house so that they shall be saved." These are the words of the Angels. Blessed are those who receive them.

We were then called up in single file. The twin sisters, who stood at least six feet tall, met us first. One had a Bible in her palms and other a Quran. In unison, they both said "Choose" to each of us. After a hand would be laid upon the Bible, he would remove a stamp from a metal box of fiery coals and burn a cross into our skins. No one uttered a cry of either objection or pain.

As they thought, I did not. Where they must have believed he was leading them up a staircase nearer to heaven, I believed he was taking us one level lower and closer to hell. That descent though was still to be traversed, and the path worried me most. What lies next, I wondered? What next do his Angels pour into his ears?

THE GENERAL ARRIVES

It was the first days of our third year that the pounding on our north tunnel wall began. Our final battle he thought, and so he readied us for the fight. Weapons and ammunition were meted out to every man, woman, and child, and yet we still had more. Rows and rows of us slept and ate behind the wall. Six across and at least fifty in length. When I could see the wall trembling on our side, I ran to his quarters.

"They are almost through," I said to him.

"And there they will be met sharpened tooth for sharpened tooth."

"They have many more mouths and many more teeth," I replied.

"The Angels have prepared us well. Are we not armed for battle, and are we not marked for heaven?"

"Please, I beg of you," I said. "We can still make a run for the sewers. We lived there once. And perhaps there are other tunnels we can find."

"I will not be ashamed if you leave," he said and stood up.

I stayed with him of course. He strapped on two belts of ammunition and hung an automatic weapon over his shoulder. As we came to the north tunnel wall, those in the middle parted so we could come to the front. A pickaxe. That is what broke through first. He raised his hands and they all stood, the barrels of our guns pointed straight ahead and waiting to be discharged. At any moment, I was expecting explosives or even a hose from which gas would begin flowing. Instead, we saw a ray of light come through. It moved around and lit up our faces like a searchlight.

"General John Danzig, United States Marine Corps, Sector 4. Identify yourselves."

"We are The Children of God," he replied, the first time I had heard him use that phrase. "You may continue the path you are on, but any weapons must be left behind."

The wall came down within a half hour of time. The General entered first, like a tank I remember. Eight others followed. Four lined up on his left and four on his right. His eyes then took a quick assessment of the situation. Our guns were still pointed ahead, but it didn't seem to instill a bit of dread in him nor those that he had come with.

"How long have you been here?" the General asked.

"The twins," he said with a look over his shoulder.

The twins stepped forward and asked only the General to choose which book he preferred. The General neither scoffed nor hesitated at the request. He put his right hand down hard upon the Bible.

"The Good Book has been chosen," the twins replied and walked away.

"Praise be to God," we all replied as had been inculcated.

"Two years and a few odd days, General," he then said.

"How many are with you?"

"All that you can see."

"You think you could have them put their weapons down? I'm sure you've trained them well. But that little girl with the twenty-two in her hands and her teddy bear between her feet, well, you never know. She might just get an idea in her head that teddy isn't quite safe with us standing here. I could probably take the slug, but nonetheless, it still makes for a fucking bad day."

"Lower arms," he said.

"Thank you."

"There is food here for you."

"Food we have. It's water that we're having an issue with. We tapped into a line when we got here. Unfortunately, it suddenly shut off about two days ago. So, we started tracing it out. And lo and behold, it led us here."

"We are the source of your spring, General. The valve we are working on."

"I brought some engineers with me. They can help you."

"I thank you for your offer, but we are quite capable. You shall drink again before the night's end "

"I appreciate that."

"Is there anything else we can do for you?"

"No, that is it."

"Then our ways our own, General."

Even here, under the most absurd circumstances and wretched conditions, it was apparent that two alpha males do not combine to share their packs. A metal door was fashioned where the wall once was. It had only one handle, and that was on our side of the divide. If I had a choice of which gray wolf to follow, it would have taken me some time to decide, even as one of those wolves was my brother.

UNTO US A GIRL

I knew it troubled him greatly that another group was inhabiting the tunnels. I can only assume it was tantamount to venturing far off to another planet and finding a cross of Jesus buried in the soil there. How defeating would that be. To find that your God once had a mistress and you were not the only one.

Months went on. He slept little. He paced back and forth, waiting for the Angels to visit him again. Strands of his hair turned white. Lines began to find his face. He was petulant, curt. Anger rose within him quickly.

Then one day, he came to me soaked in sweat, as if someone had taken a wet cloth and wiped it across both his hair and his face. Across from me he sat and took hold of my hands.

"I must tell you something."

"Please," I replied.

"The Angels have spoken once again to me. They were stern. They said, 'O ye of little faith, how soon thou thinkest the Lord hath forgotten. Thy time is but an eye's blink in that of heaven. Have thy no patience?' And my eyes I lowered in shame at their rebuke. And I said, by all of heaven and earth, I give oath that I will falter in faith no more. Then, as I was relieving my eyes of the tears, they said, 'A girl has arrived, the deliverer. Out of her shall come the one who crushes the head of the serpent that slithers above ye. Nations of new will be born and bring tribute and bow in obedience. Keep then thou watch. For she shall be shackled.' "

"We place no one in shackles," I said to him.

"Then with the General she must be. Have the water turned off. He will arrive soon after."

"You do not wish to call an assembly first?"

"It is of more importance for the General to hear than them."

In less than an hour after the valve had been closed, the General arrived. He was alone this time. At his side, a large gun, which was not asked to be removed. Once again, the General was asked to choose from which book he believed.

"Welcome, General. We have been expecting your arrival."

"You need to let us know when you're taking that valve out of service. Our sector has grown since I was last here. We need that water."

"It is not out of service. I asked for it to be closed."

"And for what goddamn reason might I ask?"

"Last night, the Angels came to me and said there is a girl among you. She is one of us, General. And I would like for you to bring her to me. This girl should be easy to find. The Angels have said she will be in shackles."

"Yeah, well, your Angels are fucking wrong. There's no one in shackles on my side. But if they want to have a look around, I'll have no objections to that. Shit, I'll even give them a personal tour. As far as handing someone over from my sector to you though, I'm pretty goddamn certain that's not going to happen. Now, you were here before us, so I'm going to show my due respect. But don't try my goddamn patience. We've got a shitload of things going on and no time to be fucking around with this."

"As I said before, General, our water is your water. We have no intention of denying your house the well of life."

"Then turn it the fuck back on. And I'm not leaving until I hear the rattle of those goddamn pipes."

"I will have it turned on when you leave. You have my word. As for the girl, in your charge I shall leave her. Keep watch of her though. She is the deliverer."

"Of what?"

"Of all of us, General. Of all of us."

That was not the last time he shut off the water to summon the General. There were, in fact, two more times before the last. One for the infant he said the girl will give birth to in six moon's time. And the other, to tell him that a good priest drinks the blood of Christ, whereas one in false robes sets it aside. I was now more worried about another return of the General than I was of the Caliphate finding us. His patience was wearing thin, and in him, I saw a man who was starting to believe that a bullet into my brother's head would solve at least half of his problems.

FOURTH REVELATION

And to me the two Angels said, "Rise up from the bowels of the earth and return with the bodies of the serpents, more alive than dead. Let them knoweth the taste of their own blood. Let it spring forth from inside their bodies and flow over their swollen tongues. Be not merciful as the serpent has shown thee no mercy. Let them get to know their skin. Set flames near so that blisters bubble, and the scent of their own burnt flesh sickens them. Bring knives to their maws and slice them like fatted cattle. Let them know pain thrice that a woman in birth knows pain. Do not bring death upon them though. Let them still breathe as the beetles and maggots take feast of their hearts, livers, and lungs. Let them wish of life no more. Let them wail and pray that they have never been conceived. All of this hath been commanded. Alleluia, Glory to God in the highest, praise to the Lord."

They all stood and shouted their allegiance. Even the young were with him. There were no words I could bring to him to reverse the course he was leading us on. The killing squads began shortly after.

Where before it seemed to perhaps be just a misunderstanding of his mind, now it had become madness. And us, being tethered to him like an umbilical cord, were being dragged down right along with. The orders he gave to them were to return with the living bodies of Caliphate soldiers so they could be strung up and made to pay for their sins. It wasn't done en masse, for he knew that would have attracted too much attention to those in Ayla. So, they were taken one or two at a time, to make it look as if the soldiers had just deserted their posts. It became apparent immediately, though he resisted the idea at first, that the bodies would have to be moved. The screams of the living he was able to suppress from our ears by shoving balls of clay into their mouths. The fetor of decay though he could not control. So, he had the bodies taken down from where they hung and moved to an area directly outside of our tunnels. The exact place where we always received the General.

THE LIGHT OF GOD

It was but two weeks into his crusade when he came to me in a most frantic state. I was thinking that he had come to say he was revisiting his decision.

"The tunnels are darkening, and I have been told that we have no more candles to be lit."

"I will have power to the bulbs restored. For the other areas, I will place the battery lanterns down," I said.

"I wish no other light. We will make our own candles."

"From what? There is no wax or anything else we can safely burn."

"I will have bodies brought to you. Boil them down and fashion candles of the tallow that remains. You will now be the candle maker, the light of God."

"I will do no such thing. Even if God Himself asked me," I answered in a firm protestation. "It is inhuman. And one that certainly heaven itself would not sanction. Perhaps not even the heaven of the Caliphate."

My refusal did nothing except to place a greater distance between us. Within hours he found another more than willing to be his candle maker. The next day I approached her as she was pouring the tallow into the molds, which were discarded cans of food. Cotton strips from Caliphate uniforms she was using as wicks. I said not a word to her, but set down by her side jars of cloves that she could use to perfume the unholy scent.

THE CRUCIFIX

We were having our morning meal together when he set his plate aside, folded his hands together, and looked straight at me. On his tongue, I knew he had important words ready to embark so I also abandoned my own plate.

"Last night, I walked among the ruins of the General's house."

"The Angels have visited you again?"

"Yes, and unspeakable horrors I was shown. Flesh of men, women, and children covered the tunnel walls, and very few wore faces recognizable. The General himself I saw upon an inverted cross."

"Is it to be soon?"

"Of that day and hour, I was kept ignorant."

"And what of our house?"

"I did walk over to it. The door was open and there was a great light of white emanating from inside. The Angels though stood guard at the entrance and told me I was not allowed."

"Then perhaps we shall be spared."

"Or perhaps to heaven we had already ascended."

I found that reply odd. And now that I think about it, I should have asked him to expound. However, my attention to the matter was released when he unclasped his hands, and on his right palm, lay a bronze crucifix that had acquired a dull olive patina. It was a curious piece, for it was obviously a locket, hinged at the side. I asked him if it opened. He said that it did not. He said centuries upon centuries of sadness had fused it together. I returned my eyes to it. The figure of Christ was smooth and almost unrecognizable, as if the thumbs of generation after generation had worn Him down. If I had to put a guess to its date of origin, I certainly would say it was at least a thousand years old.

"From where did it come?" I asked,

"The Angels. It was given right before they left me."

"Are you to wear it?" I questioned.

"It is for the girl. She must have it around her neck before the Caliphate come."

"And who to place it?"

"I will summon the General. It will be taken to her."

"You have called him here four times now. And not once did he acknowledge her existence, or even the child you said she had born. He cares only about the water."

"Speak no more of it and prepare for his arrival."

When I returned to my quarters, I wondered about the crucifix, taking doubt of its authenticity in every other thought. It seemed almost impossible for him to have constructed such an object himself. From where the tools and from where the ancient bronze? Certainly, it could not have been found within the tunnels. For its construction, by blueprints found, we knew to have begun no earlier than 1899. I thus convinced myself it must have been taken from a Caliphate soldier. A good number of them came from lands rich in ancient artifacts. No other explanation would I accept. His Angels were hysteria, delusion, manifestations of hope, but certainly not actual entities capable of gifting crucifixes. I laughed aloud. How grotesque my initial thought to believe his Angels had indeed given it to him. I left my quarters and hurried to prepare for the General.

THE PROPHECY

The general arrived within two hours. He was not alone this time. With him were twelve others, eleven of those who were well-armed.

From his mien, it seemed his patience with my brother had been exhausted, and who could really blame him. I feared the worst. My brother told the general of his vision where his area of the tunnels had fallen to the Caliphate and also of his own horrific death upon an inverted cross. He then told the general to take the crucifix and place it around the neck of the girl. The general declined the offer, and soon after his entourage began to leave. To my surprise though, a man with a gentle face and without a heavy weapon swiped the crucifix from the little girl and took it with him. I looked over to my brother and upon his face, not a change in countenance, as if he had expected the crucifix to be taken all along.

ORDINATION OF IMMORALITY

To ask only a simple question, I walked into my brother's quarters unannounced. They were all turned away from me, but I did not need to see any faces for I knew all three. Like Caligula, he was copulating with one of the twins, while the other was sitting beside him with an arm around his waist. He still had his white robe on. They were wearing nothing more than what was given to them at birth. I seemed to have no feet to flee and no air to speak. Then, the sister who was not on all fours, brought her lips to his ear and poured forth words. He turned not, but instead waved a hand for me to come and join them. My body once again found movement, and I ran out of there, knowing that the corruption of his mind had now been completed.

CONSECRATION

He was calm that day, the possession gone from his demeanor. It was almost as if my brother had returned. We ate together in the morning and separated right after so he could prepare for the words he was to deliver in the evening. I did not feel myself the entire afternoon and retired to my quarters in the hope I could find a few hours of sleep. My eyes I remember never closed, for the imminent dread I sensed was all-consuming, and neither my body nor my mind could find even a wisp of the respite I sought. I felt stiff and cold when supine. I trembled and sweated when I paced. I wished nothing more than to be done with the night to come.

The frankincense was heavy in the assembly area, the candles were breathing without a flicker, and from all of the crosses, the Jesus' now removed. An hour we all waited for him until finally, the ram's horn sounded. The twins entered and took opposite sides of the altar, standing tall like obelisks. Each had on a strapless black dress made of cloth I soon realized were from burqas stolen from Ayla. Their eyelids were obsidian shaded, and their lips were layers and layers of a crimson red. Upon their foreheads, one had the word Dies and other Irae, in what seemed to be from coal. And there before each, a metal ammunition box painted forest green. Another few minutes passed before he arrived. He glanced my way and nodded. And after I also nodded, he began to speak.

Children of God, the Chosen, it has been accomplished. In the tunnels near to us, with the Angels I huddled and we watched as a crucifix was placed around the neck of the deliverer. She is safe, and the prophecy fulfilled. Alleluia, Glory to God in the highest, praise to the Lord.

The Angels then looked right, and time moved forward. And as I looked with them, I saw lands and waters of the earth tomorrow. Battles raged. Lights of cities blazed with fire, and great peals of thunder echoed into the air. Steel birds swept through the skies to bring terror, and armies of the cross marched victoriously. And the moon then appeared, and as if it was a celestial spotlight, it showed its light on a certain patch of the desert earth. And there everywhere below, like black ants, **the soldiers of the Caliphate hurried away from that which once they had devoured.** *And though in spirit I was joyous at the triumph, my hands and teeth clenched as I watched all of them escaping without retribution. Then though, as if they knew my mind, the Angels spoke. "Anger not, for their names and their hiding places are known. For either by sword, famine or plague, or by wild beast shall each be slain.* **Yea, we say unto you, fear Him and all His power. Glory to God in the highest.** *His vengeance is swift and just."*

"Come," the Angels then said, "and before thee see the New Jerusalem." Of falsehood, I now speak not. For the night suddenly became day. Not as the darkness does by a slow retreat back to its grave, but by time faster than the blink of an eye. Standing now, we were atop the Qubbat al-Sakhrah. One Angel was pointing west toward the Mediterranean Sea, and also to the north in the direction of Galilee. The other Angel was pointing to Eilat in the south and to the River Jordan in the east. And at the sight I marveled, for the masses were all prostrating in our direction, with faces to the earth and palms to the heavens. And just as I was about to speak, the Angels said, "Quiet say we and watch as the one you saveth becomes its queen."

Not a moment after, the earth shook, and I watched as the al-Aqsa mosque fell to ruins. And out of the ruins came a lion with a crown in its teeth. And the lion walked to the one who was born in our tunnels, and she took the crown and placed it upon her head. The Angels then spoke again, "Alleluia, salvation, and glory, and honor, and power, unto the Lord our God. It is accomplished. Go ye and tell them. The Lord wishes them in His house. A dinner has been prepared at His table, and all shall be seated."

They were astonished and amazed. It was evident from their faces that they believed every word he had said. He paused long, looked over his flock as if he was a searchlight, and then spoke again.

Verily, I say unto you, from vines grown by crystal springs of living water, fruit picked by heaven's shepherds, and must from the crushing of pulp and skin underneath feet of anointed children, the Angels have given us wine to celebrate the coronation of the deliverer. So come forward now, in columns of two, and ye shall be given a cup where when all have received, all shall drink.

Footsteps slow and tongues silent, we obeyed and walked toward the twins, who from the ammunition boxes ladled out liquid into cups that were handed to us. When we had all returned to our seats, he raised his cup, signed the cross, and drank first. The little girl with the ram's horn fell first, and though I wanted to run to her, I knew it was too late. Some stood, twisted and convulsed. Others just fell forward into the mess of their own vomit. It was quick. It was final. Minutes, I suppose. Probably less. Lambs to their deaths, a mass murder. Of all that we were, now we were no more.

I swear to you. Of his intentions, I was not privy. Then ask you why I did not drink when the others did. This question I am unable to answer, to either you or myself. Certainly, I would not have wanted to live if I knew all others were to perish. For now, in the day I sleep, and at night

I wander the tunnels. It is as if I am on the earth alone. And yes, while I could summon the General or even walk into his house if I so wish, a part of me does believe that great horrors will soon befall all those that dwell there. So, I have decided to remain. And while the Caliphate will surely also discover our tunnels, I know of many hiding places. And once they have seen all of the dead laid out in the assembly area, I have faith they will search only once and then no longer.

8   A CHILD IS BORN

добре чи невдача

Y ou either have good luck or you have bad luck. There is no in between. But contrary to what people believe, it does not run in families, where generation after generation is either blessed or diseased. Rather, good luck and bad luck choose the ones they want. This I know for fact. This I give to you an example. When I was twelve, my bedroom was moved next to guest room. This turned out to be bad luck. For my uncle who came to stay with us six months later, he ended up staying in guest room. For him, this turned out to be good luck, as every night when rest of family sleep, he have short walk to his niece.

My luck continued the same when two years later I was taken to a doctor to remove child put inside of me. My father told me to shut my mouth. He said he would provide answers to everything. This was in back of pharmacy in Chernivtsi, some 500 kilometers from city of Kyiv. I was on folding table with legs spread out and my feet up on stacked boxes. I was given 5 pills, which put me in a daze. But not enough of a daze where I could not see the doctor. The same bottle of vodka he use to take a drink was same bottle he use to sterilize his hands. I bleed on way home. I bleed for next two weeks. And I bleed until they finally take my uterus away.

I never say a word to my father after this. It was not a long period of silence. His liver fail him two years later. At age of twenty-three, I graduate with degree in architecture, but there are no jobs for me. Finally, fourteen years later, I win lottery and get to come to United States to city of Mies van der Rohe. I feel new again. I feel like as if everything before had been washed away. One week following the drones came. As I say, you either have good luck or you have bad luck. There is no in between.

Дівчина

When the young man who delivered the girl to me left, I took hold of her and gave her big hug. I was warm, warm from her holding on to me. Her skin was very cool though. It was strange. Very strange. Since being in the tunnels, I have had the body of many men and soldiers up against me, and none were warm like this.

She had long hair to her waist. And it was black, black as Chernozem fields of where I came from. Her hands she had folded as if she was praying. And through her fingers, she had a black rosary, and she also had prayer beads of olive wood. They were so tangled together I could not tell which hand held which god. She did not even look sixteen. There are many things I wanted to ask her, but first I needed to get her free.

The chain around her ankles was wrapped three times and secured in front by a padlock. I pulled on it a few times. It did not release. This I am sure. So, I left her for a moment and went over to my makeup bag. I was thinking maybe I could set her free with perhaps a hairpin or maybe tweezers. When I returned, her chain was on floor like snake. She must have had the key all of the time. But why, why did she keep herself in chains. I did not ask. I had other things to say.

"What is your name?"

"I cannot seem to remember," she say.

"Do someone strike you in head?"

"I do not believe so."

"Do you know how this get into you?" I say after reaching out hand and putting it on her belly.

"You of all people should ask."

I find reply amusing and give her little smile.

"Do man who bring you here tell you I was whore?"

She shake her head. If I take her at word, I have to assume she come to conclusion by dress I was wearing. My room certainly do not advertise my occupation.

"Child in you probably do in month," I say. "Any plans on what you going to do with it when it start sticking head out?"

"Give it to God."

"Which one?" I say.

"Do you think it matters?"

"Yes, I do think it matter. Right now we have one who seem to be on warpath, and other who seem to be on vacation. So, at moment, neither seem to be good choice."

"I need to rest. May I stay here for the night?"

"Of course. You stay here as long as you like."

"They told me you would say that."

"And who are they?" I say.

"Those who keep me safe."

I said no more to her that night.

Голоси

My lies I swear on my father's grave. My truths I swear on my mother's. Only my grandmother was ever able to figure that out. So on my mother's grave, I will tell I began to believe the girl is not crazy at all. First, it was the candles. Down here they are not so easy to get. One week of work credits for two. The girl seemed to find comfort in them. So I see they are coming close to being over. I said to her that maybe we should put them out in order to save them. She said to me to just let them burn. I did so. Now two weeks later and the candles still burn as if they do not even need wax to burn.

The candles being strange are not only thing though. It is about this time the voices come. I checked the walls and I checked the ceiling. I am thinking some crack opened up to some shaft, and this is why we hear voices. I did not find a thing. So I spoke to the girl.

"Do you hear these voices?"

"Yes."

"I wonder of language. I have never hear of it before."

"It's Sumerian."

"How do you know?" I say.

"I am not sure."

"And you understand it?"

"Yes."

"And what they say?"

"They are saying a lot. But mostly they are arguing over the soul of the child within me. Those on the left say it belongs to their God. Those on the right say they are lying beasts and it is their God who has dominion."

"Why you? Why are you pick as mother?"

"I am not the mother. I am nothing but the deliverer. But to which God I still do not know."

"You are liar!" I scream at her.

After this, she gave me a bad look and brought her head up to have a look at the ceiling. Now we no longer have flames on candles and we are in darkness like I never knew darkness.

"Speak in the whore's own tongue," she then say.

I lifted my hand, and I was going to give her a slap when the talking got louder as if they were right by my ear. I fell to the ground like I am a building which has just gone to the ground. But still in my ear voices are yelling things in my own language and they are saying things even I cannot say to anyone. This I swear on my mother's grave.

Дитина народилася

The water of girl never broke. She did not even have contractions. She just awoke from sleeping, stood up, and told me the time is here. I also did not see any pain on her face. I said to her to lay back down and move apart her legs. This she did not do. She stayed standing and said this must be the way. I heated some water and brought her towels.

I got to my knees in front of her. The flames of the candles started bending like as if there was heavy wind, but there was no heavy wind. The talking in the room started to get louder, but this time like there are voices on one side of room and also voices on the other side of the room. On one side, the voices seemed like they were celebrating. On the other side, the voices seemed like they were angry. She then took both my hands and put them where the baby was to come out. She is probably 10 centimeters dilated now. I said for her to keep pushing, but she said it was not necessary. And then the baby girl came out. There was no placenta and there was no umbilical cord. So, I looked up at her to ask how this was possible. She did not say anything to me, but looked up at ceiling and lifted her arms and then she screamed. The girl she then left and did not return for three days. In those three days, my breasts became full as if I was the mother. This I also swear on my mother's grave.

Розп'яття

I removed the baby's mouth from my nipple right after the general's translator left our room. It was well fed and now asleep, and so I set it down in weapon's case he had brought us before the birth. I then walked over to the girl with a candle so I could have a better look at crucifix he just put around her neck. It was unusual, quite unusual. Not only because it looked to be thousand years old. But also because it was a locket. Whoever see such thing? I was hesitant at first, but I needed to touch it. Maybe I was hoping if I did touch it, it could also keep me safe like I assumed it was there to keep her safe.

"It will not protect you," she say, her eyes opening sudden like as if she is some doll just shaken. I am in surprise and I almost fall back.

"Do you know it going to be put around your neck tonight?"

"Like you, I only knew they had stopped arguing."

"Why is it not put around baby?"

"Because death does not know her name," she say.

"And so what, so what of all of this? What do any of it mean?"

"It means the other God will be angry. It means there is not much time."

"Until they find us?" I say.

"Yes. He will send them now."

She then took hold of the crucifix and squeezed it. When she unravel fingers, I could see on her palm the likeness of it had been burned.

I did not want to believe what I had just seen. But of all the things that I have seen and heard, this was the least strange. This was the one that made the most sense.

Вони приходять за нею

I awoke with a rushing of air through my nostrils as if like I am a racehorse. A hand was covering my mouth, and something hard was pressing into my head. He gave me a few seconds to understand what was happening, and then he removed his hand from my mouth and placed a finger on his lips. When I nodded and gave him a look to say I was not going to say anything, he slid fingers to the back of my neck and pulled me up with a hard grip of my hair.

The other man in the room had already awoken the girl. She was standing with her back to the wall, and the point of a knife was not more than 30 centimeters away. The flames of the candles in the room were now much higher, as if they also had been awoken. Neither man seemed to notice the strangeness of this.

"Take off dress," the man with knife say to girl.

The girl seem to have no objection to command and reach down with both hands to take hold of the bottom. I say something just as she begin to lift it up.

"I will do what you want," I say to him.

"And why would I trade a young whore for an old whore?"

"Because when you are done with old whore, at least you will still have life left in you."

I know I shall have give to him better explanation. I am sure he think it is me who is threatening him. After he come over and give me punch in face, he turn back to girl. She is waiting for him standing there wearing nothing but crucifix around her neck. He then starting masturbating to bring himself to erection. The girl stare at him like as if it is very first time she have ever seen man perform this act. She then place her eyes on me. Maybe she want me to look away. I do not know.

I think it must have been very painful. But the man with the knife did not even scream, even as we all watched his flesh being cut like as if someone else was in the room and cutting it with machete. The other man did also not do much better. Not long after he came over to stare down at the death of his friend, we saw his body jerk forward and then his back arch. Something must have gone through him because we watched him cup his stomach with his palms, and then we saw blood starting to come out from his stomach. The candles were going crazy at this point, dancing all over like they are happy at dying men. And then we heard the sound of wings, like one would hear same sound when someone throw rock up to tree with lots of birds and then they all fly away together.

I looked over to girl. The dress had come back on her body. I never saw her put it back on like I had never seen her take it off. She then just like that go back to sleep, like as if no men had ever come to our room. So, I then dragged the bodies out of the room and brought them to the room next to us. As anyone else would have done, I wondered why both men did not scream. It kept me awake for a long time until I finally went back to room. I only saw one mouth. I did not need reason to open the other mouth and confirm that it too was missing tongue.

Погані мрії

I do not think I have said this but after the girl came, I also move my business to room next to where I sleep. It cost me dearly. But what other choice did I have. I could not lay with men in same room as girl. It would not be appropriate. So, last night I am with soldier and we hear a scream. Soldier above me do not roll off. I do not blame him. He paid and why should he care. We hear screams all the time, and always we hear crying. Noises in tunnels we like. Noises mean people still breathing. It only when we do not hear noises we get worried. It mean people are dead, or it mean we are dead.

I let him finish. Then after, I went to her as I am thinking that maybe it was her though it did not sound like her. She was sleeping, but looking like she was having terrible dream. She was not sweating though. When I dream like this back in Chernivtsi, I remember I awake with body wet and sheets wet. I did not want to wake her at first. But after taking her pulse and finding it to be going too fast, I decided to wake her anyway. She opened her mouth and took in a big breath like as if she has been under earth and I had just dug her out.

"There there, my zaychyk, it is only dream," I say to her.

"It was not."

"Okay," I say to her. "It is not only dream. Tell me of it if you like."

"While you were in the other room, two angels came. They helped me to my feet, and we began walking through the tunnels."

"Do these angels have wings?"

"Angels do not have wings. They have golden armor. They have silver hands like scythes. Bronze feet with four spears pretending to be toes. Tongues as asps do. But wings. No, they do not have wings."

"I am sorry then. I have never seen one. Please, you go on."

"After a while, we finally came to a stop. I looked at both of them to question why. It was then that the angel on my left pointed for me to look forth. And when I did, I saw a priest."

"And this bring you to alarm?"

"Yes, because there I saw that he was being hanged on one of the pipes by his lavender stole."

"Do you see who is hanging him?"

"Yes. It was another priest."

"Do you see face?" She shake head. And I have another question for her, as anyone else would have another question for her. "Is this first time you seen angels?"

"No. They have come before and have shown me other things. Terrible things."

"How more terrible from what we already see?"

"Much more terrible. Everywhere they take me the tunnels are filled with rotting flesh. Everywhere I see none are taking breath. Please, I need to return to sleep. There are more dreams waiting for me. They would not be pleased if I did not show."

The next morning I was in line for food. Both in front of and behind me, I hear people talking of the priest who had hanged himself.

перверзія

For the last three days, the voices in our room were with us day and night. They were not loud, but more like as if someone had left radio on in other room and we can only hear little loudness. I did not remember eating. I did not remember sleeping. I only remembered sitting there and waiting for something to happen. Then, while I was watching her and her baby sleep, the candles shot up and they were like torches and suddenly the girl sat up.

"They are in our tunnels."

"This is end, is it not?" I say.

"Yes," she say.

"And I am going to die. Yes, this right?"

"Two more nights will first pass."

"Do you know how I die?"

"Of course. Do you want me to tell you?"

"No," I say. No one want to know how they die.

"We must go," she then say. And after standing, she pick up baby out of case for weapon and make walk to door. "Mariela."

"Yes?" I say.

"It was never good luck or bad luck. You were chosen."

Є багато брехні, але лише одна правда

One night has gone by. I write now by the little light of my lantern. The sounds going through tunnels remind me of way I feel when I was twelve and hear footsteps of my uncle nearing my room and waiting for door handle to turn but hoping somehow it will not open. I am weak. I am sick inside, and I am wishing I had never been born.

I have read all I have written before. It cannot be truth. The girl and her baby are of my imagination, brought to life from my wishes. She is me in a younger time, and baby is the child I was to have given birth to. Of course, how strange my mind plays trick when it wants to believe otherwise. And do not we always save best lies for ourselves? So, I will write one last final lie. I will write all escape from here. Child, baby, and old whore.

9 SEAN & AIDAN

Letter #1

Hey Sean, what's going on? A lot of people writing down here lately, so I thought I'd give it a try. I don't know if it's a therapeutic thing for them, or they're just doing it for the sake of posterity, which would be the worst damn reason to write because it's not like the Caliphate is going to archive our last days in some compendium. I guess it gives me something to do after returning from teaching these kids here and then playing daycare dad. Never should have mentioned I taught elementary. It's an easy gig though compared to the others, so I should probably just thank my lucky stars. I could be digging the tunnels or literally shoveling shit with the Department of Streets and San. Anyway, I'm not sure how it works where you're at. I mean, if I write instead of talking to you in my head, will you be able to see what's on the page? Whatever, fuck it, I'm just going to go with this writing thing for a while. I suppose you'll figure it out when you see the pen in my hand.

So, I broke up with that chick I had been talking to you about. Just wasn't working, and she really wasn't my type anyway. Not that beggars can be choosers down here, but I guess I do want something a little more meaningful. It was just fuck and run for the both of us. Yeah, you heard that right, I blew out of a relationship because there was too much screwing and not enough commitment. Damn, how things change, huh? I'm going to blame this one on you. All those things you used to say about how I was always letting the good girls go to chase the train wrecks are starting to reoccupy my head. Man, now that I think about it, how I miss our talks. Just you and me and a case of beer. Never really needed much more.—**Aidan**

Letter #2

It's a day before Christmas Eve. The people down here go all out for this. You should see it. Well, I guess you probably can see it. Anyway, it's like a contest. Every tunnel's got something different. We've got crafted reindeer and snowmen, trees made of stacked suitcases, and wreaths of real branches and leaves brought back by soldiers from raids. One tunnel even had Christmas lights strung up on the water pipes, and another had a complete nativity scene. God knows where they got that stuff from. I had my kids decorate the classroom with paper-ringed garlands, snowflakes, and angels. They were totally into it, and to tell you the truth, it was pretty cool to see their faces. All just like little elves. Damn, last night I was remembering the time we set our clock for one in the morning and waited for Santa Claus to come. What, we were seven, I think. Remember, we made those name tags because we weren't sure if Santa would be able to tell us apart, and we were afraid we would get each other's gifts.

Oh, I probably should have started out with this one. I'm making a career move. Gave my notice and in a week I start basic training. I just couldn't keep teaching those kids. Every time I came back to my quarters, I kept thinking about you and how I was doing nothing at all to avenge that last day. Yeah, I know you're pissed right now. But fuck it, it's done. So, you're just going to have to live with my decision. Well, you know what I mean by "live with" it.—**Aidan**

Letter #3

Sorry I haven't written in a while, but basic training was a bitch, and I barely had enough strength to drag my ass back to my quarters to lay it down. But I graduated this morning, and now I'm officially a private in the United States Marine Corps of Sector 4. Can't wait to get up there. Everyone's going in my crosshairs. I don't care.—**Aidan**

Letter #4

I'm a little messed up right now. And not in the way I would like to be. Last night, after a run-through of a mission we got coming up, I was walking back to my quarters and heard this really faint voice singing. Normally you hear stuff like that all the time down here, so you don't pay much attention. As I got closer though, I started to realize it was a kid's voice singing that song mom used to sing to us when we were little. You know that one: "You Are My Sunshine."

Anyway, I followed it along until I got to the quarters where it was coming from. It was a boy, Sean. One from my class. No older than five. He was just sitting there with his mother's head in his lap. When he finally realized I was there, he put a finger to his lips so I wouldn't say anything. I actually thought it was kind of cute that a kid would do something like that, so I decided to sit down for a bit and keep him company. Jesus Christ, Sean, I popped up about ten seconds later because after looking at her closer, I realized she was dead.

After a while, after he finally stopped singing, I took him to the infirmary for the nurses there to tend to him. What's killing me is that I should have brought him to my quarters. I could have looked after him. But instead, I just dropped him off. I don't know what to make of the whole thing. Is it just how messed up things are down here, or is it just how messed up and inconsiderate I've gotten? Trust me. You were the lucky one, bro. This isn't a life for the living. It really fucking isn't.—
Aidan

Letter #5

Hope you've got some time. This one's going to be a little longer than the last four. Yesterday we went on a special ops mission. Seven of us ventured twenty-five miles or so from Sector 4 by way of the Deep Tunnel project. It emptied us into the Thornton Quarry. There's a highway that runs over it, and we were on an ambush looking for small military convoys. The sergeant spaced us out about 50 feet apart in these woods overlooking a section of that highway that was a little farther down. Damn, it was just so nice to be outside again. That air tasted so good, and the scenery was great. Kind of reminded me a little of when mom and dad used to take us on those skiing trips. It was fucking cold, though, and there was about a foot of snow on the ground. The sky was one slate of gray, which was actually a relief because I don't think my eyes could have been able to deal with a full winter sun. Everyone else had sunglasses on. You'd think they'd be standard issue to recruits.

For the first three hours, we were just lying there freezing our asses off. I don't think I counted more than twenty vehicles. No military. Just families. Maybe it was some holiday on their calendar. Who knows? I don't keep up on that stuff as I should. You know, when you're staring at the same thing for that length of time you start to drift, and it's not always good. I was thinking about the little boy singing to his dead mother, and I was thinking about watching you take your last breaths. Both thoughts made me just want to waste somebody. That's probably when we heard a distant honking of horns. Five cars I counted as I moved my scope down the highway. When they came into range, I locked my scope onto the lead vehicle. There were two kids in the back, laughing and bouncing around. Upfront I could see the father bumping that horn with the palm of his hand, and his wife with a big smile on her face. It was like they didn't have a care in the world. Like this was their new home, and they belonged here.

I told the sergeant afterward that some squirrel had come out of nowhere and startled the hell out of me. Nowhere near the truth. I put that front tire in the crosshairs and fired. The car swerved right off the road and into a ditch. As the other vehicles stopped, and people started piling out, one of them pointed up to our position. We really had no choice then. I mean one call from one of their cell phones to the right person, and we'd have a Caliphate unit up on our ass in no time. So all of us just unloaded on them.

Twenty-two, Sean. That's how many we wasted. I know this because the sergeant sent me down to make sure they were all dead. Now, this is the part that's going to haunt me for the rest of my goddamn life. A kid, maybe fifteen, I think, opened the door and stumbled out. He was bleeding from his forehead, but nothing life-threatening as far as I could tell. Immediately he locked his hands over his head and started walking towards me. I told him to stay right where the hell he was. In English, of course, since how was I to know the damn Arabic phrase for "Get down on your knees." Listen, I gotta go. I'll write you later.—**Aidan**

Letter #6

Sitting in my quarters at the moment. Our unit's out on a raid up in Ayla. My ass, here, because I caught a suspension. Sergeant was a hair from making that permanent. Fuck was he pissed. Can't really blame him. Not only was I responsible for the killing of twenty-two innocents, but I also put the whole unit in jeopardy. I think the conversation went something like this.

"What the fuck were you doing out there, Private?"

"I told you, Sergeant, a squirrel ran right over my weapon, and I accidentally hit the trigger."

"Oh, bullshit, Private. I know you purposely fired on that vehicle. I asked around. I know all about what they did to your brother in the labor camp."

"I swear, sir."

"Yeah, you swear all right. Goddammit, those families didn't deserve to die, Private. They were just caught up in the same fucked-up universe we are. Jesus Christ, Private, that makes us no better than them."

"Yes, sir. I know that, sir."

"No, you don't know that yet. You haven't seen enough killing on both sides of the field to understand it."

"Yes, sir."

"And just to let you know, the only thing keeping me from sending your ass back to that daycare center is because I can't seem to come up with a good enough story to tell the General without him canning my own ass. Right now, the only thing he knows is that we went out, didn't spot any targets, and came right back."

"Thank you, sir."

"Don't thank me, Private. I did it for myself. But if you ever pull even something close to that shit again, I'm going to let the men handle it themselves."

"Yes, sir."

I kind of felt like I was being chewed out by dad again. Except now, I'm old enough to understand that I did mess things up. I swear, Sean, I'd do anything to have the moment back. Okay, I gotta put down this pen and get my head together. Talk to ya soon.—**Aidan**

Letter #7

Went up into Ayla for the first time since the invasion. Yeah, I know, you're going to say the labor camp we were in was considered a part of Ayla. May have been, but it certainly wasn't the Chicago we knew. I mean, we were some thirty miles west of the downtown area. Anyway, all the street names are now in Arabic. The few churches we passed had their crosses taken down and their bell towers converted to minarets. Didn't see any livestock on the streets but I've been told there's an area near the Grand Market that's teeming with them. The one thing that does strike you when you're up here is the smell. Chicago never really had a specific one. But this place sure in the fuck does. Can't pinpoint it exactly. Might be from the cooking that settles onto the streets. I don't know, but it's definitely a smell that makes you feel the loss and permanence. You know, it's when that scent on something you once loved changes is when you realize it's moved on and you're no longer a part of the equation.

So, back to where I was going to begin. The plan was for the seven of us to hit a small police station. Intel said that at night there would only be two there. Went pretty much as diagrammed at first. I walked into the station. The Arab sitting there behind the desk realized that while I may be dressed as a Caliphate soldier, my big Irish head isn't making a lot of sense, even with the beard. And as he reached for his gun, I lunged over the desk and put my knife right through his neck. Unfortunately, I couldn't pull the damn thing out. So, I had to spend more time than I wanted trying to dislodge it from his spinal cord or whatever the hell it was caught on. It was my only knife, and I certainly didn't want to leave it behind as a souvenir.

Anyway, I finally got the knife out and then called in the others. They spread out through the building and started collecting whatever they could find. I stayed back by the door and kept watch. Everything's still going well. The guys are dragging out crates of RPG-7s, ammo boxes, Kalashnikovs. It was like it was Christmas Eve, and we had just hit the rich kid's house. Oh yeah, the second guy wasn't even there. So I'm thinking this is great. Even better than planned. I mean, we're all giving each other the thumbs up and smiling like school kids.

Now I'm not sure why it didn't dawn on me that the reason there weren't two there is because maybe the other one had stepped out for a moment to have a cigarette or something. But it didn't. Didn't click at all until he returned. The first shot he got off went right past my head. The second one, though, grazed my leg. That's when I unloaded six rounds into his chest. One stupid move because I should have only hit him once. Now we got eight bullets ringing in the air instead of three, to go along with all those "Allahu Akbars" the dude was yelling before heading off to his seventy-two virgins.

Everyone stuffed whatever they could into their backpacks, and we headed out the rear exit into an alley. We walked that for about two blocks. Not a damn sound to be heard, and I'm thinking we got out by the skin of our teeth. I don't have that thought in my head for more than a few seconds when a 4x4 with Caliphate regulars rolled by the street we were getting ready to cross. The sergeant motioned us down, and we waited for about ten minutes before moving out again. Maybe we should have waited eleven minutes, maybe eight minutes. You think about that after the fact. All those what-ifs. Doesn't matter, I guess. We headed out when we headed out, and that was when all hell broke loose.

Two 4x4s now, one from the north and one from the south. We barely got a few rounds off before the gunners manning the truck bed mounts started lighting us up. Dropped two of us immediately. Now it's the five of us. And I guess while we could've just cut and run, there was no way after losing two of our men. So, we started unloading on them. It was just insane. The noise, the smoke, the confusion, the endless stream of bullets being fired your way. And then, it was over. Just like that. Total silence. Just want to add that the thing about fighting the Caliphate regulars is that while they're fanatics, they fight like a bunch of assholes. They all hopped out of those 4x4s and started running toward us firing their weapons. I'm not sure if they think Allah's got some kind of force field protecting them, but it didn't take long to lay them all down.

The initial plan was to take one of those 4x4s and ride it out of there so we could bring back the bodies. Wasn't in the stars though. Both 4x4s were disabled, and then we started to hear the voices of another Caliphate unit. Before we took off, the sergeant had us hide the men in garbage cans. None of us wanted to do it, but really there was no other choice. About thirty minutes later, we were all back in Sector 4. The sergeant debriefed us, and after he left, a couple of the men started huffing a can of vapors. Can't really blame them. I mean after going through a mission like that you need something, anything, just to push that adrenaline out of your system.—**Aidan**

Letter #8

Our unit had dinner with the General this afternoon. The sergeant told us before we got there it was a pretty big deal. Said he had never heard of a unit being invited like that, and we should think of it as an invite to the White House. We were hooded and then led to the command center. From what I was told, very few down here have unescorted access. The location is on a need-to-know basis. Now I'm not messing with you, the place is one-fourth surveillance station, one-fourth weapons depot, one-fourth library and den, and one-fourth music studio. Yeah, I wrote that last one correctly. There's a small stage set up with guitars, drums, and amps. Unbelievable, huh? The sergeant told us the General plays a kick-ass guitar.

We got served rabbit stew with two bottles of Yamazaki 12. The General cooked it himself. Wasn't half bad to tell you the truth. Before we ate, he led us in prayer for the two men we lost. After that, he didn't say a word throughout the entire meal. The guy's a motherfucker, Sean. Probably sixty-some years old, but still built like a tank. Tatted up pretty good, too. Had a full sleeve on one arm with some of the wickedest tats you've ever seen. Definitely not someone you'd ever want to cross, or even speak out of turn. He'd probably eat right through you before finally snapping off your neck. Kind of reminded me of our football coach, minus the tats of course. After we finished, he brought out an apple pie for dessert. It was all pretty fucking surreal to tell you the truth.

So, after we finish, the General's picking up our plates to take them away. And as he's doing it, he starts talking to us for the first time. From what I remember, it went something like this.

"I heard you guys ran into some heavy shit out there. Probably feeling goddamn lucky to have your asses back here I'm guessing."

"Yes, sir," we all answered.

"Yeah, I would be too. You get in a situation like that, and it's just a fucking roll of the dice. Doesn't matter how much of a rock star you are. A bullet's got your name on it, it's got your name on it. Anyone piss their pants out there?"

"No, sir," we yelled this time.

"Fucking liars. Anyway, you guys did a commendable job. The thing is though . . ." the General started to say when all of a sudden he took out this big ass knife and put it to the throat of our sergeant, "if any one of you assholes ever come back here again without the bodies of those in your unit, I'm going to personally disembowel each and every one of you. You got that?" We all nodded our heads. "Okay, let me try it again. You got that, motherfuckers?"

"Yes, sir."

"Good, because we're going back out there tonight. And I'm going with you."

"They're probably not in the alley anymore, sir. They could be anywhere," our sergeant said.

"Yes, they could be anywhere. But they're not fucking anywhere, Sergeant. They put their bodies on display. Both of them are hanging upside down on crosses in the middle of Al-Hayat Plaza. So, as I thought I just made fucking crystal clear, we are going to go out there, pull the nails out of their hands and feet, and bring them back. Just like that. And during all of this, we are going to leave a trail of dead so long it's going to take them a fucking week to pick up all of the pieces."

We had just started to get up when the General called us back.

"Did anyone hear me say dismissed?"

"No, sir," we all replied.

"Yeah, I didn't either. All of you. Take a Kit Kat for the road. May just be the last good thing you have in your mouth because if you get snagged up there, I guarantee the next thing is going to be the dick of some Caliphate soldier."

We all reached in the fishbowl as ordered. The sergeant waited to be the last. And just when he went to put his hand in, the General grabbed his wrist. Jesus Christ, Sean, you could have heard that snap a mile away.

"I hope that fucking hurt more than your face is showing, Sergeant. Now, I wasn't fucking there, so I don't know the half of it. But sure as shit, I can tell you that even if it was my goddamn retriever those camel jockeys had killed, I wouldn't have dumped him in a garbage can. He would have been on my back even if I had a goddamn fighter jet strafing my ass. Strip down to your skivvies, Sergeant. You are now part of the civilian population. First Sergeant Johnson, when he's done, collect his uniform and then escort him to where we're digging. As for the rest of you, now you're officially fucking dismissed. And get some rest. 0100 tonight."

I gotta admit, Sean, when I walked out of there, hooded again, I was sweating it. Seemed like a suicide mission to me. But I guess if I wanted anyone on my side, it would be that crazy son-of-a-bitch. Wish me luck.—**Aidan**

Letter #9

At that afternoon dinner, the General made it seem like it was a spur of the moment decision to go out and retrieve those men. When we arrived back at the command center at one in the morning, I realized that the General must have already had the plans drawn up long before he had started cooking the rabbit. It might have been reckless, but it certainly wasn't the suicide mission I had originally thought it would be. And I can't tell you how hard it was to keep a smile off my face when we were unhooded and standing around a mock-up of Al-Hayat Plaza (old Daley Center) with twelve soldiers of the General's elite squad. Let me just say, with the total now at seventeen, that's a massive operation for us.

We were going out at 0300 hours, and arriving at the plaza at 0345. The General said even at that time it would be well guarded. Al-Hayat Plaza and the adjacent buildings in the area, we were told, now serve as the seat for the supreme Caliphate council, along with offices for the governing of Ayla. The Picasso he said had long been torn down, and in its place, two machine gun nests and an Abrams M1A2 tank. Around the perimeter, they had stacked sandbags, which was patrolled by about twenty of the council's revolutionary guards. Those guards, the General said, all carried AK-47s. He also said to expect a few RPGs in the mix, though the intel he had gotten wasn't really certain. The two crosses were positioned behind the machine gun nests and rose about twenty-five feet high. He said when we get there to keep our eyes off of them. Said it would only be a distraction that would mess with our heads.

Since we knew that area pretty well, we were able to come out of the sewer system right at our mark. He moved his elite out first. Six took the western flank, the other six the eastern one. That left the five of us, which included the General, to take up residency on the north — placing us behind the Daley Center and also behind the Caliphate's perimeter.

At 0355, the General motioned for three of us to move out to the east of the building. I started to go, but he pulled me back by the shoulder. I took it as kind of an honor that he wanted me with him. That was until I realized I was the one carrying the duffel bag with the LAW and two 66 mm rockets. I should have realized why no one was picking up that duffel bag back at the command center. I mean, of course, the first ones to take heavy fire are going to be the ones shooting off the big bottle rockets.

The General and I then moved to the western edge of the building. He nodded to the bag. My cue to start loading the rockets. So, I started loading them. And then, he starts talking to me. And I don't mean in this hushed voice so no one can hear us. But in this voice as if he was trying to talk over other conversations like we were at a party or something.

"What did you think of the stew?"

"Good, sir," I said, one-fifth of the decibel level he was at.

"Wasn't overdone?"

"No, sir. Perfect, sir."

"You need two things for a good rabbit stew, soldier. First, you need the right seasoning. I only use salt, pepper, celery, and a touch of olive oil. Anything else is goddamn superfluous. And secondly, you need to know when to stop cooking the fucker. Rabbit has a tendency to dry out."

"No, it wasn't dry, sir. Again, perfect, sir."

"Well, I'm glad you liked it, solider. You ever hear of Metallica?"

"A few songs, sir."

"Yeah well, that means you never heard of them. Saying you only heard a few of their songs is like saying I think I fucked her. You were

254

either completely in, or she's still got her cherry."

"Sir, we have three Caliphate approaching. Twelve o'clock."

"You think I don't know that, soldier?"

"No, sir, it just seems like we might want to do something."

"And while I would love to see you put a fucking hole through them the size of a basketball, I suppose it would be more prudent if we saved both of those rockets for the tank, and I just shot all of them in the head, huh?"

"Yes, sir."

"Okay, then. We're on. Take out the Abrams, and don't fucking miss."

I swear, Sean, it was the most beautiful thing I had ever seen. Right after the General blew the top of those guys' heads off, the whole place exploded. Perfectly choreographed, too. They didn't have a chance. I hit the back of the M1A2 turret twice, and the General's men immediately took out the machine gun nests. As directed, I then moved to the crosses to assist in taking down the bodies. When I looked back for a moment, I could see the General standing in the middle of the plaza just mowing down the Revolutionary Guard. What wasn't killed, just ran off. Man, I just wanted to scream, "Take that, you motherfuckers."

Jesus, Sean. Those ten minutes or so made me feel like a winner again. The last time I felt like that was when you found me on the baseline, and I hit that three-pointer to take the state quarterfinals. All right, the adrenaline has finally worn off. I'm tired as hell and need some sleep. Write to ya later.—**Aidan**

Letter #10

Thought I'd drop you a line since our unit's in a holding pattern right now. We took out the imam two days ago, which was a big moral victory for us. The only problem is that the same day someone from Sector 4 went rogue and blew up a madrassa with about 50 or so kids in it. The whole city up there wants revenge, and so we've been grounded. These raids we do aren't going to come easy anymore. Not that they were so easy in the first damn place, but this is just going to make them basically suicide missions.

I know we haven't talked about it since you've been gone. But I've been thinking about that labor camp guard. I've been thinking of sneaking out of here and paying him a little visit. I want him to suffer like he made you suffer. I want the pain to be long, and I want it to be excruciating. Yeah, I know what you're thinking. You're saying I wouldn't have a chance in moving thirty miles up there on my own. You're saying my vengeance is better spent working these raids from here. And I'm saying, fuck that, we always stood up for each other, and everyone always knew they had to fight both of us even if they only wanted one of us. That camp knew it too. That's why they transferred me out after you were killed. They knew I'd get to him eventually. We're twins, Sean. There are no two of us. There's only one. And deep down, even in heaven, I know you're just as angry as me that they split us into parts. God, I miss you so much. God, how I wish I had been on that same train they put you on.—**Aidan**

Letter #11

Felt like I was in some fairy tale yesterday. A pretty messed up one because obviously, I'm down here. But a fairy tale nonetheless. For at least a part of it anyway. At about 1400 hours, the new sergeant pulled me out of my quarters. And let me just say, that's not the time you want your command leader to come for you since our raids we run at night. The sergeant told me to take an extra clip. Fuck that, I thought. I stuffed two clips in my pockets and then taped another two around my calves. I wanted at least to blow away a few of the Ahabs before they shot my ass up.

We picked up another soldier. Private Aiken. I was with him on another mission. Holds his own. Didn't seem too reckless and didn't seem to show any fear. That's what you really want. You go up there you don't want anyone to be a gunslinger, and you sure as hell don't want the guy next to you to be pissing in his boots. Quiet guy, too. I like that. You can tell me everything you want to tell me when we're back in the tunnels. Up there, though, I want your full attention on the game. I can give a rat's ass about how you watched your mother get raped, or your child's head smashed in. Not that I'm a completely insensitive dick. But it's not the time.

So, we get briefed. Sergeant says we're going to a safe house to retrieve something. And that was it. Except for putting on our Caliphate soldier costumes. You know, bro, it didn't dawn on me until I was looking at Aiken that I realized why the hell we had been chosen. I mean, at first, you think it's an honor. But when I looked at him and his long ratty beard, I understood the two of us had been picked because we had the longest ones. Damn, I can be such a dumbass sometimes. I was wondering why the other soldiers in our unit kept trimming their beards.

They were vets, already knew how to fix the straws to be drawn.

The new sergeant's leading the way. Like Aiken, I'm cool with him. Doesn't seem like he's going to be doing any dumb shit to get us killed. If there isn't at least a 50-50 chance of success, he's going to abort. In this world, I'll take those odds every time. We head into the sewers from Sector 4, then about a klick later we stop. I don't know how he knew when to stop, but he did. From his pocket, he takes out this homemade periscope and shoves it through a tiny opening in the manhole. He's looking around to make sure it's cool for us to go up, and then we go up. After a two-block walk, the sergeant makes a quick right turn up the steps of this brownstone. He knocks. And then this old Mid-Eastern looking man lets us in. Beside him is his wife. The sergeant speaks to him in Arabic, and the old woman gives a nod of her head toward the stairs.

Okay, so this is where the fairy tale stuff comes in. We follow the old woman up to a bedroom. She opens the door and we all step in. And there, lying on the bed is a body. Young, maybe sixteen or seventeen. A white linen sheet is pulled up to the neck, and there are rose petals thrown all over. At first, I thought it was a boy because of the short hair. But as I got closer, I realized it was a girl. Jesus, just the most beautiful face I've ever seen. Hell, I would've asked her to marry me before even asking her name. The whole thing kind of reminded me of Snow White. Except for the fact that she wasn't there because of a poisoned apple, but because of a gunshot wound to the head. Couldn't imagine she was going to wake up from that no matter who in the hell gave her a kiss.

The sergeant then got to his knees, and we did the same. He led us in a short prayer. Afterward, he pulled the sheet over her head, and we all stood up again.

"Private Aiken, go down and see if the old man's brought the car around yet," the sergeant said.

After Aiken left, I spoke to the sergeant.

"This is what we came for?"

"It's not a what, Private, it's a who."

"I'm sorry, Sergeant. I didn't mean to show any disrespect. I was just—"

"That's fine, Private. I understand."

"Where are we taking her?" I asked.

"Back home."

"Where's home, Sergeant?"

"Sector 4, Private. The General wants her back there."

"You know who she is?"

"Yeah, I know who she is, Private. Saw her in the command center not too long ago. You just had the privilege of meeting The Assassin."

At first, I thought I misheard him. But then it made sense. That was the reason she had been able to do all that damage to the Caliphate. No one would have expected a teenage girl to be the angel of death. Damn, Sean, The Assassin was a legend down in these tunnels. Everyone had different ideas about who it was. But hell, it turned out to be my Snow White. An original Grimm ending and not at all a Disney white-wash. I got a bad feeling, Sean. This doesn't portend that we've got very much longer left.—**Aidan**

Letter #12

Got some pretty disturbing news this morning. A rumor's been flying around that the Caliphate had a spy down here and he escaped. I heard some guys talking that they were thinking of making a run for the Deep Tunnel project. I don't know where the hell that would get them. I'd give it a week tops before a Caliphate patrol picked them up and tortured the hell out of them. I'm pretty sure I'd rather fight it out down here than be captured by those sadistic bastards.

All right, I'm out of here. Chow time. I'm figuring it's going to be mystery soup and rock bread again. Kind of reminds me of mom's cooking. I loved the woman to death, but as you know, it would have been better if the house never came with a stove.—**Aidan**

Letter #13

Okay, got about two minutes for this one. We just took a code red and been given our orders. Hoping it's a drill, but for some reason, it sure in the hell doesn't feel like one. Anyway, just wanted to say that if something does happen to me, I hope I'm going to the same place you ended up. That's what happens, right? You die and get returned to those you loved the most. Otherwise, what the hell would be the point of all this. So maybe I'll see you soon, bro. If not, you'll have to get through another one of my letters.—**Love, Aidan**

10 THE PRIEST

Tuesday, January 29,

"Is it too late to see me?" I asked Father Mahoney after I had entered his quarters.

"Of course not," he said, and then closed the book in his hand and set it aside. I knew it would be an Agatha Christie. Father Mahoney had become quite a fan ever since he had started reading some of the ones I had brought to him.

"What chapter are you on?"

"I have actually just begun."

"There are stirring times ahead," I said.

"Yes, I believe there probably are," he answered with a smile, and after a pause added, "You have something on your mind?"

"It may take some time."

"Then perhaps you should have a seat. I'll make us some tea. One of our parishioners slipped me a bag at Mass. We can share the bag if you don't mind. It's probably a good vintage."

We talked a little while after that. Oh, about nothing really in particular. He must have known I had something extremely important to say. But he humored me and waited with the utmost patience for me to finally drum up enough courage to start speaking of it. And that I finally did, right after I took my last sip of the Earl Grey tea and set the cup aside.

"I've been remembering, Father," I began. "And I would like for someone else to remember with me."

"I would be honored to remember with you," he said.

"I am in church. I am fifteen years old. We are standing near the front in a reserved section. My mother is on my left, looking old and ruined. My father is on my right, held up by crutches to keep him off his shattered ankle bone. He looks stoic and hardened, as if waiting for a warship to pick him up from the shore. Father John is reading off the names of the murdered girls and their murdered fathers. I am staring up at the Jesus, waiting for my little sister's name to be called.

"Her name is called. My mother's body comes down like a building on a documentary I once saw, and my father tends to her the best he can. I myself do not move. I am still staring up at the Jesus. I am waiting to see tears from His eyes. And when I realize He is not going to cry, I begin to look at the nails in His hands and feet. I am waiting for them to pop out. I am waiting for Him to come down off that cross. I am waiting for Him to walk down the nave, stop at our pew, and tell me that He is either going to return with my little sister alive or with the heads of those who took her life.

"Father John waits until all has settled down. He tells us not to hate our Muslim brothers and sisters. He says the deaths were by men not of religion, but men with evil in their hearts. He then reads from Corinthians 15, and in my head I am thinking, O' God I need a miracle to still believe in anything You have to say.

"I remember walking out after that. I remember exiting the doors of the church into a field of television cameras and ambitious reporters. My father is pushing through the crowd like an angry icebreaker. He is stepping with one crutch and thrusting the other into their chests. We barely make it to our car. We are still surrounded like rock stars. My mother is banging on the windows and screaming hysterically. My father pulls away, and the last thing I remember is our car ride home. My father spoke only once. To my mother, once she had calmed down, he said, 'When it is okay for us to hate, then we will return there. Until then, all of them can go straight to hell.' "

"Did you ever return?" Father Mahoney asked of me.

"No, we never returned."

"But here you come to Mass every week."

"Yes, but every week I feel like I'm betraying my father. And every week, I feel like I still need a miracle to believe in anything that He has to say."

"The miracle is that you are here at all. You do understand that, right?"

I nodded my head, thanked Father Mahoney for listening, and returned to my quarters. I lay awake for hours afterward, thinking about his words. I suppose he intended for them to have two meanings. I suppose it was a miracle that I still had enough faith inside to keep listening, and I suppose it was a miracle that I was still alive when so many others had perished. Father Mahoney is like that. He is not one to tell you that your suffering is God's plan. He is the one to say that after all you have been through, you are still strong enough to have faith in God and the Jesus.

Saturday, February 02,

"I have finished," I said to Father Mahoney after cleaning the chalices and cutting the bread into cubes for tomorrow's Mass.

"What is your guess?" he asked.

"I say we have thirteen."

"It is a hopeful guess you give. But it is the number of the Lord's Supper, so I say we should toast to it."

"I will get the water."

"If you like your whiskey with water, then you should pour yourself a glass," Father Mahoney said, and then from a pocket of his pants, pulled out a small bottle of liquor. "One of our parishioners slipped it to me last week. It's probably a good vintage."

I left to get some cups. And when I returned, Father Mahoney was sitting in the first row. I sat beside him, and he poured us both a drink. In silence, we stared at the Jesus. A few minutes or so passed, and Father Mahoney took hold of my hand and squeezed it. I suppose he was asking for me to forgive the Jesus. I suppose at that moment I did.

"You know, Father," I began when he suddenly put a finger to his lips. I, of course, left my thought and quieted as directed.

"Do you hear that?" he then questioned.

I admit I did not hear anything at first.

"Bells. I hear bells," he uttered while getting to his feet.

I watched him walk to the altar, and then I watched as he looked heavenward.

He was not imagining, because right at that moment, I started to hear them myself. They were ringing above our heads. There was no mistake. It was glorious, and it was ethereal as if a choir of angels with bells in their hands had gathered right above our heads. I walked over to meet him. Tears had already flooded his eyes. Mine had just begun. A sign. Yes, it was a sign from the Jesus that He had not forgotten us.

And as we stood there, tears on our faces like crying children, the bells rang louder and louder until only one who had been struck deaf would not have been able to hear them. Father Mahoney fell to his knees and began to pray. I myself remained standing and turned to the Jesus. Even through my blurry eyes, I swear He was no longer there. If, for but just that one moment, perhaps He had come down from that cross to take a look around at all the suffering throughout our tunnels.

Sunday, February 03,

"What is your guess?" Father Mahoney said to me.

"I suppose one hundred, maybe even one hundred and ten."

"Yes, I think you will be close. Please help in seating them. I have to finish preparing the sermon."

Father Mahoney hurried back to his quarters. He still had another fifteen minutes before our first Mass of the day. The bells had uplifted the spirits of most everyone in the tunnels. To accommodate the renewed faith, we had to hold four Masses. And at each, we prayed and sang our thanks in a house of God that nary had room for another soul. The Jesus was near, we all thought. The Jesus had come down from His cross and was now donning His battle gear. Soon, He would arrive to save us all.

Tuesday, February 26,

It has been three weeks and two days since those bells rang. The Jesus has not yet arrived, and this morning, like last morning, Father Mahoney was not in his quarters when I went to visit. In fact, he has not been in his quarters at all since last Sunday. It is quite unlike him to just vanish without a word to anyone, without a word to me. Perhaps he has been called into the wilderness of our tunnels to be given another sign. Or perhaps he has gone off on his own to seek rest and solitude for just a day. After all, he has been plagued with exhaustion, trying to keep up with the demands of the Services we have had to accommodate the new parishioners. Either way, I have prayed to the Jesus to keep him well and safe. The tunnels do have their dangers, even for a priest.

Thursday, February 28,

I admit I now fear the worst. We have searched the tunnels day and night. We have handed out fliers to everyone. Some have speculated he was assumed into heaven. Those same people say that soon we will all be assumed into heaven, one by one. Those same people said it was the only explanation. I suppose that is possible. I suppose that after the ringing of those bells, anything is possible.

Friday, March 01,

My heart is more than heavy. It is a ship that has been sunk in the middle of the ocean. They have told me that Father Mahoney has been found at the far end of our tunnels, one length of his lavender-colored stole wrapped around his neck and the other wrapped around a water pipe. Below his feet, they told me was a crate onto which he took his last steps before kicking it away. I told them it was a sin impossible for our Father Mahoney. They said it was the only explanation.

Sunday, March 03,

I did not need to guess at the number of those at the funeral. The number was seven, which included myself, Father Mahoney, and the Jesus. I said a few prayers and told a few stories, the other six said nothing. I have become myself again. I have become my father. I have decided that I will return here to this church when it is okay for me to hate.

Saturday, March 16,

It has been almost two weeks since I have written in this diary. I did not think I would ever write again. But we have a new priest, and I suppose I will have new things to say since I have decided to resume my role in assisting with the Services.

I still think about Father Mahoney all the time. I think of him as a kind-hearted man who wanted nothing more than to first bring a smile to those around him and then perhaps to bring a few words of God afterward. That is how I believe a priest should be. He should start first at being a man of the Lambs before being a man of God. As far as the Jesus, I am not sure what I will do. I suppose it will be like ex-lovers who, by some strange set of circumstances, once again find themselves under the same roof. I'm sure we will throw each other glances. I'm sure we will think of the times we spent together. But I do not believe there will ever be a reconciliation. There is now too much between us. I have twice taken Him back and twice He has forsaken me. I am now of stone, and a stone neither wants nor needs anything. How glorious to be a stone.

Monday, March 25,

The new priest has only given two Services, but already I am certain that he dislikes me and I the same. He is so impersonal it would make one think he was playing the role of someone impersonal. He gives Mass reading from notes as if he is a teacher's aide. His sermons speak of nothing, and he hurries through the Services as if he were in a race. We have already lost two parishioners, which brings us now to six. I swear we could serve lobster tails and brandy at the Eucharist, and still, our flock would be the same. Even the Jesus, in the few times that I have looked at Him, seems disinterested. I am contemplating a return to my full-time position of thinking about Father Mahoney.

Sunday, March 31,

"We are done," Father said curtly after Mass.

"May I walk with you to your quarters?" I asked.

He nodded. Father had his own room. He did not seem at all troubled that he had been placed in the same quarters that our Father Mahoney had resided. We did not say a word on our walk. When we arrived at where he slept, he parted the curtain that hung over the entrance and was about to walk through when I finally spoke.

"From which parish did you come?"

He turned around and stared at me. I wasn't sure if he had heard me.

"From which parish, Father?" I asked again.

"I wish not to speak of it."

Tuesday, April 02,

Today I took a walk to the Department of Occupancy and Vital Records. I have an acquaintance there. I asked her for a favor. I asked her for some information on our new priest. She said his in-processing form listed him as a relatively recent escapee from the Fawzan labor camp. I nodded my head and said thank you.

From those who have escaped Fawzan, there has been nothing but stories of the utmost atrocities being committed. A man of the cloth would surely have been subjected to twice that. I can see how the beatings could have struck him forgetful and made him unwilling to bring anyone into his confidence. With this new information, I will stay on a little longer and give him time to heal. All of this I have forwarded on to the Jesus in prayer. I thought He should also be made aware, in case He was also wondering.

Friday, April 05,

Things are changing quickly down here in the tunnels. At least once a day, we are now called upon to visit the dead or those who are at its door. The deaths we see vary widely. Some have taken their own lives. Some just seem to have willed weakness into their bodies. Others voluntarily refuse treatment for infections and such that could easily have been ministered to. Others are soldiers carried back from raids that were conducted. The hardest to say prayers over are the children who have succumbed to disease. Those are the ones who wanted life the most. Those are the ones that no matter how loud we pray to their departing souls, are unable to hear a single word of God over the wails of their grieving parents.

This afternoon though, I think was the hardest. The little girl in her strawberry-imprinted dress was gulping for breaths like a fish that had just been taken off a hook and tossed into a boat. She couldn't have been any older than seven years of age. She must have already been orphaned as there was no one else around her except the nurses at the infirmary. As Father and I stepped before her, I took inventory of the looks in those nurses' eyes. They were all spider-webbed in red. I knew then that before the hour struck, she would be at heaven's gate.

"Let us pray," Father began after taking to a knee. And as he had done before, took out a sheet of paper from his pocket. "Through this holy anointing, may the Lord in His love and mercy help you with the grace of the Holy Spirit. May the Lord who saves you from sin free you up and raise you."

He then sprinkled holy water over her body and arose. I followed him out of the infirmary and put a hand on his shoulder.

"Should we have not at least remained and waited for her last breath? She has no one else," I said to him.

"Death is on its way. There is no need for us to hold the door for it. And there are others to tend to."

It was true what he had spoken. We did have others to tend to. However, his voice was curt and callous, as if these deaths were annoying him. I am not sure what to think of this.

Sunday, April 07,

The coughing from the child awoke me. It is pneumonia, and it is progressing at Godspeed. Death is coming for him, and there is nothing that I can do. That any of us can do. An orphan he was as of two days ago. I hold my tears so that I can weep twice as hard for him when his soul departs. I look around. This place where I sleep has become a waiting room for heaven. There are seven of us now, where two months ago there were twelve. The two Polish tunnel diggers sleep head to head. Both I would guess are in their mid-fifties, and neither has much grasp of English. Whatever their reason back then for not learning, it was time well spent as it is useless now. Suffering is universal. It needs no spoken language. A woman is sitting up in the corner. I know she is also asleep because when she is not, she is either softly singing or combing her hair. The gray strands lie all about her as if she was in a stable. It is not dementia that has taken her. It is nostalgia, which is all the more horrifying of an affliction. The other two are lovers. Young men. They do not copulate here. I would not mind if they did. They are in training to be soldiers. Neither are fit for what awaits them. They will be meat to the lions.

Wednesday, April 10,

This afternoon I went to visit Father for a little comfort. My mind muddled, I walked into his quarters without knocking. There I saw him cleaning a gun. He asked what manners had I been taught that I should walk into the room of a man unannounced or unaccompanied. I said I was sorry, but still kept my eyes on the weapon.

"Has a priest no right to protection?" he asked of me.

I said that surely he does.

"Good, then. The world is still upright," he replied.

I wasn't sure what to say next. I had even forgotten the reason I had come. I said I was sorry to intrude.

I feel something is not right. I, though, will not say a word until my proof is definitive. God strike me dead if I am wrong. For who am I to bring accusations upon a priest.

Friday, April 12,

I cut my hair last night and then shaved my head this morning. It seemed to have angered Father. As we were handing out food to the breakfast line, Father spoke loud to me because I was standing at least ten feet from him. I was menstruating. My body stank. And getting any closer would have made me feel even smaller in his presence.

"Are you now a monk?"

"I am now a woman without lice," I said.

My retort seemed to have angered him even more. As if he was upset that I had even dared to return a reply. He appeared to be gathering more words for me when a fight suddenly broke out in line. That was not unusual. There were always minor skirmishes in the food lines. What was unusual, though, was that this time Father slammed the ladle in his hand down and rushed over to where the altercation was taking place. By the throat, he took one of the offenders and threw him up against the tunnel wall. If not for the intervention of other men, I swear he might have choked the man to death. When they gently released him, I looked

272

into his eyes for an answer to his actions.

"Order, or chaos. Only one of these can be chosen," he said to all of us.

"They are hungry," I said.

"Be sure we shall test you with something of fear and hunger," I remember Father saying. I remember it as if it was my own name.

Saturday, April 13,

I met with the Historian today. That is the title he prefers. Though most here refer to him as the librarian. He is in charge of the books that were found when one of the excavation crews accidentally tunneled into a sub-basement of a library. It is quite an impressive collection, and while there are no shelves in the vault where he keeps them, they are stacked high like stalagmites, and the columns are numerous. The columns are not marked, but are sorted accordingly that I know. And the reason I know is that they do not need to be marked. He has the memory of a computer. When I had come before and asked for Saint Augustine's "Confessions," he rose from the desk that sits outside of the vault and went directly to it. The book he handed to me before a minute elapsed. I looked around for a log of some sort in which he could write my name. There was none. He said he would remember. And that he did when I returned the book one month later.

"Have you come again for another book by your saint? The only other work I have of his is "The City of God.""

"I have not," I said as I stared down at him as he sat at his desk. He again had on a hard hat with a lamp affixed to it, making him look more like an archaeologist than either a historian or a librarian.

"Then what is the title you seek?"

"Be sure we shall test you with something of fear and hunger," I said.

"Ah, the Quran. We have plenty of those in stock," he replied and began to push himself up from the desk.

"Wait."

"Yes?" he replied and eased himself back down into his chair.

"Are you certain it's from the Quran?" I asked, hoping he could not see the horror stretching across my face.

"Be sure we shall test you with fear and hunger, and a loss of wealth and lives and fruits, but give good tidings to the patient. It is from Chapter 2, entitled 'The Cow.' Shall I get it now?"

"No, that is all right. I've changed my mind."

"As you wish."

"It's strange," I then said after taking another look at the entrance to the vault behind him.

"What is strange?"

"The opening seems smaller since I was last here. Perhaps it is just a trick of the lighting."

"It is no trick. I have begun sealing it in."

"So they don't burn everything in it when they come?"

"Yes, exactly. They have a tendency of doing such things. Just ask Alexandria."

"I do not understand."

"The library of Alexandria. One rumor gives credit to Amr ibn al-As, that he was acting under orders of the second caliph Umar. Umar said, 'If these writing of the Greeks agree with the book of God, they are useless and need not be preserved; if they disagree, they are pernicious and ought to be destroyed. For they are at odds with the Quran.' "

"And so," I began, "will you seal in even those books of the Quran that have been collected?"

"Of course, I am a historian. All works deserve their place in the hands of humankind. Disagreement with what is inside is not up to me or anyone else."

Sunday, April 14,

He was at Mass. And although I was supposed to be by his side to assist, I feigned sickness and asked to be excused before it even began. He chided me for weakness, but finally granted me permission to leave. I left and hurried a path to his quarters. Once inside, I rummaged quickly through all of his belongings but found nothing unusual at all. I then was about to leave when it struck me that the Bible near Father's blanket seemed quite thin, almost ten times so if I had to place a guess. It brought me to wonder which books had been left and which books had been removed.

I knelt and picked up the Bible. I paged through Genesis, Exodus, and Leviticus. I paged through Numbers and Deuteronomy. However, where I expected to find Joshua, I instead found a new god with new words:

In the name of Allah, Most Gracious, Most Merciful
Praise be to Allah, the Cherisher and Sustainer of the worlds
Most Gracious, Most Merciful
Master of the Day of Judgment
Thee do we worship, and Thine aid we seek
Show us the straight way
The way of those on whom Thou hast bestowed Thy Grace, those
whose portion is not wrath, and who go not astray

Seven verses like the seven days of my God. Seven verses and all seemed to be floating on the page like seven warships on the ocean, each with their cannons pointing directly toward me. I flipped through the rest of his bible. I flipped through another one hundred and thirteen surahs. I understood then.

Wednesday, April 17,

At night the tunnels are unlit. I imagine it is the darkness that God saw before He decided to start hanging His little stars on the canvas of the universe. At night it would be a perfect time to get up and escape if one was planning to get up and escape. That is why, for the last two nights, I have positioned myself some thirty feet from his quarters to keep a watchful eye. I am not alone, though, in thinking he is one of them. Across the way, soldiers have taken up residence in a room across from him. They have tried to be inconspicuous, but they are not so inconspicuous. Anyone sitting there in the darkness can tell they are also keeping their eyes on him.

Thursday, April 18,

Last night he came out from his quarters into that darkness. I expected I would not have to move. I expected the soldiers to come out any minute and arrest him. When they did not, I found myself with no other choice but to follow him. He walked for what must have been a mile. I walked for what must have been a mile. It's quite difficult to walk for that length in the tunnels without making a sound. I did not make a sound.

He switched on his lantern and set it down. I could see the metal ladder in its light. I could see him taking hold of one rung and then stepping on another. There was no other choice. I fired directly at his head but missed. He turned in my direction and seemed surprised. I found that odd. Why would a murderer be surprised? I fired again, and this time I am sure the bullet found his side. His hands lost their hold, and he fell. I began to walk closer when I saw his gun pointed in my direction. I did not care. Why should I have cared? I knew I was under the camouflage of God's infinite darkness.

We both kept shooting until there was nothing more left for both of us to shoot. The bullets of my God against the bullets of your God I was thinking. I am almost certain I hit him another two times. His God, though, was able to lift him up, and there I watched from the ground as he ascended the metal ladder into the sewer system.

The soldiers came running up to me soon after. The sound down here in these tunnels travels like the speed of light and must have awoken them from their slumber. One stayed behind to tend to the hole he had put in my side while the other two ran off.

Friday, April 19,

I have not slept though they here in the infirmary tell me I should sleep. My mind is a whirlpool. My thoughts are circling around so fast that even if I had the quickest of hand, I would not be able to catch any of them. I am trying to remember my little sister, and I am trying to remember when I was staring up at the Jesus. I am trying to remember the one priest that I loved and the one whom though I shot was able to escape. O' God, I need a miracle to still believe in all that You have to say.

Saturday, April 20,

They are here. There are sounds of gunfire in our tunnels, and there are also sounds of explosions. There are the cries of children, and there are the wails of men and women. Everyone has fled the infirmary except for the few of us who are unable. Unlike the others, I do not mind. I do not fear death. Gladly I wait to see my little sister, mother, and father once again. For the Jesus, though, when he greets me, I will say not a word. I will just pretend like He is not even there. There was no reason for any of this suffering, and therefore there is no reason for me to speak or acknowledge Him. In heaven, like on earth, I will be a stone. And how glorious to be a stone.

11 SYLVIA PLATH

"I shut my eyes and all the world drops dead; I lift my lids and all is born again." - Sylvia Plath

This dream, it is worse than anything I have heard or seen when I am awake. This dream, it is always the same. We are asleep, and suddenly, we are awoken. They drag both of us away. You, they kill before my eyes. It is not an easy death. Your feet and your hands they hack off. The blood it pours out from your body as if from broken water pipes. For me, I am tied to a bed. First, I am raped by soldiers and then the sons of those soldiers. It is an unspeakable horror that lasts for days. Finally, they leave, but I know I have been seeded and now cells are dividing inside of me. I turn my head to the side and fall asleep in tears of disgust and shame.

One would think that would be enough for a single dream, wouldn't one? It is not, though. I keep dreaming, and I am older, and I am still tied to the bed. In the corner of the room, there is a child of about five. He is prostrate on the floor in prayer. His words come in a whisper to my ears. Speak up, I say. He speaks up. "In the name of Allah, the Beneficent, the Merciful. Allah! There is no God but He, the Living, the Self-subsisting, the Eternal." I yell for him to stop. He quiets as I command. Then, he rises from the floor and sits on the bed. A small hand he places on my own hand and says, "Mother, believe and I will untie you."

"I talk to God but the sky is empty" – Sylvia Plath

I am losing my mind. They are above me, and they have now infiltrated my being. Each breath I take is labored and with fear. The people here think I have gone mad, and I do not blame them. I myself do not even know who I am. You have not returned from your raid in seven days. And in those seven days, I have barely taken food or water. I am drenched in sweat when I wake, and I shiver before going to bed. I am writing only to keep my hands off of my own throat. It would be easier with a knife, but I wish the strength to self-strangulate.

I have paged through Matthew, Mark, Luke, and John. I have gone the distance to the Book of Revelation and then back again in reverse order. Where is my God? I have called to Him so many times that by now He must know me by name. If He does not give me a sign that you are alive, I will find a way out of here and convert. Perhaps their God will be more compassionate. Perhaps their God can speak, whereas I find mine to be mute.

"It seemed silly to wash one day when I would only have to wash the next. It made me tired just to think of it." – Sylvia Plath

Unlike a rocket ship departure or a New Year's arrival, I count up instead of counting down. Twenty-one days is a long time to be in this state. The clothes I kissed you in at the hour of your goodbye I still wear. I stink more than those around me stink. Back and forth I rock like an old woman, but age has yet to draw a single line upon my face. In nervousness, I twist my hair and it comes out in my fingers. I am saving it in a pile for when you return. I will then put it back on my head and then once again I will be your beautiful wife.

I hear them talk around me. They speak as if I have not ears. They say it is help I need. Of their diagnosis I cannot confute, but madness is a best friend for despair. Perhaps I should prepare for my own departure. Perhaps I should conjure the souls of suicide poets and suicide writers. Of what better consultants could one have than those who have come before? Oh, my love, death would be a featherbed to this horror I lay down in.

"All I want is blackness. Blackness and silence." – Sylvia Plath

I have a new friend. She speaks to me as if I was not there. She is correct. I am not here. She says most likely you have found safety somewhere else. This new friend she lies beautifully. So beautifully that one would hardly know she is even lying. But I am not so easily deceived. I know you've been picked up by boat and ferried off to Osiris.

Quiet, my love. Do not speak to this. All that I ever was, was when I was with you. That said, I am now nearing an end. Sooner would be better, now would be best. But oh my love, death I am choosing like a wedding dress. After all, one must be particular with something worn just once and never again.

"I have taken a pill to kill the thin papery feeling" – Sylvia Plath

Let it be recorded, I do not expect our reunion. I expect an infinite sea filled with the dead. I will swim. You will swim. But together once more, that I see as an improbability. For my God is a jealous God. He does not allow us to love anyone more than Him. And that is how I loved you.

Death is here, my love. It is all around. It is in these tunnels, and now it is in my veins. By one way or the other, this body of mine will soon be lying in state. Goodbye, my husband, our time was as short as cake, but oh how I am still forever content.

12 GILLY

"Gilly, wake up," I said, standing over him as he slept sitting up in a corner of the room, a tin can of vapors and a heart-shaped mirror within his reach. The candle before him was down to its last few inches. But those last few inches were still enough to cast a shadow on the wall that looked just like him in his earlier days. If it wasn't Gilly, I would have thought it quite insane. A cough I then feigned, and the lashes of his eyes fluttered like butterfly wings. When he finally drew his lids open and spoke, I swear his words reached my ears well before his mouth began to move. If it wasn't Gilly, I would have surely thought my mind had been blown.

"Is my dress still stained?" Gilly asked.

"Yes," I said.

"I was washing it off in my dream. I thought it would come clean," he answered. By now, both his shadow and voice had caught up with time so that they were once again old and in synch. Just a rip in space-time, I could only assume.

"It looks fine, Gilly. No one will ever notice," I said as I gave another look at an inkblot on one sleeve of the floral-patterned velvet dress he was wearing.

"Do you remember a guy that's been in such an early song?" he then asked.

"Yes, and I can still see him inside of you."

"I would like to sing one last time. Do you think they will still come?"

"Of course. They've never forgotten you."

Before I could reach down to help him to his feet, he was already lifting his body by moving up the wall like a mime. His veins were coming through his jaundiced skin like rivers in Braille and colored dead blue. His hair was short, slicked back and gray, devoid of the fiery red that used to make both boys and girls swoon. His eyes still pierced, though. One ice blue and the other the color of a carob pod.

"I'll need my boots," he said, standing an inch or two shorter than me. "What's a queen in bare feet?"

I looked around, and by his guitar, I saw them, block-heeled and suede. After retrieving them, I carried them over to him and got down on my knees. His toes were prominent, age and starvation had made them ugly and long. I remember the first time I was there like that it was fifty years or so back. His feet were beautiful then, and they were small, as if he had purposely bundled them as a China girl would. I gave him my mouth and I gave him my love then, but I don't think he but blinked. I don't even think he knew it was me.

"You want me there?" I asked as I looked up at him.

"How's my makeup?" he asked to avoid answering me.

"You could use a little," I said. And with that, he put his arms akimbo and threw back his head. From my pocket, I took out a crimson lippie and smudged it on the apples of his cheeks. When finished, I stood back to take a look at this aged rock queen.

"My looking glass," he requested. When I gave it to him, he put a finger to his cheek and traced it around his face. "I'm quite engraved. Like ancient river beds of Mars, don't you think?"

I said nothing. I just kept staring at him. He then spoke, and the words put another one of his fissures in my heart.

"Your eyes are the worst of mirrors. In them, I can see all that you love and disapprove of. No one wants admiration and rebuke in the same look. Take my scarf and tie it over my eyes. I don't want to see them looking at me like you are looking at me now."

I did as he said. He then requested a sniff from his can of vapors. After that, I led him by the hand, and we walked out of our quarters and into the tunnel. I counted sixty-nine steps before I turned him around, and we returned from whence we came. Onto my tortoise-shell suitcase that was now his stage, I helped him step. He wasn't even a foot above the ground, but he always had such a presence that it still looked like he was sixty-two miles high. His fingers slipped through mine, and I prayed he wouldn't fall.

"The curtains are parting," I said to cue him to begin.

Three songs he sang. All were new. All were a cappella. And none were what they would have wanted. Gilly didn't care. He was never one to rest his head upon yesterday. I had tears rushing down my face. I had my eyes looking ahead at our funeral scene. After easing him to the ground, I returned him to his corner. He took a few more sniffs, and I watched him for the length of consciousness to sleep.

Journal #14, Gilly and Me – Day 1070

"Gilly, wake up. I've brought you something to eat," I said, shining the flashlight upon him as he slept curled up like a dog. He was wearing a silk waist-length white kimono inked dark green with bonsai trees. When he failed to stir in my voice, I took a match and lit the candlestick that was a few feet before him. The light cast a butterscotch haze over the two open books that were just out of reach from his outstretched hand. The writing of one I could see was in Arabic, the other in what looked like Old English script. It was then I noticed that in one corner of the room he had drawn a black signpost. High above in white chalk, he had one street Heddon and the other Regent.

"Are the books still here?" he asked, and it startled me that he was awake all along.

"Yes."

"I was dreaming they were the last copies on earth. Suddenly I felt this great hunger pang, and so the pages I began to eat. It wasn't long before I grew wings and turned into a beast."

"What do you think it means?"

"From gods come monsters is of course what I think."

In his words, I remember I immediately took to a knee and closed the covers to both books. There a King James Bible and there a Quran. There in opposition, like a black queen and white king were they. The only thing I was not sure of was which one was which.

"Where did you get these?" I asked, my body recovering from the freeze that had occupied it after his last words had rolled off his tongue.

"I was given them, or they appeared. I haven't the faintest idea."

"Shall I burn them?"

"What good of that would come?" he said and slowly sat up. "Man would only recreate them in a manner worse than the first time he tried to coin immortality."

I picked both books up and hurried them to another corner of the room. Then, I sat cross-legged before him. In the candlelight, he looked alabaster. He looked like an x-ray.

"You should have some of the bread I've brought you. I can almost see your bones."

"No, thank you. When you lived too long, you should not eat," he said and fed himself with another sniff of his vapors.

Arguing with him would have been pointless. Taking away his vapors inadvisable. I slid the plate off to the side. It was then I noticed the trail of dried blood that stopped at both his wrists. I leaned over and unfurled his fingers, which were curled to his palms. The nails were so long that they were cutting into his skin.

"Can I clip these?" I asked.

He turned his hands over and nodded. I was quite surprised, a new coat of permanent marker he had put on them. Except for the length, they looked perfect. They looked as if he was ready to go dancing.

"Are there many of us left?" he asked as I started to pare them down to something less than eagle talons.

"Less than when we last spoke. And most likely lesser when we are done with this conversation," I replied.

"They took our books and they took our paintings. They took your god and they took my earth. Worst of all, they took our thoughts and left no one with a mind of their own to think."

"It will all be returned to us someday, Gilly."

"You were always Eleanor Porter's orphan child. Their hands are like chalkboard erasers on humankind's blackboard of creativity. They are the dawn of ignorance and the pirates of freewill. They are the subjugators of hope, the oppressors of love's vagary. They'll return us to apes. An ordained de-evolution. We'll be rewound millions of years in a flash. I pray for a starman to intervene. But then again, what would be left to see? Name me one distant visitor who would possibly travel light years for this?"

"We are not yet defeated. I still have faith."

"Faith, you understand, is not wanting to know what is true."

"Do you not even wonder how it is you lived so long without some hand of providence to intercede?"

"No, there is nothing arcane in a heart that still beats and lungs that still breathe."

"And so there is nothing you believe?" I asked, now moving on to his right hand.

"With age comes decay and reality. Hopefully, one will have no fear of that."

"You're a liar if you say you have no fear," I said as I decided to fight back.

"Of the pain and putrefaction, of course. But in most circumstances, you can always change the length of that."

"I must leave, Gilly. I cannot hear any more of this," I said as I returned his hands to his lap.

"Prior to that, and of course before our deaths, I want you to take me up there. They have shattered the stones of the pyramids and leveled Petra and Greece. I would like to see the hills and trees before they get their hands on them."

"We would get no more than thirty feet before they tore us to pieces."

"Look at this body. I am now its inmate. Lucky I would think one who could unlock the time to set themselves free."

"That key I cannot give you. And for myself, I am not yet ready."

"Then you are not only weak, but a conspirator with the breaths I take."

I then watched as he picked up his can of vapors and brought the opening once again to his nose.

"Gilly, you need a respite from those vapors. Can't you see? They are destroying you. There will be nothing left when we are set free."

"Please, no more of your words at my door. My brain hurts like a warehouse. It has no room to spare for another one of them."

I soon left and took a slow walk around the tunnels. I was in despair. If I didn't intervene, I knew he would be dead before me. And then I could call him my murderer.

Journal #14, Gilly and Me – Day 1075

"Gilly," I said as soon as we walked in. He was standing in a corner with his back to us. He had on yellow parachute pants and a matching suit coat. He was painting on the clay wall with the oil pastel crayons he had asked me to bring before we entered the sewers. From what I could see, he already had earth, a star, and a moon.

"Can you go find them and bring them back in?" he said after laying down another stroke.

"Who?" I questioned.

"The lovers. They were just here. They must have had backstage passes."

"We didn't see anyone on our way here, Gilly. Maybe you were dreaming."

"If that was so, they appeared more real than the two of you."

"Okay, maybe they were here, Gilly. But I have someone more important for you to meet. I brought the priest."

"Is it the one from before?" he asked.

"No."

"That's good. The other one was one of them."

"How did you know?" I asked.

"His hands and feet were always clean."

The priest and I glanced at each other.

"Gilly, please turn around. We would like to speak with you."

"If it's my last rites, it will have to wait. I still have death and lovers to paint."

"No, he is just visiting."

Gilly set the oil pastels to the ground and turned to face us. In what could have been no longer than an instant, he looked fifty years younger and then as quickly returned to his dying face. It wasn't only me who took witness to this trick of the light. I saw it also in the eyes of the priest.

"How are you feeling?" the priest asked.

"Upside down and inside out, but I am becoming quite used to it."

"Have you prayed tonight?" the priest then asked him.

"Aye, my Lord," Gilly replied.

"Then you have accepted Jesus Christ as your savior?"

"If you bring him here to save me, then he will be well received."

"Gilly, just say that you do accept Him. I want you in heaven with me."

"I have been kinder than you. By that alone, if I am not with you, it is because your heaven is a level below mine."

"Perhaps I should leave," the priest said as he placed a hand on my shoulder.

"Gilly," I pleaded. "Say it goddammit. Say He died for your sins."

"I must get back to my painting. Time may be infinite for you and your god, but it is not for me."

I collapsed to my knees, and the priest walked away. The cross around my neck I removed. For a moment, I was thinking of tossing both it and my soul across the room. For a moment, I was thinking of following Gilly right into hell. That did not last, and I returned it to around my neck. I felt drained and I felt I had lost. I felt as if my birth meant nothing at all. Gilly, he must have felt something beyond me.

Journal #14, Gilly and Me – Day 1077

"Gilly, wake up. I think God has finally left, and we should follow Him right on out of this place," I said, whispering in his ear as I lay next to him. I was shivering in the thought of dying as he was twitching in his sleep. I was thinking of all the things they would do once our tunnels were completely overrun. All night while he slept, I listened to the sound of sporadic gunfire and small detonations that were now taking place. It was only a matter of time now before they would find us, two old queers nestled in our death scene. I was thinking it was time for us to travel on before they stole the breaths right out of our mouths. And then as if he had been reading my mind, he squeezed the wrist of the arm that I had wrapped around him. He was wearing a pleated, white tuxedo shirt and nothing else. He had blindfolded himself with two turns from an elastic bandage, and for eyes glued on black buttons taken from the cuffs.

"All the nightmares came last night," Gilly began. "And it looked as if they are here to stay. There will be no room for me, and it will be no fun for you."

"Yes. So we should get ready to leave this stage."

"If you unwrap your arm from me, it will surely be easier for me to make an exit."

As he requested, I withdrew my hold on him. He crawled like a cat to the wall. When he turned around, he was sitting there like a rag doll. He was sitting there as if the only life left in him was being borrowed from mercy's chest.

"My vapors, please," he requested.

"You're a junkie, Gilly. The world is dying all around us, and all you can think of is getting high."

"I am sorry, but for most of them, I was dying here first."

I was never the one to deny him anything, and so I brought the can over.

"Do you even know what's going on right now?" I asked.

"Your god has left and been replaced by one with less patience for our frivolousness."

"And don't you think you were part of that banality?"

"And if all my life I just sat around and prayed, they may have been able to call me Peter Pious, but I would have been more the liar."

"Gilly, I have something for us. We can drink it at the same time and leave together."

"How nice and naïve to think we can take a friend with us on the way out. Unfortunately, I must educate and enlighten. Death, you see, has no other passengers. We all ride with it alone. Each in our own cars. You in yours and me in mine," he replied and then returned for another long inhale from his can of vapors.

"Gilly, I beg of you, if not with me then before or after. I do not want their hands to be the last things that touch you."

I called his name again. I rattled his body. I slapped his face. My words and actions though were of no more use as he had already found the cave where Hypnos lives. All the while, death was marching closer, the inevitable parade of battle cries and wails. I swear I did what anyone else would have done for the one they most loved. I gave him a kiss, and then I broke his neck with a swift benevolent twist. In death, he looked no different than in life, so of what charge could I be accused.

Journal #14, Gilly and Me — Day 1078

Gilly, wake up. Their weapons are firing not more than a few quarters away. I have hailed down death's car and you were right. I am looking inside, and it looks like I will be riding alone. You may have had a one-day start, but I will ask the driver to go all night if he has to. I will see you again, Gilly. Because ha ha. We are forever entwined.

13 AGNES DAY

My Last Testimony,

I must tell this story. I must tell it not only because my death is most certainly near but because He wants me to tell it. Why else would He let me live for another three days? There could be no other plausible explanation. For not too long ago, I was shot. Through the heart. Yet here I sit with a pen in my hand. I beg of you not to think insanity has befallen me, or at the time, I had merely drifted off to sleep. Neither would be true. For I was God's witness. I swear to you I was.

Three days ago, they finally came. As we all knew that one day they would. Why they could not have just poisoned us with gas I do not know. Why they did not just flood our tunnels and drown us all I am not certain. It would have saved them maybe a thousand or more. But I suppose as in the beginning, as they have proven, they have no respect for life, not even their own. That I have always found inhuman. And oddly, that has brought me solace as I would rather have my death come at the hands of those outside God's dominion than from one of His own children.

When our area was finally breached, they immediately began to fire upon us with their automatic weapons. And we, we began running toward the other end in one great stampede. There was no courtesy. The young and the old were trampled into the ground, and I could feel their bones breaking under my feet. I wanted to stop to help those who had fallen, but you must understand it was impossible. There was not even room enough to cover my ears from the deafening sounds of their bullets and their explosions ringing out in the tunnels. It was horror, unimaginable, and ineffable.

To what place were we seeking refuge, you might be asking? It is an easy question for me to answer. None actually. We were just trying to run to add a few more minutes to our lives. Soon we came upon a line of soldiers waving us along. They were getting ready to topple a few of the coal cars in order to stop the advance of the Caliphate. After crossing by, I stopped to catch my breath, and then for some reason decided to stand beside them and wave my arms along with them. The rush of those fleeing soon began to thin out. Instead of three of four running down the tunnels at the same time, it was now a single file. I should have continued on, but I was transfixed. Inside I was cheering each of them as if it was the finish line to some race, and I was the only spectator who had not left.

Finally, the soldiers determined that the coal cars had to be pushed into place. It would have allowed no one else through. I could not bear that, so I jumped on the back of one of them, but it was to no avail as he threw me off. After picking myself up, I bit down on the hand of another one. He was not as kind. He grabbed me by the hair and whipped my body into the tunnel wall. My head did split a little from the impact, but the pain or blood I did not think of.

As I knew would be, another wave of us came down that tunnel. And now twenty, maybe thirty were stacked up on the other side with no route of escape. Minutes later, the Caliphate finally came. Their bullets tore into the backs of those we had forsaken, and I had a clear view of all their death faces. And where their bullets did not find flesh, they found the first coal car so that it sounded like a hailstorm raging down upon a tin roof.

With a view now unobstructed, our soldiers started firing their weapons. They were screaming like mad, and I was covering my ears and thinking of how war could not have possibly crossed God's mind when he created Adam and Eve. It was five minutes at most before they had shot all of the Caliphate dead. I was not joyous. I was thinking of how they had all been led astray and of all the beautiful things they would miss.

The living among us were now seven. The soldier near to me handed over a spare weapon and I refused, telling him I am here with but prayers to defend. We heard nothing for an hour or so. Our hopes rose with each passing minute. None of us spoke. I think that is true. I can't remember now. Fear is an odd emotion. It silences your tongue but fills your head with all these loud and terrible thoughts.

The sound of running footsteps. That's what we heard. Faint at first, then building from there. A crescendo, I suppose. The next sounds came from the soldiers clicking off the safeties of their weapons. Not long after, an avalanche of voices. We all knew it. None of us would be saved. The second wave of the Caliphate had arrived. I made the sign of the cross, bestowed upon myself my own last rites, and waited.

A girl came first, fifteen or sixteen years on this earth. She was carrying an infant close to her bosom. She was twenty or so yards from us. The soldiers aimed their weapons around her. And then the gates of hell opened as the first faces of the Caliphate could be seen. Still ten yards away, neither her nor her infant had a chance. I saw flesh and blood explode right out of her left shoulder. The pieces of flesh hit one of the soldiers in the face, and he had to wipe it away. She stumbled a bit but kept running. Then the bullets opened up more holes in her body and she fell, her elbows skidding across the railway boards as she lay the baby in front of her. I stood up and cursed God in a voice that ripped my vocal cords. I told Him to do His own work and not let others kill for Him. One of the soldiers must have heard because he turned around and shouted at me to get down. A bullet found him next, and then I saw smoke rising from a hole in the upper left part of my chest. There was no blood and there was no pain. I then put a finger to it and felt the casing. And then I thought, how possible was that? How does a bullet go no farther after it enters the skin?

The last soldier remaining reached around and grabbed a grenade. It had just left his hand when he too met his death. The grenade rolled toward the infant. At that moment I should have lunged for cover. But the grenade changed into the shape of a red ball, and I was both mesmerized and paralyzed. I know you are thinking that it was my mind playing a trick on me. My mind wishing that the soldier had mistakenly thrown a red ball instead of a grenade. I swear though, neither my eyes nor my mind was deceiving me. The light that came next was not a flash, but a bloom of the most brilliant white I had ever seen. Soon it enveloped everything in the tunnel. I felt peace. I felt warmth. I felt this infinite love spread throughout my entire being.

For how long I was asleep, I am not sure. It could have been a minute, an hour, or a day. I now lay where I had once stood, curled into a ball with a thumb to my mouth as if in the womb of my mother. I did not move at first. Instead, I listened. But there was not a sound to be heard. So, I arose and immediately looked out to where the girl and the infant had fallen. To my utter astonishment, the coal cars were no longer there and so also had the girl and her infant disappeared. Inside of me, a fury swelled. How dare they steal the innocents.

I then stood up and walked to the Caliphate's side of the battlefield. The first Caliphate soldier I came to was lying face down. By his hair, I grabbed him to turn his face to me. I wanted to scream so loud that on his walk to hell, he would still be able to hear me cursing him. But as I looked at him, a horror shot through me as his eyes were missing. To the one next to him I looked. The same. I then began to wade through the rest of their dead. Another one. The same. One more. The same. The same. The same. All of them had had their eyes removed.

A sound of fluttering of wings turned me around. And there I saw the girl holding the infant close to her breast. The sight weakened the pulse of my heart and drew my skin pale. She gave a smile to me, and tears rushed out to wet my cheeks. She spoke not but gave a nod of her head for me to follow her. And I did so, following her to this room. A room well concealed. A room with an old desk, blueprints, and dust from at least one hundred years ago.

"We must go," she then said, meaning her and the infant.

"The Caliphate will eventually find me here, won't they?"

"Yes, but you have an extra three days. The angel He sent cannot hold the bullet any longer than that."

"Why me? Why was I given more time than the others?" I then asked.

"Because He saw the light in you, Agnes Day."

There is a clock here, atop the desk it sits. Somehow it still keeps time. The devil, or God, or both of them I assume have given it back its life. After the girl and the infant left, I turned it to face the other way. I did not want to watch the hands go around. Outside I can hear the crusaders running down the tunnels screaming like savages and uttering words incomprehensible to me. It is only a matter of time before they discover this room and then me. There is a God that I know. There is only one true God that I am certain. I have seen His works, and I am amazed. If this is His plan, then I accept it. Who am I to question His will? What right have I to ask for more time? He has already shone His light upon me. He has made me His witness, and for that, I gladly accept His decision.

Agnes Day

14 THE HISTORIAN

April 18th (15th Day of Dhul-Qa'dah)

It is most interesting that in those early days of the Caliphate crusaders, we sniffed for their crude weapons at our transportation hubs and arenas, locked down our generating stations and high-risk chemical plants, surveilled telecommunication networks, and kept a vigilant eye on our busy streets and schoolyards. But the one threat we had forgotten to prepare for was the most obvious of all threats—one that got its start more than 3500 years prior when sheep with tularemia were sent into enemy cities. It picked up again as wells, rivers and aqueducts were poisoned, corpses with bubonic plague were delivered via catapult over castle walls, and blankets used by smallpox patients were distributed to unsuspecting tribes. So, a worldwide coordinated attack utilizing a similar tactic of warfare should not have come to anyone's surprise.

It must have been like splitting the atom to them when they created it. It had to be a perfect pathogen, and it was. Perfect in the way that transmission through human contact was certain. Perfect in the way that in the soil it did not remain long. And perfect in the way livestock was unaffected. It was a silver bullet, targeting only the human immune system. Hemorrhaging occurred within the first hour, complete immobilization at the fourth, and certain death not more than two hours after that. More perfect, though, was that it had an antidote. The only way it could have been improved upon was if it had the means to discriminate between Muslims and the kafirs.

Beware of the sword you kill your enemy with, for it is with the same sword that the children of your enemies will kill you. The squadrons of drones that flew that Christmas Day were a wondrous sight to us, as they must have been to all of the other cities that they flew over. As they came in low, you could see attached to some of those miniature planes a banner reading "PEACE ON EARTH." A Christmas greeting from some company, I thought. Others must have thought a gesture of goodwill by a humanitarian organization. Still, more must not have given it any thought at all.

Those drones flew not only over Chicago. They flew over Sydney, Tokyo, Seoul, Shanghai, Guangzhou, Ho Chi Minh City, Bangkok, Delhi, Mumbai, Sao Paulo. They flew over Moscow, Jerusalem, Johannesburg, Kinshasa, Berlin, Rome, Paris, London, New York, Lima, Toronto, Mexico City, and LA. Over all of those and then hundreds more. Network news, radio play, and social media fanned the flames. En masse to the breaking news, people left their Christmas mornings and Christmas nights to come into the streets to take witness of this glorious sight. As the payload of what everyone imagined to be snow fell from the skies, children stuck out their tongues, lovers twirled about and embraced, the old closed their eyes and unfurled their fingers to let the deadly pathogen gently come to rest upon their skin. Bewitching a sight was it to watch. As so it must have been for those inside the city of Troy when they opened their gates and in rolled a great wooden horse. Praise to those who remember the deceits of the past, death to those who do not.

With swiftness, the offensives followed, backed by more pathogen-carrying drones. And by the end of the first month, civilization as known to those countries of a non-Muslim majority had, for the most part, ceased to exist. Governments went underground to regroup and search for an antidote. It was all useless by then, though, as the major cities had become immobilized, and once-mighty military bases became ghost towns. The Caliphate was already established and orders issued to begin the cleanup. They at first were overwhelmed with the task of removing the deceased. The lesser cities were burnt to the ground. The greater ones required much more care and ingenuity. Crematoriums operated twenty-four hours a day. Rotting corpses were transported by trains to the outskirts of these greater cities. Black smoke was the new canvas to the sky over the metropolises that once dimmed the stars with lights from their steel-and-glass monoliths.

For two years following, fighting in the rural areas still continued. Where resistance was encountered from bands of paramilitary groups, it was met with uncompromising brutality and overwhelming force. They too were then vanquished.

Within those countries where the pathogen had been spread from above, tens of millions of Muslims were unaffected. While they claimed that this was by the intervention of Allah, it was later ascertained it was by human design. For years they had been delivering food to their mosques infused with the antidote. The faithful ate unaware that they truly were being saved and retained for the Caliphate. Even nature must have been jealous. Even nature in all its complex wonder could not have been that selective.

That was three years and four months ago. Tonight, as I write, it is the fifteenth day in the month of Dhul-Qa'dah. I am composing this from Sector 4, the largest of 5 autonomous sectors of the Alliance in the city of Ayla, which they the Caliphate have renamed, which once we called Chicago. We inhabit a system of freight tunnels, forty feet below the streets above. There are 47 miles of usable tunnels in a mostly rectangular grid right under what was the heart of Chicago and is now the heart of Ayla. The grid is just a little less than 4 square miles. There are access points to the city above, both from the sewers and also from the sub-basements of a few select buildings. From these points, we run reconnaissance and conduct our raids. We prick them when we can. We let them know there are still a few thorns left.

I came here thirty months ago, five months after the freight tunnels of Sector 4 had been discovered. Before that, I was a slave in the Fawzan labor camp. When my middle-aged body had withered away under the toil of an 18 hour, seven-day-a-week workload, they were about to execute me. It was only by fortune that I was spared and reassigned to the Ministry of Labor. There, I became an accountant, an accountant of men. When I finally escaped, the slave labor force in the city of Ayla and its surrounding suburbs numbered exactly 137,353. That number I reduced by two to account for my own departure and that of a man called the General. He is the one who engineered our escape. He is the one with whom I credit my freedom.

When the General and I arrived here, the freight tunnels were a disorganized sanctuary with less than 200 inhabitants. It was lit by dying cell phone flashlights, fed with stolen food from the brave that ventured above, and armed with knives and sharpened sticks. Human waste was piled into abandoned coal cars and rolled to remote areas. Bathing was not an option. Within a year, the General had organized the tunnels so that we were a fully independent city with a hydroponics lab, infirmary, school system, streets and sanitation group, records department, excavation team, and militia. Water and electricity we tapped into from pipes and cables that ran through the tunnels. Weapons we gathered in raids conducted during the night.

Near the end of the first year of the General, we numbered over 1000 men, women, and children. The increase of 800 was due to our active recruitment of escaped slaves from the labor camps, and those who had somehow been able to avoid detection by the Caliphate. By the second year of the General, our zenith, we numbered nearly 1700. Now, as I write, we have been reduced to less than 1100. Soon though, we will be less than that. And then, within days I presume, most certainly eradicated as they have finally found our city.

Yesterday I sealed the vault. After doing so, I sat cross-legged outside and bowed my head in thought. Oh, how at that moment did I feel like an Essene in a Qumran cave. And, as they must have, did I then begin to wonder whether the writings would ever be found. For surely, the earth holds within its womb many more writings than have been discovered. But if they are found, would it be a few years from now or perhaps five thousand years in time. And as I reflected upon the latter, what then would the world look like. Would our texts be like hieroglyphics to them? Would they doubt their authenticity? Would they believe anything of which I have seen? Could they even conceive that such mass destruction came from the human race?

I am not of the courage to draw my own blood. It surely is a weakness, but then again, what historian wants to shorten the past. So, I will remain here in my quarters and await my fate. I have always understood empires rise and empires fall, gods are created, and new ones take their stead. But never until this hour has it dawned upon me that fortunate those who are born neither at their beginnings nor at their ends. Oh, how I wish my death would just hurry, and then someone else could write about the past. Oh Anna, my sister, my dreams are terrifying and leave me hanging.

To the one who happens upon this, I pray that the world you come from has by God's grace healed its wounds and found peace. I pray that those above me have long ago consumed themselves with their own hatred. I pray that either mankind has abolished religion, or has united all of the gods we once worshipped. Ultimately, I pray that no longer have you the need to pray.

15 MAJOR CALEB ADAMS

Thursday Morning
Day 15 in the month of Dhu al-Qa'dah

I have received a message from Sector 4. It stated that their location has been compromised after a Caliphate spy escaped. They are requesting we proceed expeditiously with the digging of the tunnel linking our sector with theirs. After placing our own troops on high alert, I ordered around-the-clock excavation teams to the site. In addition, I ordered that where we can, a doubling up of our quarters in anticipation of their evacuation. I also ordered our infirmary to begin preparation for the possibility of wounded. My response to General Danzig's request has been composed, coded, and now in transit. My assessment is the same as his. We will need another ten days.

Thursday Evening
Day 15 in the month of Dhu al-Qa'dah

A message from Sector 2 arrived at 1905. They acknowledged receipt of our transmission, wished us our best, and stated their prayers for

Sector 4. They have also written of promising news from the Russians and Chinese. Their forces have met up in the city of Blagoveshchensk. Now, they hold that city along with the city of Heihe. It is the first major victory that we have heard of, and a significant one if indeed it is true. Unfortunately, it is of no relevance to the plight of Sector 4. We are still monitoring Caliphate troop positions and have not noticed any unusual activity. I would have expected an immediate response by the Caliphate. Perhaps they were in error, and it was not a spy. The General, though, does not seem like the type of man who would raise the alarm if he was not certain. I will therefore take him at his word that the days of Sector 4 are indeed numbered.

Friday Morning
Day 16 in the month of Dhu al-Qa'dah

At 0400, I visited the excavation site. When one of the men fell from exhaustion, I took his place and continued digging for an entire 4-hour shift. The clay is intransigent. It does not easily separate from Mother Earth. Nine days I now firmly believe is optimistic. Ayla is still quiet. It is a good sign.

Friday Evening
Day 16 in the month of Dhu al-Qa'dah

Good news has reached my ears. We have gained 5, perhaps 6 days. On our side, the tunnel suddenly opened up into an abandoned construction area. Our excavation team moved through it unimpeded for 2000 or so meters before encountering another wall of clay. This places us 3 days at best from Sector 4. I am now more hopeful than before, which does in itself begin to worry me. War is not hope. It is a certainty.

Saturday Morning
Day 17 in the month of Dhu al-Qa'dah

Intelligence units in Ayla have now detected Caliphate troop activities above Sector 4. Due to this, I had no other option except to recall all units save one. I cannot deny that it is now quite evident they are preparing to enter.

Saturday Evening
Day 17 in the month of Dhu al-Qa'dah

2115 hours. First Sergeant Markham has just left. Stethoscope monitoring of the tunnel has picked up the sounds of automatic gunfire and detonations of small explosives. It has left me with no doubt that the Caliphate has begun its operation. I ordered our teams to keep digging, though I am now considering rescinding that directive. The decision is weighing heavily upon me. We are still two days away, four if I consider that most likely Sector 4 has halted the excavation on their side. We will not reach them in time for an evacuation. And, as my responsibilities lie first with Sector 3, I must take into consideration that the closer our shovels and pickaxes get to Sector 4, the more likely it is that our sector will be compromised. I have begun to pray. We are all anxious. I myself cannot sleep for more than an hour at a time. My thoughts I cannot put to rest.

Sunday Morning
Day 18 in the month of Dhu al-Qa'dah

There is no longer a need to monitor the sound by stethoscope. The reverberations of explosives and firing of automatic weapons can be heard from the excavation site. I have ordered the excavation teams to cease all further activity. We have stopped digging, approximately one and a half days away from Sector 4. I am both sick in body and sick in faith.

Sunday Evening
Day 18 in the month of Dhu al-Qa'dah

The tunnel we have dug collapsed one hundred yards back from where we halted excavation. Two of the lead teams, which requested permission to remain at the front line, are now trapped or under the rubble. I should have been more adamant in my order for all excavation teams to pull back to Sector 3. Their fate weighs heavy upon me.

Monday Morning
Day 19 in the month of Dhu al-Qa'dah

The rubble has been removed. None of those from the two excavation teams were found alive. It is a sad day, like most of our days.

Monday Evening
Day 19 in the month of Dhu al-Qa'dah

I write now from the excavation site. Alone, of course. The wall of clay which separates us from Sector 4 is filled with rolled up pieces of paper stuck into the crevices. They are the writings of prayers and notes to loved ones from the teams that last dug here. I have read every one of them. I am sickened and I am distraught.

Tuesday Morning
Day 20 in the month of Dhu al-Qa'dah

The fighting is the most furious I have heard. Sector 4 has held up for two and a half days. I do not expect a victory. There is nowhere for them to go as I have failed them.

Wednesday Morning
Day 21 in the month of Dhu al-Qa'dah

The gunfire has slowed and has become erratic. It is reminding me of my daughter's breaths as I held her dying hand. And as I was then, I am now, waiting for the silence to tell me that the suffering is over.

Monday Morning
Day 26 in the month of Dhu al-Qa'dah

Cement trucks have been spotted at the site above Sector 4. I have no doubt they are going to entomb it. After the last truck has pulled away, I will order the excavation teams to begin digging again. I will abandon none of them. For each, a prayer I will have read over their body, and then there let them rest in eternity. It is not to say I do not hope for a few survivors. But I must be prepared for that in all likelihood, we will find none.

Thursday Morning
Day 29 in the month of Dhu al-Qa'dah

It is irony that defines our lives. It is ironic that once we began digging again, another hole opened up and we entered Sector 4 only six hours later. If we had only known, what joy it would have been to save them all. What a glorious victory to write down for all of those to be born of us.

I was the first to enter. The stench was immediately overwhelming, but it was nothing compared to the silence. There are three types of silence I have always believed. That which you hear when you are alone. That which surrounds you at the moment of triumph. And that which you hear when you are in the presence of death. It is the last one that speaks the loudest. It is the one that reverberates around your head and reminds you that someday you will also be dead.

We had to walk only a hundred or so meters before we started meeting them. The fortunate ones had just been bullet-ridden or made unrecognizable by explosive ordnance. Others it was obvious to tell had suffered all along their way to heaven. They, the Caliphate, were not discriminate at all. The old and young met fates in the same manner. Heads were hacked from children just as they were hacked from the elderly. They spared none the pain. All the horrifying thoughts of death were engraved upon their faces. With our blood, they wrote on our walls. With our girls and women, it could be seen they first had their way. Like the others, my sadness was quickly replaced with rage. Like the others, I wanted to go up there and exact a vengeance one thousandfold of that which we had seen.

Twelve hours or so we spent in the tunnels of the apocalypse. The two priests had become exhausted. The volunteers had become exhausted. And I myself could no longer continue. I ordered a stop. I knew that we needed to let both our sorrows and anger rest. Tomorrow I said we will return and bless the rest of them.

<u>Thursday Evening</u>
<u>Day 29 in the month of Dhu al-Qa'dah</u>

I admit I had been looking for him. Like one looks for a fallen king after a great battle. You are certain he has been slain, but you want to know whether the victors took him back as a prize, or they showed respect and left him where he fell. And if they had left him where he fell, you want to know how he met his end. You have scenes of preternatural bravery in your head. You have him as the last one standing. Hundreds of the enemy he has already laid to death. He is screaming that they can all go to hell. He is ready with his knife and his hands when the ammunition runs out. If you only had two hundred of him, Sector 4 would never have fallen, and Ayla would have been in dear peril.

I did not realize how large an area Sector 4 actually covered. Easily I'd say it was of a size more than four times ours. So when I set out on my own to find him, it took a while. It was a city unto itself. From cables and pipes routed long ago, they had their own electricity and running water. They had a church, but who does not have a church right outside of death's door. They had a school and a training center. They had an infirmary, a hydroponics lab, commissary, daycare area, reading room. All this they had, and so I knew they must have had a command center.

I walked a little farther and suddenly no longer was I stepping over civilians, but bodies of soldiers. This made me realize I couldn't be too far away as I understood the retreat by the units of Sector 4 would have been in the direction of the command center. The sounds of the blowflies soon intensified. And no matter how reverently I tried to tread on the ground beneath me, I could not avoid stepping upon charred flesh, a limb, a torso, an errant head. Rarely could I now find some soldier I could deliver to the mother who would be able to say that yes this was my son or daughter? The last line of defense had been met by such a barrage of machine-gun fire and explosives that I wondered if even any of their DNA remained in recognizable strands.

The sign on the partially rusted steel door had a metal plate affixed with the words "High Voltage" and nothing more. It lay about twenty feet from the entrance. It had put up a good fight. Battered and pockmarked, it probably stood for a good half hour before they were finally able to detach it from its hinges and remove it from the command center. I shone my flashlight in. And like I was projecting it down the nave of a devil's church, the beam lit up a figure disrobed and inverted on a cross. The body had been left untouched, but the head was charred as if it had momentarily been dipped into a blast furnace. To keep from vomiting, I had to look away and so I swept the light around the rest of the room. To the left and to the right were those who had fought beside him. All were pinned to the wall through their shoulders with railroad ties like one would pin butterflies.

I knelt and said prayers for all of them. To whom I prayed even now I am not sure. There certainly isn't a god who I would worship that would let this happen to any of his children. I walked over to my king. Below his head, neatly folded, was the uniform he had once worn. Next to it were his black combat boots and then his silver forty-five. I took to a knee and swatted away the flies perched upon his face. And then, just as I was about to say one last prayer for him, in a low guttural voice he said, "Kill 'em all."

How long he had kept himself alive, I would say perhaps seven or eight days. How he had kept himself from death, I have no idea at all. For those first few days, the pain must have been excruciating. After that, I am assuming he just drifted in and out of consciousness. I took out the gun from my holster and flicked the safety. Men like that know the sound of their own weapon. It must have taken him great effort to move his head to the side. I knew what he meant. I picked up his gun. I fired once and finally let him travel on to another great battle. I admit I stood there and cried like a little boy who had just lost his father. I admit, except for the death of my daughter, I felt the most hopeless I ever had in my entire life.

I walked out of there a different man. For three years, I had led Sector 3 as if we were there only to survive. I led it as if I accepted our lot in life, destined from one day to the next to keep ourselves hidden from those who ruled above us. Now, I swore, we would assume the mantle as Sector 4 had. We would build up our own war machine, and we would train everyone to become soldiers. We would wreak havoc in their homes and in their streets. We would destroy as many of them as we could, even if it meant destroying all of us. Defeat, as he must have believed and I now realize, is a fait accompli if you never come to the fight.

Sunday Morning
Day 17 in the month of Muharram

We found no survivors. Sector 4 had been breached and overrun. It did for a moment cross my mind to occupy the area. And while it was better suited than our sector for living beneath the earth, I couldn't be certain that the Caliphate hadn't left a secret passageway for which they could return. So, in the end, I decided to entomb them for eternity, leaving them there like those who had perished on a ship that now rested on the bottom of an ocean's floor.

Before sealing the hole up that separated us from Sector 4, I assembled a team to make one last sweep to gather up any provisions that we might have missed. Flashlights, utensils, copper wire, batteries, and anything else that could be of use. I told them to be respectful. I told them to think of every dead body as if it was someone from their family. Personal belongings were strictly prohibited. A few hours later, the team began trickling back. I did an inventory of the men. Specialist Smith still had yet to return. I was just about to go look for him when we all heard the sound of footfalls running toward us. We all took positions and drew our weapons.

"Major Adams," the voice said to me as it cleared the darkness and came into the light. "Two. I've found two. Alive."

"Say that again, Smith."

"Two, sir. At the far end of the tunnel. An infant and her mother."

"Jesus, Smith," I returned. "Why didn't you bring them with you?"

"I tried, sir. The mother refused to come with me. She told me to go get you."

"She asked for the commander?"

"No, sir, she didn't ask for the commander. She asked for you. She told me to go and return with Major Caleb Adams."

"Did you search her?" I asked. Asked because I knew of no one in Sector 4 except the General. Asked because I thought it was a Caliphate trap. Asked because I thought she was strapped with explosives and waiting for me.

"No, sir, I did not."

"And of their situation?"

"Sir?"

"Smith, are they well, or do I need to summon a nurse or doctor?"

"They have not a scratch on them, sir. Nor do they seem to be hungry or in need or water."

"Considering what we have seen, Smith, you don't find that a little odd?"

"I find it quite odd, sir."

"Would you go to her and her infant if you were me, Smith?"

"No, sir, I would not."

"But yet you didn't shoot her."

"She presented no threat to me, sir."

"Take me to her," I said, not even knowing why I had said it. "After we get to within ten meters, I'll walk the remaining steps alone."

"I'll go with you the distance, sir."

"It's an order, Smith. Not counsel."

We walked a good eight hundred meters. For the first half of that walk, I asked the questions I had to ask.

"When we come within ten meters, Smith, what I am to look for?"

"I'll point to it, sir. It'll have a white cloth panel covering its entrance."

"Is there a hidden room within it?"

"No, sir."

"Then just an ordinary room? Like the rest of them here?"

"Yes, sir."

"Is it possible we missed them on our first walk through?"

"No, sir. This was my area. We searched all the rooms. We wouldn't have missed them."

"So, she and the infant must have moved to it from another hiding spot?"

"It seems so, sir."

"How were they positioned when you found them?"

He answered and I asked a few more questions. For the last four hundred meters or so, I was quiet in voice but my mind was loud. I was playing out different scenarios in my head. By the time we got near, I had settled upon two. The first was to come upon her quickly and empty one bullet into her head. The other was to not even look upon her face and roll a grenade into the room.

Specialist Smith halted my movement as if he was a crossing guard and I the child heading across the street. He pointed off to his left. I checked the clip in my weapon again. I removed the safety and I finished the distance. As Specialist Smith had said, she was sitting there with her arms wrapped around her knees. The infant was beside her in a 240 transport case. The two small candles to the right of her were giving off an extraordinary amount of light considering their size. I'm not sure why I didn't shoot her because, in my mind, I had already pulled the trigger.

"Who are you?" I asked.

"I am nothing. But she, she is the one who has been sent to overcome."

She turned her head to look at the infant. I did not turn mine. I was not about to let my eyes stray from her person.

"How did you know my name?"

"I am not sure."

"Where were you hiding before this?"

"We have been here since they entered the tunnels."

"And yet while we checked all of the other rooms in these tunnels, yours was the only one that we missed? I find that hard to believe."

"You think that I am one of them?"

I nodded, or I said, "I do." I can't remember now. My gun was still aimed at the middle of her forehead. Her arms were still wrapped around her knees. The infant was still asleep in the 240 transport case. The strangeness of it all for a moment made me think I was in a dream.

"I will need you to pay attention to my next words. They are very important to your life." She nodded and I continued. "Your position there means there will have to be steps. Each one you are ordered to take will have to be slow and deliberate, so I do not mistake them for anything else."

She nodded again, and I then directed each of her movements until she was standing in front of me. In the great light of the candles, her dress was more than translucent. I could see her breasts, her stomach, the black tuft of hair between her legs. I could see she wasn't fitted with explosives or concealing any other weapon. Yet I still, for some reason, uttered my next words. As if I was destined to utter my next words.

"Take off your dress."

She offered no objections and soon stood before me like Eve. I nodded, and she returned the dress to her body. She spoke then. And her words were terrifying. Terrifying not because of what she said. But terrifying because I was starting to believe someone had handed her a book in which the future was written.

"In three years from this day, you will once again ask me to take off my dress," she said. "We will laugh. And it will be our first time as man and wife."

I took her and her infant back with me. We did not speak the entire way. I put them in the care of Specialist Smith and stayed on to help the sealing up of Sector 4. All the while, understanding that in all likelihood someday one of the other sectors would be doing the same for us.

I suppose it was after coming upon the journal entries from the general's translator that I decided to disobey my own orders about returning with personal belongings. Of course, a moment after taking them, I was already having regrets and reservations. But after coming upon another notebook of writings, this one from young lovers whose story broke me at the knees and had me weeping for hours, I no longer had any qualms about collecting any other personal accounts that I could find. After all, why should their voices be as silent as their bodies? They all lived extraordinary lives and deserved to be heard. So yes, it was I who stole their testaments and compiled them herein. Editing I have done, but liberties I swear I have taken none. This I would say of what you have read. Believe none, believe some or believe all. But this was Sector 4, in both its rise and its fall. This was Sector 4, triumphant in will and inspiration for all to continue on with the good fight.

Major Caleb Adams
US Army, Sector 3
City of Ayla